Also b

A

VIRTUAL

REALITY

Mark Harris

Matador
9 Priory Business Park,
Wistow Road, Kibworth Beauchamp,
Leicestershire. LE8 0RX
Tel: (+44) 116 279 2299
Email: books@troubador.co.uk
Web: www.troubador.co.uk/matador

ISBN 978 1789015 928

British Library Cataloguing in Publication Data.
A catalogue record for this book is available from the British Library.

Printed and bound in the UK by TJ International, Padstow, Cornwall
Typeset in 11pt Bembo by Troubador Publishing Ltd, Leicester, UK

Matador is an imprint of Troubador Publishing Ltd

"The distinction between the past, present and future is only a stubbornly persistent illusion."

Albert Einstein
(1879-1955)

One

AFTER Diva – and that's how she spelled out her name to me – had performed a certain weird if not incredible act before my disbelieving eyes, the boggling peepers of a writer and early retired newspaper journalist, I kind of knew for sure that she was telling me the truth about not being an "Earthling". On the odd occasion previously, I'd heard or read about Alpha Centauri being the nearest star system in the Milky Way galaxy to our sun. And I soon became convinced that my exceptional and unexpected new acquaintance – whom I'd thought on first meeting was a rather attractive Chinese tourist, one of transient hundreds to be seen on any one day in my home town of Cambridge – was, in reality, another sort of visitor altogether. One from an Earth-like eco-planet, some 4.37 light-years distant from our solar system, and whose civilisation is far in advance, scientifically and technologically, of our own so-called culture.

My first knowing experience of Diva didn't seem to make much sense, to say the least... it just wasn't appearing at all real to me. Maybe I shouldn't have been so astonished, my many years as an investigative journalist having taught me always to expect the unforeseen. But this was something else entirely, something out of everyday comprehension... something out of this world! And I definitely wasn't wearing one of those virtual reality gaming headsets when this woman, boasting a crown of jet black hair arcing into her cheeks, emerged suddenly from my blind-spot zone. She looked really cool – on an unusually mild, even without considering global warming, and sun-splashed February afternoon – in a tight-fitting red anorak with a faux-fur-rimmed hood, non-seasonal tartan miniskirt and knee-high, black leather boots. This quite youngish-looking female - relatively tall for an Oriental lady, I thought – approached me in a provocatively lithe fashion then tilted her radiantly green, almond eyes in the direction of my seated and over-coated figure. Surprisingly expressing herself in fluent and excellent Queen's English, the woman asked politely whether she could "utilise" my cigarette lighter - actually I refer to it, unconventionally, as "my spasmodic cheroot illuminator". The old and stainless steel Ronson lay, fairly conspicuously to a real smoker with a nicotine urge, beside my equally shiny metal, cigarillo case. The rarely employed puffing – maybe more likely, I think, posing – apparatus rested, alongside a half-demolished pint of good Dutch lager, atop my compact wooden table. This stood on The Anchor pub's paved terrace flanking the picturesque, and now sparklingly sun-dappled, Mill Pond area of the River Cam. The ugly brownish remnant of my finished little cigar, the first I'd smoked in a few weeks, lay flattened in a glass ashtray.

I was leaning against the protective and glassed-in low railing separating me from the sun-reflective, constantly in wispy motion and seemingly impressionist-painted water-pool. I'd just been observing closely a dozen, variously-aged Chinese men, women and children boarding a punt under the watchful eyes of its young tour-chauffeur gripping a pole. The flat-bottomed craft was one of several moored by chains to a nearby little pier. Once the passengers were comfortably seated, in four rows of three, they covered themselves briskly with the colourful winter blankets provided. Also within my concentrated field of vision, and paddling close to the famed Cambridge riverboats, was an eclectic assembly of waterfowl. The silent, feathery gathering comprised a stately, though inquisitive, swan with its accompanying trio of attentive, grey-plumed cygnets; a pair of bobbing mallards - the male characteristically sporting rather prettier plumage than his mate. And what, at first perplexing glimpse, may've given the impression of a floating, headless chicken was, of course, a beak-dipping, white call duck. My focus on both forms of the city's usual river traffic was now overridden, brusquely, when my auditory sense kicked in and detected the sudden, footfall-sounding movement to my left. My final blue-sky image before turning towards the resonance of heel-clatter on stone slabs was of a squadron of purposeful seagulls swooping low across the water.

I've got this phobia - had it for as long as I can recollect, and for various reasons - about strangers touching my personal belongings. So when the lissom, possibly 30-something eye-candy smartly popped a super-long cigarette between her pouting, crimson-enhanced lips, held out a slender-fingered, gesturing hand then requested use of my lighter, I responded: "S-Sure… but please allow me." In my abruptly diverted state of thinking, I was amazed to have caught the evidently outgoing woman's words first time round. She nodded twice, supplementing her double affirmation with a coy smile. Next, she curved her body slightly in towards me when I raised the lighter to her apparently cosmetically bronzed, appealingly elliptical face. As I ignited a tiny plume of bluish flame, she tentatively half-cupped one soft and smooth palm around my Ronson-clasping hand; while between the first and index finger of her left hand, she held the fag firmly in her mouth. The woman inhaled through the thin paper tube of a noticeably aromatic tobacco, the outer end of it flickering momentarily with a fiery glint. My lighter-grasping hand fell away as she straightened her slender frame and, with eyes closed, blew a spiralling column of grey smoke skyward. After that, she made eye-to-eye contact with me again. "Thank you," she said evenly; then, lowering her gaze to my glass, she added: "Can I get you another beer?"

Needless to say, I was taken aback by her kind offer – sincerely meant, I was sure; but my response was somewhat delayed. Naturally, I wondered about motivation; hers and maybe mine, too. And the notion flashed through my mind that a pint of lager was a comparatively hefty price to pay for the mere act of combusting a cigarette. The woman hovered over me patiently, awaiting my reply and puffing away whilst I dithered.

"That's very thoughtful of you…" I remarked at last, staring benignly up at her, "though really not necessary."

She shook her head grinningly.

"But I want to," she stated with a whimsical persistence. "And by the way, my name's Diva… spelt, D-I-V-A."

"Okay, Diva," I uttered, a tad too emphatically as I wondered why she was telling me. "I'll take you up on that… and by the way, my name's David."

At that moment, and all of a sudden, I became aware that the erstwhile brightness of the afternoon had vanished. I glanced over my right shoulder and, with a touch of dismay, noted that the sun had just disappeared behind a not insubstantial and sadly looming cloud. I spotted a high-flying passenger aircraft, probably climbing from Stansted airport, as it headed for the huge and expanding bank of dark grey cumulus, a lengthy white contrail gradually dissipating in the jet's wake. After a swift look around us, I took aboard also that the only other people sitting on the terrace, a young man and woman who had been conversing in French and obviously a couple, were departing now by the steps leading up to the short span of bridge that carries Silver Street over the Cam. Here they would likely be approached by some rival punt-company touts, a clipboard with the illustrated river tour waving in their hands as they vied to sign up new customers. But if the Gallic twosome evaded the competing business calls, transited the narrow thoroughfare and peered over the balustrade, they could marvel at the proximate, quaint and 18th century 'Mathematical Bridge'. The criss-cross, wood-planked footbridge linking two areas of Queens' College, one of the oldest and largest of Cambridge's 800-year-old university, was held together originally by statistical logic, not nails.

"Would you mind if we went inside the pub, Diva?" I enquired of my uncomplaining bystander. "It's not as fine out here as it was earlier… and, anyway, the terrace seems to have lost the unusual winter buzz it had this afternoon."

"I agree with you," was the prompt verbal reaction.

Intermittently, the Chinese woman had been flicking ash from her diminishing cigarette into the small glass dish. Now she stubbed out little more than the filter-tip. I downed the remains of my Amstel and got up from my chair. I grabbed my man-bag from the neighbouring vacant seat, where - I supposed, a tad immodestly, and still mystified by transpiring events - Diva might've parked herself in an alternative scenario.

My companion - and I felt that to be a reasonably apt description – took the lead and advanced into The Anchor's lower-deck bar, holding the glass door open for me to enter after her. But as she walked the few metres to the entrance, Diva enacted a very odd move. Quickly, she pulled the anorak's hood over her head, virtually obscuring the upper half of her charmingly oval face. And I thought: Wouldn't you more likely do that on exiting a building, particularly at this time of the year? On entering the warm cosiness of the partially wood-panelled room, with its framed old sepia photographs of Cambridge and neat bar-counter up a few steps, I felt a momentary and involuntary, spectral shiver zip down my spine. It appeared that only one of the many compact tables was occupied, and this stood beside the window overlooking the river pond. The couple of middle-aged, Chinese women sitting there seemed to be engaged in a rapid and intense conversation with each other. But they stopped and looked at me in a startled way when, a trifle noisily, I closed the terrace door. As we passed them, I detected two pairs of almond eyes pursuing us with perhaps overly disgruntled expressions. This time I preceded Diva, leading her to a corner table, a snug niche out of sight of the two Far Eastern women. She held onto her handbag as I removed my coat and dumped it, then myself and accompanying shoulder-thing onto the relaxingly padded, wall-side seat. This was below a black and white, photographic mural-tribute to Syd Barrett, the founding member of 'Pink Floyd'. Apparently, and I'd learned this on one of my early visits to The Anchor, the inn was one of his hangouts and where he would play his music fairly regularly during the sixties… a bit before my time.

"Would you like the same again, David?" Diva enquired, breaking my yet puzzled reverie and turning to head for the bar.

"Yes, please… but you don't know what I was drinking. It was…"

"But I do," she interrupted smilingly, and moved off without more.

How could the woman know precisely what I'd been imbibing? I pondered in the instant. My glass wasn't a promotional one bearing the name of the lager-beer or its Dutch brewer. It was just possible, I speculated, that she'd been loitering around the bar area, somewhat unobtrusively, earlier on and happened to overhear my order. I doubted whether she could've figured out my tipple from the Netherlands solely by its colour; or even by taking an inspired guess. I was dubious also about whether Diva might've asked a bemused barmaid to recall what draught beer she'd pulled for me. Although the state of affairs was intriguing, it seemed more than a little peculiar; but nowhere near as extraordinarily strange and mind-blowing as it was soon to become.

With nobody else seeking alcoholic refreshment at the bar, it wasn't long before my second pint of Dutch lager was set down in front of me. And the bringer of beer, clutching also what appeared to be a tall glass of orange juice, sat down opposite me. Disconcertingly, the anorak's hood still was hiding in shadow much of Diva's upper facial features. Then it happened, the first of many coming moments that I'll never forget for the rest of my life. I was swallowing a mouthful of lager while watching the unspeaking Diva place her glass on the table. I followed the movements as she reached up and, in what struck me as slow motion, withdrew the hood back over her head. On later calm reflection, I failed utterly to understand why the lager glass hadn't plummeted from my trembling handhold to the flag-stoned floor, and shattered into a thousand tiny fragments. I was so bewildered... no, stunned by what my eyes were conveying to my brain, that an attendant medical professional might've been astounded I hadn't passed out from the shock. Yet contrary to any potentially resultant and objective assessment of the scene that confronted me, I managed to retain sufficient residual capacity to return my glass, albeit very shakily, to the table and in one piece. Even today I find it difficult to remember, anyways accurately, the chaotic thoughts tumbling around my racing mind like clothes in a washing machine. But at the time, I couldn't deny the living image that confronted me. The woman now full-facing me - who I knew for certain had to be Diva, the Chinese woman I'd exchanged a few brief sentences with on the pub's terrace, and who'd just bought me a pint of Amstel - was now an Occidental! She was quite obviously a Westerner, boasting a swathe of strikingly blonde hair and a penetrating pair of azure-blue, non-almond-shaped eyes...

Two

STRANGELY, I *can* recollect a particular notion – a one-liner, of sorts – that had transited my wobbling grey stuff after Diva's very apparent and mind-blowing metamorphosis… maybe she has concluded that gentlemen prefer blondes. Now she was just staring at me wordlessly across the table, or rather at my undoubtedly extreme facial antics; though that might've been regarded as a contradiction in terms. What about her extreme facial antics? The profound hush between us continued awkwardly, to say the least, for what seemed like several minutes. But I could've been wrong about that; I was losing all sense of time passing. At last, I managed actually to put together and even utter, in an uncharacteristically stammering fashion, a hesitant couple of brief sentences. Possibly in the odd, potentially yet comic circumstances my innate sense of fascination assisted me in formulating them.

"H-How d-did you… d-do… w-what you j-just d-did, D-Diva? A-And w-why d-did you d-do… w-what you j-just d-did?"

Generally, I considered myself a fairly level-headed kind of guy, certainly not one given to blabbering histrionics. But having just about registered what was verbally escaping my mouth, I had to self-confess that this was a unique and quite incomprehensible situation. Nonetheless, I was sort of regaining my wits and seeking hesitantly to analyse and assess the current situation. So before Diva, or whoever she was, could answer my fairly straightforward though babbled queries - assuming she ever would - a series of linked-up ideas entered my thought-system. Perhaps she's a con-woman seeking to take me for the proverbial 'ride'... maybe she's a professional magician, and the quickness of her hand has deceived my vision... or, possibly, she'd been wearing a brunette wig; and her eyes had been cosmetically or otherwise disguised. But what was it all about... and why the hell?

Then, suddenly, Diva did respond... though with more questions.

"You're thinking I'm pulling a fast one, aren't you David," she said forthrightly, and expressing my name as if she'd known me for years. "You believe I was wearing a readily removable black hairpiece, don't you? And that I rubbed off, surreptitiously, some highly convincing make-up... or sneakily disconnected a sophisticated film of artwork from my upper visage?"

Could be my formerly flabbergasted brain-network was entering its recovery stage. I was now feeling slightly more upbeat, mentally speaking.

"Am I correct in supposing you're a mind-reader as well as a quick-change artiste, Diva?" I countered, with a sense of one-upmanship and optimism that my speculations had been rather in excess of such.

All she came back with was a simple but questionable, "No comment".

Maybe I was asking for that with my whimsical searching after verification. But instead of affording me some, Diva intertwined her hands and touched an index finger to each of her temples. As I observed - in total amazement, horror or otherwise influenced - her stunning blonde tresses swiftly altered their startling hue from the roots upwards, re-morphing to glossy jet-black locks. And her eyes transformed again to their earlier exotic almond shapes, the pupils swapping the heavenly light blue for their former jade green. With a bewitching sparkle in each of them, and a smug grin, she said: "Not bad for, what did you think, a conjuror... eh, David?"

If nothing else was apparent to me at that moment, at least I knew - and almost with certainty - that she *had* read my mind. Although I remained in a cloud of warranted incredulity, it was a state of mind I seemed to be adjusting to now. So in that conditioned status, I put a few more interrogatories to the reconstituted Oriental young woman now sitting smilingly opposite me.

"I suppose I need to accept that you've proved a point, or whatever. But please tell me what this is all about? Who are you... for real? And why am I the apparent focus of your attention, for whatever reason or motivation?"

The two middle-aged and still heatedly jabbering Chinese ladies were departing, via the far stairs, to the pub's upper-deck level. The barmaid was no longer in evidence, possibly taking a short break during this very quiet, afternoon period. Diva was staring silently at me. Although sorely tempted to stay with her and continue my attempts to seek more information, especially because I seemed to figure significantly in her calculations, I decided that enough was enough. I turned away and reached for my coat.

"Please don't leave, David... I need you to help me," she said imploringly, and further mystifyingly.

I swivelled on the padded bench-seat to face her again. In a way, and had that been the only consideration, it was no real problem gazing upon her compelling features.

"You say that you need *my* help, Diva," I said, with a growing curiosity, then adding the inevitably specific question: "How come?"

"Please allow me another moment or two, and I'll explain... I promise, David," she reacted with an acceptable degree of sincerity.

With that, she re-performed her hand, index finger and temple motions of recent activation; and again she transmogrified, virtually instantly, into a Westerner... a fair-haired and azure-eyed Diva. I threw her what must've appeared the most extraordinarily resigned look ever produced by a human being. But she did keep her promise.

"I'm really sorry about just before, David," she began. "When I arrived in Cambridge today and started walking towards The Anchor, where I knew you would be located, I considered there might've been a miscalculation on my part. There were so many Orientals in the town that I thought perhaps I was in Hong Kong or, perhaps more significantly, in Cam… Cam… Cambodia."

Needless to say, and even though I was still pretty peeved and befuddled, I couldn't resist chortling at her comedic effort. Diva also creased her cheeks with a correspondingly gritty chuckle. My immediate reflection, that she seemed altogether human, proved to be a somewhat premature rumination.

"What exact form does your facial appearance normally take?" I interrupted earnestly; and, I considered, quite fairly in the bewildering circumstances.

Diva nodded with a hint of understanding, I should've thought, of my not unexpected and baffled predicament. But, at the same time, she ignored my probing intervention and continued her original explanatory train.

"I've now received confirmation that my present location is precisely where I should be. Consequently, I feel much more comfortable and relevant as an Occidental Earthling in this European environment. And, therefore, I can assure you that there will be no more physical transformations today, David."

Hallelujah! I exclaimed, internally. I resolved, maybe comically, not to enter into a discussion about *Brexit* with the woman; though she might've been more knowledgeable than me about all that political nonsense. But her puzzling reference to the adjective *relevant* and the noun *Earthling* instigated for me even further puzzling pause for thought.

"For the final time, Diva, please tell me what all this is about, else I'm going… and right away!" I announced firmly, and with as much frustration as I could pack into my voice.

Diva nodded but rather equivocally, I pondered without much hope.

"I'm going to do just that… and immediately, David," was her surprising riposte. "I come from a broadly Earth-like planet in the star system your astronomers and astrophysicists know as Alpha Centauri. It's the nearest to your sun, in what you call the Milky Way galaxy, at a mere four point- two-two light years away…"

Three

AN "Earth-like planet" I pondered whilst also hoping, perhaps too cynically, she meant physically and not psychologically. At the same time - on rapidly recalling Diva's very recent back-and-forth, hair-and-eye transformations - I speculated, and maybe too whimsically, whether her home in the galaxy might be a world of highly-evolved and super-intelligent chameleons. After all, I was totally and somewhat frighteningly ignorant about the bodily appearance of her home sphere's inhabitants or, more materially, what Diva truly looked like facially. With her last unbelievably astonishing - to say the absolute least – utterance, I should've been cerebrally self-pummelled to the pub's lower-deck floor. Though, as might be said proverbially, a developing familiarity with people, places or events will lead almost inevitably to a kind of situational contempt. In any case, I was sort of glad that her planet's indigenous population – well Diva, anyway – possessed, or could readily take onboard, a canny sense of humour. Her "Cam… Cam… Cambodia" witticism was, I considered, well up to standard… okay, I reflected further, down to *my* standard.

The pretty decent quip matched my favoured, pun-orientated one-liners. I've never been able to grasp the comedic value of those drawn-out, quite tedious and largely unfunny anecdotes so beloved of most stand-up comedians nowadays. I feel their audiences are laughing more out of pity at the alleged comics' painful life disclosures. So, for a moment or two and in that connection, I found myself deliberating on whether Diva's wisecracks were purely coincidental. Or if she somehow knew of my joke-material likes and dislikes – knowledge, she might believe, that could assist her in a premeditated, softening-up process directed at me. And particularly, was she aware about my having mentioned, rather infrequently and entirely in jest, that "I come from Alpha Centauri"? Generally speaking, I would assert this when I happened, by a fluke hopefully, to predict what someone was about to say. In the current context, and as I faced Diva, I gulped with the utterly strange applicability of my recollection.

"That's fantastic," I offered, rather than declared, at last; and in a surprisingly controlled voice. It seemed like I was going with the flow.

Doubtless I was being supported, both intellectually and emotionally, by subliminal thoughts emerging from my decades as an investigative journalist, an inveterate globe-trotter in the cause. And one who was well used to meeting, even confronting, individuals from all walks of shady life; and in countless intriguing, suspicious or even risky circumstances.

"At present, Diva, there are literally hundreds of potential questions besieging my mind, and wrestling with each other for triage," I went on, "but I'm sure you know that. I'll try my very best to hold back more than a couple of them for the time being, assuming I've got the strength of will."

The woman, if such she plausibly was, from Alpha Centauri nodded, and quite benignly.

"Tell me, please… why are you here on Earth?" I went on. "And why and how do you think insignificant me, Cosmos-wise or indeed anywise, can assist you in your, and presumably I'm adopting a reasonably appropriate term, 'mission'?"

Diva's gorgeous blue eyes burrowed – metaphorically, I should add quickly and thankfully – deep into mine. At that instance, I felt an oddly ambivalent sense of comfort-cum-discomfort. Then she spoke again, saying something I wasn't quite anticipating.

"I'm just going to the loo… and on my return I shall answer your justified questions."

Then she *did* something that also I wasn't expecting. Yet again, Diva performed the now familiar hands, index fingers and temples manoeuvre. Though, on this occasion and completely, she disappeared. I stood up instantly, my mind spinning; and, with palms flattened on the table to steady myself, stretched over it for a full look-see. This anxious movement was just in case I'd been 'taking five' – which I hadn't, in fact – whilst she was doing the 'something' and I'd missed seeing her collapse to the hard floor. A moment later, I was slumped back down on my padded seat. No, Diva hadn't taken a dive… she'd actually vanished into thin air, as I'd observed unbelievingly. I was on the point of grabbing my coat and bag, ready to presume I'd been asleep and dreaming outlandishly - had it not been for the barely touched glass of orange juice just beyond my Amstel – when, in the flash of a blink, Diva reappeared opposite me. She seemed fairly relaxed, as if she'd been sitting there consistently since bringing back our drinks from the bar.

But in that staggering, stand-still fraction of time when she ceased to exist before my startled eyes, it should've been I who plummeted to the stony ground; and even though I've always considered myself to be a reasonably strong-minded and firm-willed character. Well, my long ago and one-and-only wife - and ages since 'ex' - had certainly thought so. How could I handle this literally alien behaviour any longer? Everyone possesses a tolerance limit, including me. Then Diva opened her mouth.

"I regret what happened just before, David," she said with apparent sincerity, though I did wonder about that. "But I wanted you to be sure in your mind that I'm not performing any magic, or any other trickery, before I go on to respond to your questions. I have to say that I'm full of admiration at your comparatively tranquil perseverance in what must be, for you, a downright inconceivable and mind-smashing situation. Believe me, David, I can comprehend and readily accept that there are countless questions you would wish to put to me. Who on Earth wouldn't?"

There she goes again, I thought to myself with an inward smile.

"I like your grin, David," she said, though not entirely unpredictably.

"Look, Diva, it's scary to know you can read my mind," I remarked, and with what I felt was a hint of panic in my voice. "I don't think I need tell you that. So I'm thinking, as you're doubtless aware, is it worth my while actually saying anything to you?"

Diva adopted an unusually serious expression.

"In fact, David, I can't read your mind. With all due modesty, I can say that my civilisation is rather more advanced than yours. But, as yet, we're unable to peruse entire minds like reading what you know as books. We would need to pursue other avenues of research in that connect. But what I can do is read a thought imminent to its being expressed verbally, if it is so expressed... and also, as you've just witnessed and amongst other things, I can make myself invisible to the naked eye."

"Interesting," I uttered, with a slow vocal delivery and almost without deliberation. But I added quite consciously: "And I'm fairly confident in saying that your memory is indubitably excellent. So I'm taking it that there's no need for me to reiterate the couple of questions I put to you before your recent, amusingly introduced few moments of not being here... or more specifically, not being visibly here."

Perhaps I did detect a little chuckle emanating from the other side of the table. But I could've been wrong about that, too.

"You take it correctly, David," Diva commented laconically. "So here we go then... no, hold on a moment..."

What now? I thought, with maybe a detectably impatient sigh, as Diva closed her eyes and placed the tips of her index fingers on her temples.

"I'm really sorry, David, but I've got to go now. I need to do something very urgently…"

In a smutty way, I supposed, I thought about loos, knowing that my companion would be aware of it… or possibly not, if she was distracted by some kind of incoming message from whomever and wherever.

"Could we possibly meet up tomorrow, Friday morning… beside the Great Pond in Emmanuel College's grounds at, say, eleven o'clock?"

"Alright, Diva," I responded after a few moments' thought, and feeling that tenterhooks mixture of annoyance and disappointment again. Though I was certainly impressed – should I have been? – by her spot-on terminology for the college's main area of lake-like water.

"And, David, I know that I can trust you…"

"What do you mean, 'trust me'?"

She looked at me pointedly, as she adjusted her striking red anorak and stood up.

"I'm aware that you're a respected journalist, and I appreciate that all this would be a terrific scoop for you… out of this world, so to speak! Having met you, I like you, David… I believe you're a good guy and will keep all this confidential, that's just between the two of us. And I hope you'll accept that I wouldn't even consider applying any pressure. In the end, it's an indisputable fact that there's no actual evidence to prove what has been said or done by me this afternoon, here at the warm and cosy Anchor inn. So cheerio for the time being, David, and I look forward to meeting with you at Emmanuel tomorrow."

With that, she turned and walked towards the stairs to the upper-deck and the exit onto Silver Street, her heels click-clacking on the stone floor. The returning barmaid thanked Diva as she quickly ascended the few steps, then looked in my direction. I nodded, gathered up my belongings, donned my overcoat and left the pub. On exiting, I looked left and right. I hadn't anticipated seeing my erstwhile sidekick again that day. But I did, catching a glimpse of her as she turned left into the narrow Queens' Lane; though not before swivelling sharply and waving a hand at me.

I followed her route but deliberately slowly, not spotting Diva a second time but taking the self-same shortcut – past an entrance to Queens' College then through a deliveries alleyway alongside King's College – to the misnamed and quite level Market Hill at the centre of town. I stopped off at Sainsbury's in St Andrew's Street to acquire a few necessaries, before walking the five minutes or so to my flat beside the Cam. And I realised suddenly that my mind had been a virtual blank canvas since taking leave of The Anchor.

Four

MY second-floor apartment is at a substantial but not unattractive, late 20th century development overlooking the Cam and adjoining the narrow, riverside Richmond Terrace. That pedestrian-only walkway, though you can never tell with cyclists, extends the few 100 metres between touristy Quayside - with its bustling bars, restaurants and punt moorings - and expansive Jesus Green, which boasts tennis courts, a bowling green, a summer lido... and an annual Beer Festival. I moved into the two-bedroom flat on separating from my wife of 20 years; but that was some while ago. My comfy abode affords great views across the river to the beautifully austere, light red brick but darker roof-tiled Magdalene College, topped by its lofty and distinctive Elizabethan chimneys. And it's directly opposite the Fellows Garden, many bowing willows lining its waterside edge. Sonia had remained at our large detached house, situated in one of Cambridge's picturesque satellite villages, until the divorce went through. Afterwards, she made *Aliyah*... that is, she settled in the land of Israel and with her new partner. When sporadically in that country, likely staying in Tel Aviv or Jerusalem, I've popped along to see them briefly, on invitation, at their home in the popular coastal resort of Netanya. So, implicitly, it can be noted that the final break with my spouse of longstanding was quite amicable.

I'm nowhere near as religious as my ex was becoming during the latter period of our marriage. She would regularly attend services at the orthodox synagogue on the Sabbath, and on most of the High Holydays and festivals; even staying at a nearby hotel overnight, so as not to contravene *Halachah* or Jewish Laws about driving on these occasions. While I continued as a mere twice-a-year adherent to the Faith, attending the house of worship on Rosh Hashanah, the Jewish New Year, and on Yom Kippur, the Day of Atonement. These eventualities represented just one of the irreconcilable differences that had developed between Sonia and me. Michael, our only child, is an unmarried 'Jewish' atheist and lives in New York, where he's a senior accounts executive for a big advertising agency. From time to time, he visits me in Cambridge – that's why I'd acquired a two-bedroom flat - and his mother and step-father in Netanya; and independently, of course, I and they would go see him on a similar basis.

But all this was far from my thinking when I arrived back at the apartment that amazing Thursday afternoon. I put away my overcoat in the built-in wardrobe of my light, airy and spacious main bedroom, switched on the heating and stored my recent supermarket purchases in the fridge-freezer and cupboards of my newly re-fitted, designer kitchen. That quite compact area was open-planned to my adequately dimensioned sitting-dining room. On entering the relatively homely space – with its several wall-mounted, framed, black and white photographs of the 'Big Apple' given to me by Michael – its largish window provided me with an initial vista of the sky, then a charcoal grey. Automatically scooping up my metallic black laptop from the square wooden table, I flopped onto the yielding, brown-leather settee with a soporific feeling of achy weariness verging on exhaustion. I didn't need to wonder overlong about why that might've been the case. Then I placed the laptop beside me, leaned against the head-supporting sofa and closed my eyes. Unsurprisingly, I fell into a deep sleep laden with some confused, if not chaotic, dreams that I couldn't recall in any detail on awakening. When I did raise my eyelids, accompanied by a shivery start, I glanced at the digital clock on my swish, post-modern sideboard and noted that I'd been in the land of nod for a tad in excess of an hour. My abbreviated, 60-minute-plus rest cure – even though a disturbed one – seemed, nonetheless, to have pepped me up somewhat. Indicatively, and at once, I lunged for the latest edition 'Small Apple' computer lying conveniently at my side.

Straightening my body, I levelled and centred the exceedingly slim laptop on my upper thighs, lifted the cover and switched on. At the same time, I thought oddly about something Diva had said to me. Indeed, our encounter would've won first prize for the international media story of all time. I envisaged the sort of tabloid newspaper headline it might've prompted from an excited sub-editor: "Earthman enjoys a pint with alien visitor to

Cambridge'. But, joking aside, she was absolutely right in her subsequent polite, though dogmatic, comment. For sure, I didn't possess a single shred of corroborative evidence that anything earth-shattering had transpired that afternoon at The Anchor. Even the duty barmaid could've testified only that she'd seen me and a youngish woman having a quiet drink in the pub's lower-deck bar during the afternoon.

As the laptop rapidly fired up, my mind veered in yet another far-fetched direction. I couldn't really remember when or why exactly I'd first said to someone: "I come from Alpha Centauri". Possibly it was to Sonia; and that would've happened, if it had, some time back. I really couldn't recall my motivation or rationale for saying it initially, and to whomever I'd said it. Probably, it was a combination of context and my leaning towards whimsicality. I do recollect, however, that at some point I did say it to my son. He kind of smirked and responded that, as a member of the Jewish Faith and a traditional believer - albeit a rather non-implementing one - I shouldn't actually be saying something of that ilk. When I asked him why, I was surprised he referred me fluently to the opening words of Genesis, the first book of the Old Testament: "In the beginning the Almighty created the heavens and the earth." My comeback to Michael was that, although the opening verse of chapter one of the Hebrew Bible alluded specifically only to the "earth", of which details were provided subsequently, no reference – other than, implicitly, to the creation of the sun and moon – was made to the wider composition of the 'heavens'.

It went without saying that I didn't know whether I was the only individual, in the entire history of the Earth, ever to have mentioned personally coming from Alpha Centauri and for whatever reason… except, naturally, for Diva. But I did conjure up a pretty balmy speculation. Perhaps my fanciful, if not quirky, statement on a particular cosmic origin had been registered as unique in the galaxy-listening annals of Alpha Centauri. In consequence, it might've been one of the prompts, logical or otherwise, for Diva or whoever to pick on me. I was fairly certain that I'd half-learned something about Alpha Centauri way in the past, encouraged by my intermittent references to the star system. When my laptop impatiently bleeped its readiness for input action, I endorsed a notion to remind myself - and to bring my knowledge up-to-date - about the nearest stellar neighbour to our local sun.

There were loads of websites about Alpha Centauri, which was first recorded in the second century by Ptolemy in his star catalogue. They brought back to mind that it's a triple star system, comprising Alpha Centauri A and Alpha Centauri B - which together are said to form the binary star Alpha Centauri AB – and Alpha Centauri C. That's otherwise known as Proxima Centauri; and, as its name implies, it's the nearest of the trio of stars to our solar system at 4.24 light years. The binary A and B are relatively close together so that, with the unaided eye from Earth, they appear to form one star and one point of light. But it doesn't require exceptional astronomical technology, like the Hubble Space

Telescope, to separate them; that can be accomplished with a tolerable pair of binoculars. Alpha Centauri A is the largest and brightest in the multiple star system. And together with its very close solar companion, they form into the most brilliant 'star' in the southern constellation of Centaurus; and the third most radiant in the night sky, after Sirius and Canopus. Proxima Centauri is a smaller and faint red dwarf star that can't be observed with the naked eye, and which orbits AB at a general distance of 13,000 astronomical units.

Alpha Centauri A is clearly the primary star in the system; its radius is some 20 percent more than that of our sun, making it some 10 percent heavier. But, above all, I became especially over the moon to take onboard a variety of comparatively recent analyses. In 2012 and 2013, two possible planets were thought to exist in the AB area. Although no firm evidence of Earth-like planets exists, as yet, it's estimated at an 85 percent probability that such proof will be discovered. I noted that the Alpha Centauri system has been listed, by NASA's Space Interferometry Mission, as a 'Tier 1' target with the aim of detecting the necessary proof. In 2015, the Hubble scope apparently observed an Alpha Centauri B transit event. This could've meant the existence of a planetary body; but it may've been too near to its sun to be capable of sustaining extraterrestrial life of any kind. A slightly larger than Earth-sized eco-planet, termed Cb, is said to have been found in the "habitable zone" of Proxima Centauri in 2016.

I was more than interested to learn that crossing the phenomenally huge distance between Earth and Alpha

Centauri would, with our present spacecraft technologies, take several millennia! But I read also that nuclear-pulse propulsion, or laser-light sail science, could potentially reduce the galactic travel time to mere decades! So, inescapably, I wondered about how long it had taken Diva, and any accompanying colleagues, to transit the 40 trillion - 40,000,000,000,000 – kilometres; and the means by which they had done so. I gathered that consideration, by the Breakthrough Starshot Initiative, would be given to sending a fleet of ultra-fast and light-driven 'nanocraft' to explore the Alpha Centauri system. In 2016, the European Southern Observatory announced that Proxima Cb might well be a target for such an exploratory effort. Finally, I discovered that, in January 2017, there came into existence between 'Breakthrough' and ESO a collaboration "to enable and implement a search for habitable planets in the Alpha Centauri system".

After digesting all that information, I did ponder – justifiably, I perceived - whether any powers that might be in the Alpha Centauri system could be becoming rather intrigued by the attention being given to it by scientists, astronomers and astrophysicists on Earth. As a consequential, I wondered whether this might explain Diva's arrival on my planet. Though if my speculations were relevant - highly unlikely, I considered – why was I being added to the baffling equation? I was looking forward to hearing the promised answer, to that and my several other questions, from Diva in the lovely grounds of Emmanuel College the following day.

Five

MY sleep was unusually dreamless that Thursday night into Friday morning, so far as I was aware on waking at my normal and not too indulgent time of 07:30. Lingering for a brief while, wrapped in the snugly warmth of the duvet before sliding out of bed, I reflected that my serene slumber could've been due to a temporarily numb subconscious incapable of producing any moving, snooze-time images. Who could blame its subliminal paralysis and inaction after my recent experiences? I got up, removed my pyjamas and padded into the en suite. That morning, I really did need my 10 well-spent minutes under the invigorating rain-shower head to exorcise some demonic notions infiltrating my mind. Shortly after the refreshingly drenching soak, I ate and drank an habitual light breakfast of fresh orange juice, yoghurt, banana and crucial black Americano - made by my treasured coffee machine - whilst sitting at the living room table with my lower half girdled by a bath towel. As at most such times, I watched the latest and generally depressing international and UK reports on Sky News via my wall-mounted, flat-screen TV. The succinct, national weather forecast - in which I had a special interest that morning, whilst appreciating it could be off-beam locally

– predicted a four-degree drop in temperature from the previous day, though largely sunny spells. After washing up the cups, glassware and dishes, I carried out my regular ablutions and dressed more or less recognisably as I'd looked to Diva at the Anchor pub; save that I donned a thicker, turtle- rather than V-neck, woolly jumper.

Bearing in mind I'd arranged to meet my new alien friend on Emmanuel College's beautiful campus around 11:00 that morning, I quickly calculated my apartment-leaving time as 10:40. Slightly on the early side for a moderately paced, 10 to 15-minute walk; but I wanted to get there before Diva, just in case - I thought with curiosity, and doubtless foolishly – her manner of arrival would be of particular fascination for me. Before leaving the flat at my planned time, I performed a few routine though unnecessary chores; and really only to take my mind off its persistent focus on Diva, and what she would tell me that day.

I used the most direct route to Emmanuel along Bridge Street, Sidney Street and St Andrew's Street and into the bustling heart of the 'Town' - rather than, generally, the 'Gown' - area of Cambridge with its retail emporiums, restaurants, pubs, bars, coffee shops and other 'consumer' amenities. Not quite exceptionally, the venerable 1584-founded college I was heading towards is situated on the fringe of the city's commercial sector. Its entrance is a mere stone's throw from John Lewis. The department store comprises a major element within the then decade-old and modernistic architecture of the Grand

Arcade shopping mall which, on its St Andrew's Street side, preserves an earlier frontage. After entering my collegiate destination through an archway in its classic façade and passing the Porters' Lodge, I circuited the cobble-edged and manicured lawn of Front Court. At the same time, I peeked up at the golden clock-face centred above the colonnade fronting Sir Christopher Wren's appealingly designed chapel. Almost 11 o'clock, it informed me. I quickened my step, outflanking the church, and entered the expansive, lake-dominated area known as The Paddock. The college grounds host an eclectic variety of plant and tree species; some are fairly exotic, like the Great Oriental Plane in the Fellows' Garden.

I recalled that the late 16th century, scholarly institution had been established on the site of a Dominican Priory. The elongated and lake-like stretch of water - known as the Great Pond - that occupied the left half of The Paddock, facing me, was once the friars' fishpond. It still contains fish; and is also home territory to squads of ducks: mallards and moorhens, for the most-part. The right half of the precinct, separated by a pathway, is an open grassy section flanked by the Old Library, a building which had held originally the college's chapel. As I passed, on my right, a small flotilla of male mallards - displaying distinctive, satiny dark green heads, yellow bills and purple-brown to grey feathers - resting beneath a wintry-branched tree, I spotted Diva. She was standing on the edge of the Great Pond closest to me, and gazing at the single tree on a small island in the gently rippling water. From my earliest exploratory visits to Emmanuel, I knew the tree to be a swamp cypress. Around the base of its trunk is a number of what look to me like wooden nesting boxes. But what I couldn't quite understand was why I hadn't noticed the woman when I first strolled into The Paddock. Or perhaps I could. As she turned slowly and waved an arm in my direction, I walked towards her along the path.

Diva was wearing faded blue jeans, black boots and the same anorak as she'd worn at The Anchor. The bright red, closely fitting waterproof was like a beacon. You could've identified her a mile away. As I approached, she said:

"Aren't those nesting boxes under the swamp cypress really cute?"

I glanced askance at them, and wasn't at all phased that she knew the name of the tree.

"Yes," I replied with perhaps a trace of impolite terseness at, I thought, her misplaced priorities. "But tell me, Diva, how long have you been here… at Emmanuel, I mean, not Earth?"

"Only just arrived," she noted, rather peremptorily.

"Me, too, but I didn't notice you when I first entered The Paddock."

She would definitely know what I was talking about, nomenclature-wise and otherwise.

We began strolling together along the periphery of the extensive water feature, as if we'd agreed unreservedly on that course of action.

"How come you opted for Emmanuel as our meeting point, Diva?" I asked, as a pair of gulls swooped low over our heads like in strafing mode; but, in fact, descending for a skim-landing on the sun-sparkled surface of the pond. Both of us ducked involuntarily, her timing somewhat speedier than mine.

"Well... as you know, David," she responded, "there are so many wonderfully ancient colleges in Cambridge, with gorgeously landscaped grounds and gardens. I was undeniably spoilt for choice in the matter. But I thought we should meet somewhere quieter than the tourist-overwhelmed, seemingly even in winter, and perhaps better known star attractions like King's, Trinity and St John's Colleges on the river side of town. Appears I was right in my thinking... since it looks as though we're the only people wandering around here this morning. Plenty of lovely waterfowl sprinkled around... and I do adore those dinky nesting boxes."

At that moment, I needed to restrain myself from declaring, pointedly but unforgivably, words like: *Enough already about those bloody nesting boxes!* But what did *I* know? That aside, I now considered it was time to get down to the nitty-gritty agenda of our arranged encounter.

"How long did it take you to get here, Diva?" I enquired purposefully, as we strolled onwards, but I thought to add: "... Earth, of course, not Emmanuel."

"My problem, David," she replied, "is formulating an answer that would make sense to you..."

I nodded with a certain deliberation, possibly to signify a growing feeling that she had no intention of answering any of my significant queries. Of course, I understood now that Diva would receive my immediate thoughts; but I wasn't especially distressed by that knowledge, at least regarding my present irritation with her.

"Look, David, I'm really very sorry," she continued, "but even Earth's top scientists and astrophysicists, in their current and relatively primitive technological state of play, wouldn't be capable of grasping the complex intricacies concerning our methodology of journeying across the galaxy. And please note that we were at their present level of progress some thousands of your years ago."

I could do little more than gulp.

"Well let me repeat two more, hopefully straightforward questions I asked you yesterday at The Anchor... and really important questions, too," I countered with intent, as we carried on ambling the pond's perimeter. "Why are you here on planet Earth? And potentially even more astonishing for me, why and how do you believe *I* can help with your business here? Maybe I can say out loud, even if it's a superfluity but at least for my own benefit, that I did some very basic research on Alpha Centauri last night. I read briefly about our boffins' fairly recent deliberations and analyses relating to your triple star system. To cut the story short, because you know it in any event, I noted that early last year two groups of space scientists got together to collaborate on the possibility of launching *nanocraft*, whatever they might be, to confirm the existence of Earth-like planets orbiting Alpha and Proxima Centauri.

May I ask you, Diva, whether all that has anything to do with your visiting Earth at this particular time? And how could you, in your wildest dreams, ever think that *I*, a mere journalist by profession, could possibly assist you in any remotely conceivable way?"

Well, I'd got that off my chest. This gave me some feeling of relief in a totally bizarre situation, if ever there was one! Diva stopped suddenly in her tracks, and I followed suit. We'd now - and so crawlingly, too - reached the far end of the Great Pond. Beyond the trees skirting the lake round to our right lay the railed and gated Fellows' Garden, with its own luscious array of vegetation. This included its celebrated Great Oriental Plane Tree. Diva stared silently across a shimmering lake surface, scattered with ducks, appearing to focus on the swamp cypress islet near our start point. As I gazed expectantly, but with some trepidation, at the womanly form close to my side, I couldn't help thinking she was quite beautiful.

Then she turned slowly to face me and, wide-eyed, opened her mouth to speak.

"That's funny, David... what you said just now."

"Are you now confirming that there's some coincidence here?" I asked with an acute inquisitiveness.

"No, not at all," she replied at once. "I mean it's funny... well, amusing that I've got you to do some homework on the subject of Alpha and Proxima. That's really great!"

"I'm glad to give you some entertainment, Diva," I said. "But can you now give me some answers, please? I think I've waited long enough for them and, I have to say it, my patience is wearing pretty thin."

The good-looking woman checked momentarily over her shoulder, down the length of the Great Pond; then she turned back to me, her full lips sort of pouting sexily but sufficiently enough so as to make me quiver.

"Are you feeling cold, David?" she enquired. "I've noticed that there aren't so many ducks paddling around in the water now. Perhaps it has become a bit too chilly for them. The sunny blue sky could be tempting you to believe that a February day is warmer than it actually is. And I just caught you shivering slightly... so are you, like perhaps the local feathered creatures, feeling the cold a bit now?"

I shook my head, possibly a little unconvincingly.

"No, not really," I added for good measure.

"Look, I know we were proposing to deal with certain matters here at Emmanuel, but what about my buying you a coffee... a black Americano? Where would you fancy going?"

For some seconds, I struggled against my inclination; but, in the end, I succumbed to Diva's persuasive offer.

"Okay then, let's go to Starbucks... the branch near the entrance to Downing College. It's only about a five-minute walk away. But understand this, Diva, and I'll speak directly. If you do want me to aid you in some way, and clearly only if I feel able to oblige, you need to explain things soon and in a language that I can comprehend. In light of all that, I'm not sure I get what may be duly perceived by me as deliberate procrastination on your part. Anyway, thanks for the hot drink invite… and I'm looking forward to getting some answers at the coffee shop."

"You will get your answers, I promise," she said, and almost solemnly. "Don't worry, David."

Famous last words, I thought and Diva received instantly.

Six

EXITING Emmanuel through the arch I'd entered by, we now faced museum-flanked Downing Street. Crossing St Andrew's Street at the traffic lights, we turned southwards to thread our path along the not overly wide, pedestrian-busy pavement. We were passing Wetherspoon's pub - long ago The Regal cinema, and next-door to the popular Arts Picture House - when a terrifyingly obese young woman, totally engaged in working her mobile phone, collided with Diva. The possible student didn't apologise, just waddled awkwardly around my companion and obliviously onwards, silently demanding that people get out of *her* way. Instantly, the head-on encounter prompted me to wonder what would've happened had the alien visitor been pushed - as a result of the abrupt and heavy contact - into the road, knocked down and killed by an oncoming vehicle. For a moment, I questioned whether my use of the word 'killed' would be appropriate in Diva's case. Quite likely, she would've got up from the roadway, waved on the thankful motorist to the astonishment of bystander spectators of the impact, brushed herself down and continued walking with me to Starbuck's. If my provisional analysis wasn't correct, the alternative scenario would've involved, undoubtedly, her automatically alerted colleagues at once removing her prone body elsewhere and working some futuristic DNA-cloning technique. Marvellous what a writer's imagination can conjure up in seconds, I pondered. I was already turning to Diva; and found her nodding at me, though with an element of glinting ambiguity in her lovely blue eyes. Fortunately, she looked fine.

"Are you alright?" I asked her to confirm.

"Yes, thanks… no problem."

"Are you sure? That was quite a hit!"

"Sure I'm sure, David… and thanks for your concern," she said, tapping my arm with a flat palm. "It's much appreciated."

We continued on our way, and as carefully as possible, for a few more minutes. After passing the open-gated, main ingress to Downing College - possessing its own stately buildings and attractively landscaped grounds - we arrived at our targeted coffee shop. I pushed against one half of the glass doorway to allow Diva's entrance ahead of me. Rather gentlemanly, I felt; though she might've taken my pseudo-chivalrous act as a suggestion she should get the drinks… in any case, she *did* do just that.

"Go find us a couple of seats, David," she urged with an apt hand wave, whilst joining the end of a short queue at the serving counter.

Easier said than done, I mused, peering around the fairly spacious café with its many diverse - and largely student - customers bent over their open laptops and electronic notebooks. From past experience, I knew a significant number of these occupants would likely have been *in situ* for some time, evidenced by the dried-up dregs in their cups and mugs. This would be true of many of the city centre's coffee houses. Often, I would wonder how they could make a profit; unless takeaways were a significant contribution. Anyhow, I was lucky to spot an almost unbelievably vacant little table diagonally ahead of me in the far corner of the room. Speedily, I negotiated a few long tables with benches and claimed two empty chairs in the name of the Milky Way... but not loudly, naturally! I kept my coat on, even though it felt fairly warm. Flanking me were undergraduates concentrating invariably on glowing screens. So probably they wouldn't have the time or penchant for listening to the private conversations of other customers. A couple of the nearest guys and girls had earphones clamped to their heads, so they were well out of it in any event!

I could see Diva still hanging on for *barista* service, so I sat back and drifted languidly into some thoughts about how she felt I might aid her inter-planetary assignment. The notion struck me that, possibly, she nurtured the aim of persuading me to interview her for a worldwide media story. It could amount to a feature explaining succinctly the history of Alpha Centauri, its governing body's delight in the interest currently being displayed in the star system by our astronomers, astrophysicists and other scientists; and its peaceful intentions towards Earth. In my wild imaginings while waiting patiently - if not desperately - for my coffee, I considered she would need to leave something with me, likely an artefact of some kind, as proof that my otherwise unbelievable story was true. Needless to say, I would never consent to assist in any manner that might betray or compromise the loyalty I had for my country, my faith or my planet. Diva might well be a galactic fifth columnist for all I knew!

Suddenly, there she was before me in all her red and light blue glory with, I was certain, a large cup of black Americano for me and a glass of... yes, orange juice for her. I leaned forward to grasp my much-needed caffeine-shot, as the belated bringer of refreshment set her cold beverage on the table. She slipped off the anorak to reveal a figure-hugging, grey turtle-neck sweater, hung the favoured waterproof over the back of her chair then sat down opposite me. After taking in the active environment for a few seconds, she swallowed some of her drink.

"Busy in here, David," she commented.

"Always is," I responded, equally superfluously; and even though this was doubtlessly Diva's debut visit.

Carefully, as per usual, I took a sip of my piping hot Americano then looked directly into her über-appealing eyes, determined not to be sidetracked by them.

"So Diva," I began, with a firm resolve, "why on earth are you... on Earth?"

I realised at once that the subject-matter was far too serious for me to be making light of the question. But, at the same time, I didn't think I was exceeding our gradually developing familiarity, tangibly supported perhaps by a quick recall of extra-terrestrial arm-touching near

Wetherspoon's. Maybe the notion behind my jesting, and hopefully encouragingly human approach, was right after all; because my phraseology seemed to bring a minimal smile to Diva's lustrously smooth cheeks. So job done, I felt. Or not, as the case might be... and I couldn't have been more correct about that, even if I'd tried a lot harder!

All of a sudden, and once again, Diva placed digit tips on temples. Her now not unfamiliar action, and its virtually foreseeable consequences, were becoming very much like the derogatory two fingers' gesture to me.

"I'm really, really sorry, David... but I have to go," she said. "I do hope you can accept that it's not *my* fault. Please try to forgive me..."

I was certain the woman couldn't have failed to notice the extremely annoyed, if not exasperated look moving across my face like an advancing shadow.

"Look, can we meet some time this evening?" she offered. "Even though you may be thinking the contrary, I do want sincerely to keep my promise... and today."

"Okay, we can arrange for that," I reacted fairly evenly. "But do forgive me for just saying *this*... It's your last chance, Diva!"

"Understood, David... and, believe me, you won't be disappointed. You have my assurance on that... so, where shall we meet?"

Thinking fast, and in view of the wild goose chase to date, I didn't see why we shouldn't meet conveniently near to my flat.

"At The Pickerel Inn," I suggested decisively. "It's a pub close by Magdalene Bridge, and opposite the college of the same name."

"That will be good for me," she said, somewhat culpably.

All the same if it isn't, came my next thought… knowing gladly she would get it, of course.

"Can we agree on seven o'clock?" she asked, but in a now oddly alluring sort of way.

"Okay," I replied, "but please remember…"

I was convinced she hadn't caught my last few, somewhat dilatory, words. Immediately on my "Okay" she got up, grabbed her anorak, waved diffidently at me then wended her way between the still fully-subscribed tables to the exit and departed. All I had left for company was a barely touched glass of orange juice. I stayed to check my smart-phone, which first I turned back to *sound* from *mute*, for any incoming e-mails and also to finish my cooling Americano. There was just one message, from the editor of a magazine I'd written a couple of articles for over recent months. She wanted to commission another feature on one of my preferred topics, and asked me to give her a call in the next day or two. Whilst I was so-called retired - in the accepted official sense - from my journalistic career, I still accepted some independent writing propositions that interested me. Basically, I'd supposed, the formal withdrawal from employment would amount, predominantly, to a retreat from my constant globe-trotting in seeking out captivating stories. But I could now pursue any requisite internet research and face-to-face Skype interviews - for the kind of newspaper and journal copy I was producing - more comfortably working from home, relaxed on my settee, within striking distance of a decent cup of coffee and with the laptop where it was made to be… on my lap.

Seven

AFTER finishing my Americano, I glanced at my wristwatch. It was 45 minutes past noon and I recalled, with just a modicum of hesitation, that it was Friday. Normally, and if I've got the time to spare on this weekday, I'll nip along to the free lunchtime concert - during Term-time - in the Mumford Theatre at Cambridge's Anglia Ruskin University. I like the variety of music arranged by its Department of Music & Performing Arts, ranging from classical to rhythm and blues and everything between. The standard is generally high, whether from advanced ARU music students or semi- to fully-professional instrumentalists and vocalists, often the university's own graduates of recent or more way-back times. I was fairly sure I'd read the programme for that day in the Cambridge Concert Calendar, a booklet published at the beginning of each university Term; but I couldn't remember the scheduled performers or pieces.

If I moved now from the coffee shop, it occurred to me, I could probably make the usual 13:10 start time. There was virtually a full house every week. But I couldn't guarantee I'd even be close to heading the long corridor queue, as sometimes I did, on this Friday. Nonetheless, I flew out of Starbucks, scooted across the road as the lights kindly turned red against the traffic flow and power-walked the broad diagonal pathway, legitimately used on this route by cyclists as well as pedestrians, across Parker's Piece, the city's central area of tree-edged greensward.

At different times of the year, the expansive square of parkland is utilised for a variety of popular events, from farm and country shows to food and drink festivals. They culminate in December's seasonal, 'North Pole' extravaganza with a host of family-friendly fairground rides, a cool – that is, trendy – ice-rink and a fairly authentic 'Alpine' bar serving mulled wine and other traditional winter warmers.

Having now passed the city landmark of the celebrated Cambridge Arms Hotel on my left flank, I made full-speed ahead towards the grassy flatland's far corner. This pointed at the western end of bohemian-style Mill Road, acclaimed locally for its numerous ethnic restaurants, atmospheric and buzzing pubs and cafés, lively bars and a popular annual street-fête. I reached the entrance to the main building on the spreading ARU campus with time to spare; though not enough to percolate my customary, pre-concert black coffee from one of the handy dispensing machines. Just as well, I reckoned, having downed my caffeine ration already that day.

So at a now more moderated pace, I headed for the theatre through a passing stream of some of the university's internationally diverse, student population making its way, at that time of day, from lectures and tutorials to the variety of campus food outlets.

I found the prospective concert audience already on the move, snaking along the broad and bustling passageway into the auditorium. I joined the serpent's tail end, and took a proffered copy of the printed programme from one of the student ushers at the door. As chance would have it - and chance, I was once told by a Cambridge philosopher, is part of the Almighty's creative design for the universe – my regular front row, aisle place was still available.

I slumped down onto the firm seat, dropping my arms onto its arms. Without reading the sheet of notes dangling from my hand, I could readily ascertain from the set-up that we would be revelling in a jazz session this lunchtime. Great, I thought, as to rousing applause the blue-denim-donned quartet tramped onstage. Two of the bearded young men were carrying electric guitars, which they plugged in, one a saxophone and the fourth group member, the most facially hirsute of all the instrumentalists, taking his seat behind the plethora of drums and cymbals.

The house lights dimmed. The guitar-brandishing leader introduced the now lime-lighted foursome then timed them in, with clicking thumb and forefinger, for the first of half a dozen rocky modern, jazz numbers. At the same time I noticed, though with some surprise, that the single seat next to mine was still free. For the entirety of the foot-stomping session, I failed to focus on the gig as I would normally. My mind seemed wholly monopolised by thoughts of Diva. Constantly, I was imagining her sitting beside me and thoroughly delighting in the jam set. Strangely, I wondered about where she could be at this time, where her spaceship, flying saucer or whatever might be located and where she was laying her head at night… as if. But above all, I deliberated on whether she would show up at The Pickerel Inn, as arranged for later that day, and even whether *I* would.

After the nearly hour-long show plus a much-demanded encore, which I was disappointed not to have absorbed fully, I felt a trifle peckish. So I resolved to have, assuming I could achieve it, a relaxing snack and a pint at the Bath House, another of my frequented, city centre watering holes. It would be a 15-minute stroll to reach the cosy pub, built into a later extended 17th century house on charming Bene't Street with its lovely old church. The turning also hosts The Eagle inn, opened in 1667. The walls and ceiling of its 'RAF Bar' are smothered with the graffiti of Second World War airmen, based in East Anglia; and the pub is famed also for Francis Crick's announcement of his and James Watson's DNA discovery. So I dragged my butt off the not uncomfortable seat and headed back to town.

My target hostelry couldn't have been more centrally situated, so far as concerns Cambridge's political, commercial and cultural activities. The pub's a mere stone's throw from the Corn Exchange, the Arts Theatre and the Guildhall on historic Market Hill, with its colourfully stripe-canopied stalls and kiosks selling just about everything: from street-food, plants and flowers, through handcrafted souvenirs, glassware and pottery to hats, handbags and hosiery.

The Bath House was much quieter than it would've been a short while earlier. So I slid easily onto a yielding padded seat in one of my favourite, wall-side niches. I plucked a menu card from its table-top gripper, glanced up at a news broadcast on a nearby, wall-mounted and angled flat-screen TV then searched the familiar menu of pub food. I got up, approached the counter, mentioned my table number to the young barman and ordered the vegetarian baked camembert 'small plate' that came with crudités, bloomer bread and red onion chutney... and a 175ml glass of Merlot. I returned to my little alcove with the poured red wine, leaned into the cushioned seatback whilst taking a longish sip and sought, too optimistically perhaps, to calm down.

For a very short few minutes, I succeeded; but then I looked up again, but without thinking, at the TV screen a few metres away. It was tuned to the Sky News channel and, as always, was muted with subtitles. The blonde female newsreader was announcing the headlines to be discussed including, internationally, a catastrophe somewhere in the Middle East, a terrorist suicide-bombing somewhere in France; and, domestically, the return of Victorian diseases to England and the huge increase in rough-sleeping in London and other cities around the country.

Even Cambridge was mentioned; and although I was somewhat taken aback by its possibly cynical, illustrative selection, I wasn't wholly surprised. Maybe I shouldn't have jested, even internally, with the hope that Diva wasn't resorting to a cardboard-box bed in some shop doorway overnight.

I averted my eyes from the TV's news and comment broadcast, mindfully questioning — against the seriously depressing bleakness of our world's continuing, and seemingly endless and insoluble, troubles – whether it was, in fact, actually *news*. Then my food arrived, and I needed to focus my mind on simply cutting, dicing, forking and consuming; and apparently on something else, too. By the time I took my leave of the Bath House to return to my flat, someone – rather than something - was compelling my concentration. I did conjecture whether this had always been the strategic aim of Diva's possibly deliberate, delaying tactics. Nonetheless, I decided… I would definitely be turning up at The Pickerel Inn that evening.

Eight

WHEN I got back to the apartment I made myself an Americano, took it to the low coffee table beside the settee, grabbed my mobile and sat down. I called the magazine editor who'd invited a couple more articles from me; and had a longish conversation about what specifically she wanted. I never met the woman, though I've seen a photo beside the by-line in her journal's editorial comment page. She looked to be quite an attractive, 30-something brunette. My fellow writer possessed an appealingly sexy speaking voice, so I was more than happy to discuss the projected features' terms of reference with her at some length. We settled, finally, on deadlines and fee then signed off at the end of our 15-minute discussion. Not long after that, my son called me from New York on the landline. I noted his international number on the shiny black and cordless handset, quickly plucked the gadget from its base on the hall cabinet and spoke into the mouthpiece.

"Hold on for a second, Michael. I'm putting you on speaker-phone… got to do something in the kitchen."

"No problem, Dad. Go ahead."

My ears were telling me that he was getting more of an American, possibly Brooklyn accent each time I conversed with him. I set down the receiver on the dark granite work-surface and started to give my precious coffee machine its weekly wipe and clean. Somehow, it felt like I needed to be engaged in some simple manual task; and despite being at the receiving end of a phone call from my beloved son.

"How's it going, Michael dear?"

"Fine, Dad… And you?"

"I'm okay, thanks. So what's new?"

Generally when my son called, and that was about once a month and normally on a Friday, there wasn't anything 'new'. Life just seemed to be drifting along for him, and was mostly work-orientated. I didn't expect to hear anything different from him this time round, but I was wrong.

"I've met someone special, Dad. Her name's Dinah…."

"Jewish?" I interrupted whilst noting not only the sincerity and earnestness in Michael's voice, but also the coincidental fact that I could've said the same thing. Except that the *special someone* I'd met, but in a wholly different sense, was named Diva.

"Yeah, Dad… she is. She's a copywriter here, one of my colleagues you could say."

"Is she a religious Jewess, to any extent?" I enquired, perhaps hoping to see a potential conversion for my atheist son.

"Sorry, Dad, but Dinah isn't like that… she's more inclined towards my way of seeing life, the universe and everything."

"Have you told your Mum about her?"

"Yeah, I was speaking with Mum before I got on the phone to you."

"How is she?"

"Keeping well… she asked after you, too."

"So are you and Dinah a serious item, then?"

"Actually, Dad, although I haven't mentioned her previously, Dinah and I have been seeing each other for a while now. And the relationship has been developing to our mutual satisfaction. Just… you know, wanted to be sure of things before mentioning anything to you and Mum."

"Understand, Michael," I responded pondering parentally, but unwarrantedly, what my son meant by *mutual satisfaction. "And I'm very glad to hear about you and Dinah. Hope things work out well for you both… and please do keep us updated."*

"When are you going to find someone, Dad? It's a long time since you've had a relationship."

I ignored his question. But I was absolutely itching to inform my son of the 'someone special' that I'd encountered, too. I really couldn't bring myself to do that, and for good reason. In any case, and had I ventured to spill the beans on my recent and beyond extraordinary experiences, he would've reacted, doubtlessly, with some comment akin to:

"You didn't tell me you were moving into science fiction writing, Dad… since when?"

So probably I was right to remain completely silent on the matter. We went on to speak about the usual general matters then Michael finished off with his old chestnut of a query.

"Going to synagogue tomorrow morning for the Sabbath

service, Dad?" he asked; and, if he was on videophone, I could've perceived his naughty boy grin. *"It's not that far from your flat, after all."*

He was, of course, accustomed to hearing my standard, semantically equivocal but trenchant reply.

"I believe, son," slight pause, *"you know the answer to that one."*

I heard the usual little chuckle at the other end of the line.

"Lovely to talk with you, Dad… will speak again soon."
"Shabbat shalom, Michael."

And that was our traditional, telephonic endgame.

My coffee machine looked so sparkling and spotless now that I almost had to shield my eyes from the radiance of its glossy surface. I put it to one side on the draining area, picked up the landline phone, switched it off and moved into the hallway to slot the device back into its holder. Having cleaned my cherished Americano producer, I decided to have a bath - rather than a shower in my en suite - before going out. I turned on the water in the so-called family bathroom, stripped bare and caught a glimpse of myself in the large mirror before it steamed up. I was humbly and genetically thankful - as a male not far off the culmination of his fifties - for the tallish, arguably slim and firm physique and thick crop of dark grey, wavy hair.

Leaning back in a resolute effort to jointly rest and soak in the lulling warmth, I closed my eyes and thought of… Diva. Who else? Where was she now? And how was she preparing, perhaps artfully, for our agreed assignation at

The Pickerel Inn that evening? I harboured a notion she may've been onboard a huge and powerful mother-ship, hovering somewhere above the dark side of the moon. But surely, I thought, that wouldn't necessarily conceal the mighty galactic craft's presence from the 'eyes and ears' of even our current technology on Earth? I didn't have a clue on the subject. Inevitably, I speculated, my vision of a 'mother-ship' means of inter-stellar transportation could've been hysterically laughable to the likes of Diva and any accompanying colleagues from Alpha Centauri.

Following my bath, and possibly nodding off for a while, I got out of the tub, vigorously dried myself, drained the water, brushed and polished the white enamel and shuffled into the bedroom to get dressed. Having looked at my chronograph watch en route, I could hardly credit the time. It was just after six so, hurriedly, I put on my underwear, socks, a dark-blue shirt, a near colour-matching, slim-fit, ribbed and roll-topped jumper then, finally, a pair of navy-blue corduroys. Happily and unlike Diva's back-home 'local', assuming nonsensically that she had one, The Pickerel Inn wasn't trillions of miles from my flat!

Nine

THE Pickerel Inn is typical of extant old English hostelries. Towards the end of Magdalene Street nearest the River Cam, the roadside pub is built into one of a quaintly picturesque row of architecturally higgledy-piggledy, medieval houses. These line the traffic-constrictive thoroughfare opposite its eponymous university college. The pub itself, bearing its currently distinctive blue liveried façade, dates from the early 17th century; though a predecessor tavern is recorded as having occupied the site from about the mid-15th century. Its remarkable history tells us that, variously in the past, it was a gin palace, an opium den and a brothel. The two-storey, terraced building overlaps an adjacent archway, indicative of its former coach-house status; and that presently leads into a compact, flag-stoned beer garden for warm-weather usage.

The inn's interior is atmospherically antique and cosily welcoming, with dark wood-panelling covering its walls, ancient timber beams spanning the ceilings of its various snugly rooms that boast tables, chairs and stools to match. The floors are wood-planked and, in places, overlaid by reddish-patterned carpeting. Serving each wall-separated area, the bar extends through the premises from close to the windows overlooking the street and part of the river to the less illuminated, and perhaps more intimate, rear salon with its old-world open-hearth oftentimes glowingly employed in cold weather. At night, when it gets dark, the staff light candles on the tables, which give the interior a sensitively romantic touch, much loved by the many student and other local couples; and the small chatty groups of good friends that frequent the old pub.

Being an averagely regular patron of The Pickerel, I was well-acquainted with the male and female bar-people and they knew me. When I arrived that depressingly black, cold and rainy Friday evening at around six-fifty, the place was still fairly quiet; but I was strangely ambiguous in my thoughts when I took in the many shimmering candles. Speedily, I closed the front door behind me – to the approving nods of a pair of lovebirds sitting close together in the first section of the pub. I made for the bar and leaned against it purposefully, after my canter across Quayside and over the old stone-arched Magdalene Bridge.

"What can I get you, sir?" asked one of the amicable young servers on hurrying to me from the innermost end of the bar. I knew this one, hefty and hirsute, to be a bit of a joker and, true-to-form, he had a one-liner ready for me.

"You know, the chef here threw a big lump of cheese at me earlier today… How *dairy*!"

"I like it," I reacted cheerily; and he waited hopefully for my own addition to his collection.

I didn't wish to disappoint him.

"What did the woodworm shout out when he entered the public house?"

My fellow one-liner aficionado rested his palms on the counter and shook his head expectantly. I rounded off with the snappy punch-line:

"… *Is the bar tender here?*"

The barman chortled fulsomely. Trouble was, once you got him started…

"Ah, sir, you chose an appropriate context. So, I'll see you and raise you one…"

Which he did

Enough already, I thought edgily… and so did the joker.

"Sorry, sir… What can I get you?"

"Well, I'm waiting for someone and…"

At that moment, I was distracted by the pub door opening then closing behind me. I turned and knew at once it was Diva, even though her head was mostly covered with the inexorable red anorak's hood. She pulled back on its fur trim, stood transfixed for a second or two then noticed me and waved smilingly. As she approached, quickly unbuttoning her shiny waterproof en route, I turned to the affable bartender and said something about our finding a seat in the back room before I returned to order drinks. He would've seen Diva signal to me so - and just before I faced her again - he gave me a smiley nod and wink.

"Hi, Diva," I greeted, and unbelievably cheerily, my alien companion for the evening. "Is everything okay?"

"Hi, David… and yes, thanks," she replied, removing

her coat to reveal a quite formal frock this time. The dress looked to be well-fitted, fine woollen, dark blue with a high, rounded neck and a hem perched flatteringly just above the knees.

"Let's go grab a table," I said, maybe with a noticeably decreased amount of cheeriness, bearing in mind the proposed content of our get-together.

I led the way to the rear room which, at that time, had only two other occupants; they were sitting near its entryway. We headed for a two-seater table tucked away in a niche corner.

"What can I get you?" I enquired, as Diva swung her topcoat around the chair-back and sat down facing the wall. I removed my raincoat and performed a similar movement with it. "I hope you can have more than an orange juice this evening."

The lithe and lissom extraterrestrial spoke to me after a few moments of apparent deliberation.

"Okay, David, I'll have a gin and tonic, please… no ice. This does seem to be the right place for it, and thanks."

I moved off smartly to that stretch of bar counter in the middle section of the pub to order and fetch our drinks, not at all surprised at Diva's choice on the assumption she'd 'read up' on The Pickerel's gin history. I returned to our table as hastily as possible after paying my amiable jester of a bar person for the alcohol.

I set down the glass of gin and tonic, a slice of lemon stuck precariously over its rim, and my glass of rum and Coke, both drinks containing no ice and mine devoid of edible furnishing. As I parked myself across from Diva, she plucked up the lemon slice, plonked it inside the well-filled glass and sipped at its rim.

"Cheers! *L'Chaim*. To Life!" I declared, with an element of vocal restraint in the context, and raised my glass.

"Yes, I do know you're Jewish," she said, "and, anyway... L'Chaim, David!"

This is all total and utter madness, I cogitated in frantic-mode.

Diva was shaking her head.

"Can I ask you a personal question, David? You see, I don't know everything about everything... if that's what you've been thinking about me."

"Depends on how personal it is," I answered, shrugging my shoulders.

"Have you had any sexual relations since your divorce?"

I started to breathe a tad heavily. What was this all about? I hesitated; and for what seemed like several minutes, but was more like moments.

"I know it's none of your business, Diva, but the answer is... yes, and a couple of the relationships involved were fairly lengthy," I responded at last. "But I'm single at the present time... and have been for a while now."

"Thank you for being so candid with me, David... it's much appreciated."

After taking some more of her drink, she smiled then asked another question.

"If you could do something not otherwise possible for you to accomplish as your world stands today, scientifically or otherwise, what would that be?"

This time, I considered the enquiry less confusing and more interesting, if not fascinating; and I was pensive even longer than for Diva's preceding and somewhat suggestive poser. She continued to partake periodically of her gin and tonic, while waiting patiently for my reaction.

"Ever since coming to Cambridge, and although not being very religious, I've become engrossed in the history of the Jewish community that lived in the city, Cantabrigia as it was then known, during the medieval era. Primarily, that was across the 12th and 13th centuries. So far as I've understood events from my reading and research, most of the original Jewish population here came to England from northern France, especially from the city of Rouen, after the Norman Conquest in 1066. They based themselves initially, and naturally... geographically speaking, in London and the south-east of the country. Subsequently, they moved north into the near provinces, including East Anglia, settling in towns like Norwich, Huntingdon and Cambridge. I've been fascinated to study several archaeological excavation reports. And whilst there's a dearth of finds in the way of *Jewish* artefacts, it's fairly certain, for the most part, where the Jews resided and worked in Cantabrigia during the relevant epoch."

I halted my lecture at this point, even though I could've gone on *ad nauseam* at some enthusiastic length. But it looked to me that Diva, who gave apparently close attention to my discourse, was poised to ask another question. Just before she put it to me, I gulped some more of my drink; although, after hearing the enquiry, I could've swallowed the lot.

"David, does what you're telling me, and how keenly you're telling it, mean that you would've liked to be able to travel back in time... say, to be with the Jewish people in medieval Cambridge?"

I gave my new friend a double-take.

"S-Sorry..." I uttered, more than a little confused, "but did I hear you correctly about time travel... s-sorry, yes I did hear you aright, Diva... pardon me, and no... what I was saying doesn't mean what you just said. If anything, it would've been marvellous if the archaeologists had dug up some artefacts that specifically identified the medieval presence of the Jewish community. B-But now that you've asked what you've asked, I-I'm rather taken with the idea. S-So why *did* you ask me the question, if I may ask?"

All the while, Diva appeared to be wearing a distinct grin, no doubt due to my babbling on. In my perplexed reverie, I happened to notice that a few more people, mainly young men and women, had entered the room and sat down with their alcoholic drinks.

"I asked the question, David, because I'm going to present a proposition to you."

"Will it possibly be an offer I can't refuse?" I felt obliged to say.

"Permit me to put it this way, David. I don't believe you would wish to refuse it, for one reason or another... and I mean that seriously."

"Okay," I said, "let's hear your *proposition*, then."

Diva looked around at the now dozen or so other

customers occupying the room, largely composed of huddling couples, drinking their mostly wine or beer choices and chatting pleasantly in low tones. Then she turned back to me.

"If you help me, David, I will assist *you* to travel back in time to medieval Cambridge, to whatever date within that period you would prefer."

My doubtless startled and staring eyes exposed the depth to which I was stunned by Diva's amazingly incredible but, to some extent, maddeningly half-expected offer. It took me a while to gather all the senses I needed in order to respond.

"I-I'm taking it that time travel isn't a problem for someone from Alpha Centauri, but can *I* really take advantage of the attribute, and how? Besides, I can't get my mind around the notion that journeying to the past, or the future for that matter, is a real and practicable rather than a theoretical or virtual possibility. Maybe you can explain the concept to me in words of one syllable, Diva."

"Of course I understand what you're telling me, David… and I'll certainly try my very best to enlighten you," she reacted reassuringly. "I'm totally aware that what I've been saying is, and quite literally, completely alien to you. And I know also that, although you're an intelligent human being, you're also a layman in these matters… and that I do need to elucidate in words that are honestly meaningful to you…"

I nodded my grateful thanks, and she continued.

"… I appreciate that we're thousands of years ahead

of your Earth, scientifically and technologically speaking. And, naturally, we don't think of time travel in the same terms that your mind might be engaged in imagining it at this very moment, such as via H G Wells' fictional time machine with its rows of ornate gear levers, multi-coloured buttons and numerous brass dials…"

I bobbed my head again.

"… Look, David," Diva went on, "even today, your astronomers and astrophysicists make use of some, for them, really sophisticated, extra-terrestrial telescopes and ground-based, radio-wave formats to view, or listen to, the heavens. The Hubble Space Telescope can provide superb views of space, and well beyond our shared Milky Way galaxy… indeed, even to the edge of the expanding universe…"

Why couldn't I stop moving my affirming head?

"… And as I'm sure you know," Diva carried on, "light travels at the speed of 186,000 miles per second…"

I secured my warming cheeks firmly between bunched hands, my elbows rooted on the table.

"… Today," my alien friend went on, "light has brought to your space scientists on Earth a view of the beginnings of the universe, a time not long after the Big Bang and some fourteen billion years ago. So, David, think of it this way… If one can actually see what's occurring millions and millions of millennia back, why should one not be able to visit the place where it's happening?"

I would've nodded yet again, if I hadn't restricted my head movement; and, I supposed, if I could've comprehended fully what she was talking about now. But I did follow her, to me, fantastic explanation to some extent.

"I don't think I can put it to you in non-technical language simpler than that," Diva added resignedly. "And for sure, I don't need to say that the science involved is beyond complex. So in the final analysis, David, you'll have to take my word for it that we, in the Alpha Centauri system, can both space and time travel. But maybe I can add that the closer the destination in terms of time, such as medieval Cambridge compared to the Big Bang, the quicker and easier the journey, as you might express it. And, to put your mind at rest on the topic, I can pass the capability to you without any invasive procedure or pain whatsoever."

Why did she need to mention *pain* at all, I pondered with some spectral trembling, as Diva shook her head like a school ma'am.

"But what about the paradoxes that are said to interfere with the notion of time travel?" I enquired further. "For example, what if you travelled back in time and killed your father at a time before you were born?"

"My direct answer would be, don't commit premature patricide… but it would take me far too long, David, to explain the technicalities disproving these inconsistency theories."

Physically, I freed my head and nodded, ironically, with due contrition.

"So if I accepted your kind and unique offer to enable me to visit long-ago Cambridge, can I take it that you would provide me with… a return ticket?"

"Of course, David… that goes without saying.

66

And you'll be able to contact me, not only when you want to return but also if you encounter any significant problems."

"That's very comforting... even to an adventurous bloke like me," I remarked. "So tell me, Diva, what is it that you want me to do by way of earning this phantasmagorical prize?"

She hesitated for a few moments, imbibing another dose of her gin and tonic and kind of studying my face quite critically.

"I want you to give me a baby," she said very quietly and evenly.

Is that all, I thought; then realised, like I'd suddenly been hit on the head by a falling coconut, what she'd just asked of me. In the first instance, I decided conclusively that she didn't want me actually to kidnap and deliver a baby to her, whatever its gender. In the following rapid series of second, third, fourth and fifth instances, I recalled her earlier incongruous query about by my sexual relationships. I remembered oddly the contextually immaterial fact that, in a former existence, The Pickerel Inn had functioned also as a house of ill repute. I understood now that, if Diva meant what I now thought incredibly she did mean, I was being requested to sexually impregnate her. And finally, I wondered whether that was too high a price to pay for a return ticket to *Cantabrigia*.

But I was absolutely flummoxed, to say the very least. Why was Diva asking what I believed, and indisputably, she was actually asking of me? So I posed a question to her. In fact, I put a number of rapidly occurring interrogatories to her; though only after I'd downed most of the remains of my alcohol. As I drank, it was noticeable that the back room was at its optimum capacity now.

"T–Tell me, Diva," I began, clearing my throat, "why are you asking me to have sex with you? Even if I did, how can you guarantee that a baby would result from our, I presume, unprotected coitus? Is this the only route whereby I would be eligible for a voyage to the past? And why on earth am *I* the one in a billion, or rather more, men you've selected to copulate with?"

That would be enough of a grilling for the time being, I considered benevolently. Diva nodded, gazed vaguely about her then faced me again.

"David, I don't find the vibes here as conducive for our conversation as I felt them to be a bit earlier. But I do wish to answer your several understandable and justified enquiries. Is there somewhere else we can go right now?"

I focused upwards momentarily at the wood-beamed ceiling, then around at the mostly couples huddled together familiarly at their candle-lit tables.

"We can go to my place… it's just a five-minute walk away."

I felt that I knew what I was suggesting. It didn't amount to much verbally. Nevertheless, there was so much inherent in the semantics that I couldn't meaningfully extract before Diva's prompt response.

"Fine," she said. "Let's vamoose!"

Ten

DIVA and I got to my flat in fairly short order. The rain had stopped, thankfully, by the time we left The Pickerel Inn. It was a moonless evening, but the wet ground reflected the glow of the streetlamps and lighting from the bars and restaurants around Quayside. Before we departed the old pub, having threaded our way through its now teeming, standing-room-only spaces, my one-liner pal caught my attention from behind the well-besieged bar-counter. It appeared like he was pulling a pint of beer, lager or real ale. But he found the time to give me a military salute - though I've never told him I was in Her Majesty's Armed Forces, because I never was – and another little wink, but not without a motion of the head in the direction of my unseeing, golden-haired companion. We crossed the bridge and walked alongside the Cam, then turned right through the short alleyway flanking The Riverbar restaurant. It was just a few strides now to my apartment development's principal entrance.

Once inside the apartment, I turned on the lights, took Diva's anorak and told her to make herself at home on the settee; though I certainly wasn't thinking too accurately in my phraseology. Saying I would be back in a jiffy, I went to my bedroom, dumped our coats on the double bed and relieved myself in the en suite. When I returned to the living room, Diva was actually at the window and slightly parting the curtains for a view.

"I can't really make out the river down below," she said, still peering outside. "But I can just about discern the silhouette of Magdalene's distinctive tall chimneys against the night sky."

"Yes," I said, as she turned back into the room and settled on the sofa, "the vista from the window is brilliant. It's what attracted me to this place. And so far as concerns the Fellows' Garden directly opposite, the aspect changes remarkably with the seasons…"

"Sounds great," Diva said.

"Would you like a drink or anything, before I sit down?" I asked.

"No, thanks… I'm fine, David," she replied, in a matter-of-fact tone. "Why don't you sit beside me here, and I'll try to answer the questions you posed at The Pickerel to the best of my ability and your satisfaction."

So I sat down next to her, but with a few modest inches between us.

"I know that I've been putting you through excruciating mental turmoil, David," she began. "Though I've got to admire the way you seem to be taking what must feel like a shocking intervention in your life. Or rather maybe dealing with the situation as if everything is normal… when, clearly, it isn't."

I nodded slowly, recognising her reasonably correct description of my current and extraordinary *limbo* condition.

"I can tell you, Diva… this isn't a situation easy to digest!"

She gazed at me with lovely blue eyes that seemed to absorb my angst, and the incipient despair of my coping mechanisms.

"Please forgive me, David, but let's hope we can do something good and worthwhile together."

I seemed to be developing into a habitually nodding individual, like one of those ubiquitous plastic toys.

"Well it would be a *good* and *worthwhile* start for you to answer my questions, Diva," I commented, perhaps a tad insensitively.

"Okay," she declared. "I'll start with the baby, if I may. I do appreciate my proposal must've come as a truly astonishing, if not outrageous proposition to you, David…"

"You're not kidding, mate." I interjected, thoughtlessly misusing words again.

"… Anyway," she continued, "I hoped it wouldn't be too appalling a prospect for you, especially once you heard and comprehended the rationale behind the request I'm putting forward…"

"Do tell me, please," I urged with an extreme curiosity.

"… In our Alpha Centauri neck of the Milky Way we've known about the planet Earth, our nearest solar neighbour, for a very long time. And now, as you're aware too, Earth is beginning to become interested in seeking to discover whether there are any habitable planets in our star system. For many thousands of years, we've lived peacefully and productively together in our segment of the galaxy. Sadly, we recognise that isn't, and never has been, the case so far as your inhabited planet is concerned. We know that it would take a literal age, and much more, for your astronauts ever to arrive in our zone of space. However, we do believe fundamentally in contingency planning. So the idea of being able to engage in a study of a human being from the embryo would be both appealing and beneficial to us. And you never know, in time to come it may be possible for us to help humanity in so many different and advantageous ways, not least in comprehending how to achieve, and live together in, a peaceful and productive world... and for us to do so benevolently, with sincerity and without instilling fear or apprehension. I don't want to exaggerate but, using terms adopted here, your world is sadly filled less with love than its antonym. The extent of depression and anxiety, apart from wars and destruction that exist in all of Earth's cultures and societies, is well beyond the pale. But rest assured, David, that the child will live a long, healthy, happy, loving and fruitful life."

Then Diva remained silent for a while, contemplating the facial expression that must've represented my determined efforts to inwardly absorb what she was saying to me.

"Okay," I said after a short while, "but what would you... I mean, the people of Alpha Centauri get out of assisting Earth in achieving what might be called a Golden Age?"

She focused witheringly on my eyes.

72

"That's a very good and logical question, David, and eloquently put. Please accept I'm not being patronising in any way when I say that. I don't suppose you would think much of my answer if I replied, in a word, *satisfaction*. So I'll add that helping Earth will also help us... and in several ways, too. Not least, in a prospective exchange of ideas that could see the development of our shared galaxy's huge potential."

I decided to change tack slightly.

"You're very beautiful, as you appear to me, Diva," I said softly. "Naturally, I'm not aware of your innate appearance in actuality, assuming it's in any ways different from what you're revealing to me now. Nor do I know precisely how old you are in, say, Earth years. And that, in turn, raises the fascinating question of life-span and longevity on planets in the Alpha Centauri system at this stage in *their* 'evolution', if I can use that terminology circumspectly. Having said all of that, I ask again... Why *me*?"

Diva requested me to let her have a cold drink, perhaps an orange juice or something like that.

"Of course," I said, getting up to head for the kitchen area. "I won't be two ticks... and I think I'll brew up an Americano for myself."

As I prepared our refreshments, I couldn't quite persuade myself that Diva would still be in evidence when I returned to the living room. But my half-expectation was, indeed, wrong... she *was* still there. Her head, eyes closed, rested against the sofa back. I positioned the juice and coffee on the accessible low table and sat down beside

73

her again. The slight sounds I was making nonetheless prompted Diva to become alert once more. She smiled, we took a sip of our respective drinks then replaced cup or glass and turned to face each other.

"So why have *I* been selected for this experiment, Diva?"

"It's not an experiment, David… I thought I'd explained, not in endless detail but adequately enough," she countered, though with an element of beguiling empathy.

I bunched my lips, aptly checked.

"There's so much hubris on Earth," she went on, "and I've been thinking your world couldn't be run without it now. But I'm not aiming that barbed thought at you, David. Maybe you would say you've just won first prize in the National Lottery. Or not! Perhaps you would believe this is happening all over your planet today. It isn't! And in that connection, you might be speculating that there's some sort of fertility crisis in our star system. There isn't! You might even be considering that your occasional, allegedly witty remark about having personally "come from Alpha Centauri" has had an unpredictably mind-boggling consequence… or otherwise. I could go on and on, but shall we just jump off this whirling philosophical carousel, and end good-humouredly by saying the last idea mentioned could be nearer to the truth or essence of this matter than you might imagine."

I nodded wistfully, hoping I wasn't blushing immaturely, feeling I was getting quite some ride for my money but quickly shaking off notions of gambling wins and children's fairground roundabouts.

We each took some more of our drinks, my attention possibly focusing excessively on this guest's agile physique.

"And if we... you know what, Diva... then I'll get the chance to travel back in time to medieval Cambridge?"

"Yes, I can confirm that's the deal on offer. Please don't see it as a bribe, or even as a kind of promotional incentive. We know you've been greatly smitten by your researches into the Jewish aspects of that period here in this world-renowned, university city. But also that you've been frustrated and somewhat discouraged by the lack of identifiably physical, as opposed to manuscript, evidence of the medieval community's existence. We just want to help make it come alive for you, David. That's not too nefarious, is it now, David?"

"No, Diva... it isn't," I commented equably. "I do realise that it would be difficult, if not impossible, for you to explain to yours truly how this will happen... and the technology, or whatever, involved in transporting me to the past. But I'm presuming the transition process will enable me to blend in with the people and circumstances I could be meeting or confronting including, importantly, language and communication, dress code and contemporary cultural habits."

Diva smiled, swivelled and tapped my arm.

"Absolutely so, David," she said very firmly, persuasively and reassuringly. "If you're ready, say in a day or two's time, we'll meet up at the spot where you would wish to reappear in *Cantabrigia*. But, if possible, can you let me know now the year and climactic season in which you would wish to manifest yourself there..."

"Spring of 1275," I stated instantly, "and I'm sorry for interrupting you so sharply. I've been thinking about this subject... no, not necessarily time travel... for quite some time now."

"No problem," Diva said, "and thanks for your very prompt and useful indication."

"I can show you on a map, and right now, precisely where I would like to be around seven hundred and fifty years ago," I added for good measure.

"Okay, David."

I went to the sideboard and withdrew from the top drawer a well-thumbed copy of the AA Street by Street maps of Cambridge, its environs and villages. I brought the slim volume to Diva, opened the paperback book to the Central Cambridge page and pointed to the place I had in mind. Carefully, she focused immediately beside my fingertip indication of All Saints Passage.

"That's exactly where I want to be standing, Diva," I said, aware in a dazzling moment of disbelief that I was agreeing implicitly to her sexual, baby-making proposition. "The spot I've chosen is just outside the lofty, side-entrance gates of St John's College Divinity School. The area beyond the gates was once the compact heartland of Cambridge's medieval Jewry area. Archaeologists refer to it as the 'St John's Triangle'. At one time, it was thought the site of this old Divinity School had held an ancient Jewish cemetery. But numerous skeletal finds, alongside artefacts such as crucifixes, at the location earlier this century proved irrefutably that it was a Christian burial ground during the

Middle-Ages. Nobody knows where the Jewish *House of Eternity* was situated. Whenever I'm walking through this narrow pedestrian passage, as a short cut between St John's Street and Sidney Street or vice versa, I generally stop in front of the Divinity School gates, peer through the tall railings and ignite my imagination…"

"Wonderful!" Diva exclaimed keenly, but this time resting the palm of a delicate hand on my shoulder. "I'll see you at the very location you've indicated at, I think, seven this coming Sunday morning. Bit early… but will that be alright for you, David?"

I hesitated for no more than a few seconds then nodded my assent. It seemed like a dream, but now I knew for certain that it wasn't. And I hoped it wouldn't turn into a nightmare.

"Please remember to bring your smart-phone with you," she supplemented her instructions in a kind of after-thought manner.

Diva took the AA city atlas from my hand and set it down on the coffee table. Leaning towards me, she clasped my cheeks in her silky smooth hands and kissed me lingeringly on the lips. Another of those spectral shivers transited my backbone as, somewhat hesitantly, I began slowly but surely to wrap her upper body in my arms. Soon afterwards, she detached herself from the embrace, stood up and grasped one of my hands to get me upstanding, too. And as if she'd visited my pad previously, Diva led me directly to my bedroom.

Eleven

I DON'T know what time exactly Diva departed my flat, but she was gone when I awoke from a dreamless slumber around three o'clock in the morning, according to my bedside, digital clock-radio. As I turned, feeling quite exhausted, onto my back with my head against the firm pillow, I could recall only a few details of our lengthy and diverse love-making that night. But the two episodes that seemed to be filling my mind at that unearthly hour occurred as we came into my bedroom some hours back. The first was when Diva undressed me, the second when she disrobed herself. What followed was more or less a mystery to me now as I lay on the bed, my pervading sense of fatigue affording some post-coital testimony to the vigour and endurance of our passion. But what I did know for a fact was that I'd fulfilled my part of the bargain, the consideration for it to be met by Diva in a day or so. I could feel my eyelids drooping, and a kind of wooziness coming over me; so I rolled onto my side and flattened a cheek against my barely compliant pillow. The last and almost desperately light-headed thought, before I drifted into the worse nightmare of my life, formed itself into a momentous question: How the hell will I prepare for my forthcoming journey to *Cantabrigia*?

Emotionally speaking, it's not easy to describe the indescribable, particularly if one is personally involved. And even if the scenario, which cannot readily be put into words, has played out in a horrific night vision that, nevertheless, has an amazingly heartening context.

My first reminiscence is of being led by two people into a large, clinically white-walled room. At its centre stands what looks like the table, under powerful arc-lights, at which surgical procedures are performed. Was this a hospital operating theatre? I wasn't sure about the answer, as the two individuals - maybe a pair of nurses, I wondered - in matching white overalls, headgear, face-masks, gloves and slip-ons sit me down on a chair at a small side-table and facing a mirror affixed above it. Then both of them leave me all by myself in the spacious white chamber. After their departure I gaze at my reflection, surprised to note that I'm dressed similarly to my former escorts. I couldn't gather their gender; and they hadn't spoken to each other so as to give me a, possibly garbled, clue. And for that matter, I wouldn't have been able to identify my own sex, had I not known it, merely by looking into the mirror. But what *am* I doing here? I ask myself, at least twice, each time feeling more terrified. Quite justified too, I thought; unless I was about to be interviewed for the kind of job my two former guardians were doing.

Then I hear the door opening and another person entering the room, with its white-tiled floor and little in the way of furniture, apart from the large and small tables. I can't fail to acknowledge that the individual, now steadily approaching me, is likewise garbed totally in white. Sitting down beside me, this one removes the facemask. I'm so glad and relieved to see that it's Diva. She smiles, leans across the table, unties and removes my own facemask. I glance at my reflection and am a trifle unsure about what I'm viewing exactly. It's obviously my face, but that part that I couldn't see previously appears to be spread with a gooey brown substance. I'm in the process of lifting a hand to touch the sticky-looking stuff, when Diva quickly grasps my rising digits.

"Please don't do that, David," she advises. "It's not irritating is it?"

"Not in a physical sense," I reply, reaching up again.

Once more she stops me sharply, and looks worryingly serious as she does so.

"I must ask you not to touch your face, David. If you try once more, I'll need to ask my colleagues to restrain your hands for the time being."

And now I'm taking on my own very concerned expression.

"May I ask why, Diva?"

"Yes… you may ask, of course," she says with a frown, and utters nothing further on the subject at that juncture.

Then she gets up, walks to the table in the middle of the room and waits there. A few moments later, another fully white-smocked personage, but minus a mask, enters the chamber and begins talking with my so-called friend. After some minutes, she returns to my table and sits herself down.

"I need to explain something to you, David," she says. "I don't wish to distress you in any way, and I hope you'll understand this. A procedure is going to be performed on you in a short while. I would add that you should feel no pain whatsoever. And to that end, although you'll remain conscious, a certain liquid will be dispensed into your mouth. Do swash it around and swallow before you're placed on the operating table."

"Please tell me what all this is in aid of, Diva?" I ask tremblingly. "Am I ill?"

Diva shakes her head.

"No, you're not ill… at least not in the sense I believe you mean."

"In what sense am I sick, then?"

Diva touches my arm sympathetically.

"It's a long saga, David, but I'll need to be brief and succinct," she begins. "An extremely long time ago, the planetary inhabitants of Alpha Centauri were very much confronted by the same sorts of endless troubles that afflict those living on Earth today… war, terrorism, wanton destruction, widespread violent crime of all kinds, rape and sexual abuse of women and children, drugs-induced carnage and robbery, suicidal depression. And just as on your world today, the list could go on and on. Many thousands of years ago, the people of our star system enjoyed playing electronic games similar to the ones your young folk, even adults, like participating in prolifically on Earth nowadays. The machines you use aren't too different from those in our far distant past, including those that engage with a virtual reality or VR headset…"

Diva pauses briefly. I was becoming hooked on what she was telling me.

"… Then one of our great ancient philosopher-scientists had a startlingly unique and creative inspiration," she continues. "After much reflection on his fantastic notion, he came to the astonishing conclusion that we weren't seeing our worlds as they had been intended originally. The reason was because, over time, our visages had evolved in such a way as to become virtual reality headsets. So, he contended, the VR sets, which in that far off era in the Alpha Centauri system had recently been invented, were nothing new. They had already existed in the form of our facial features or countenance. When you wore a VR headset, you could see, hear and, in some of our then advanced models, even smell and touch whatever was apparent within the 360-degree ambit of the contraption strapped around your cranium…"

This was becoming so much more fascinating. But where was it all leading?

"After many centuries of, and if I can put it in this accessible way, humanitarian research and experimentation, our scientists were agreed that peeling off the face would enable us to see, to comprehend and to act, as had always been intended. Initially, it was necessary to perform what you might possibly refer to as ritual surgery to achieve the aims. And such became almost traditional, a significant part of the developing culture in our society. Over millennia, and using Earth terminology to make it easier for you to grasp, a mutating genetic and evolutionary process took place. And gradually that progression, which was partially engineered, avoided the necessity to carry out any facial procedures whatsoever…"

Now, as I look in the direction of the operating table, maybe I'm beginning to understand where all this was leading; and the sudden realisation is mind-numbingly horrifying. I consider running away. But to where would I flee, even assuming that I can escape? I don't actually know where I'm situated! Maybe on a mother-ship, I ponder… then, unbelievably relevant perhaps for this nightmare, I think of a pregnant Diva. Two characters - possibly the same ones as previously - enter the room and walk purposefully towards me. This is it, I ponder unnervingly. They each take hold, firmly though not at all harshly, of one of my arms; and, as Diva watches quietly, they accompany me to the light-flooded, surgery table; and there we wait.

In a mere second or two a tall, white-clad and masked person enters the theatre and approaches me, clutching a kind of syringe in one hand. As my two guards grasp me securely but gently, the third colleague raises this device - which looks to contain a dull red liquid - and with the fingers of a white-gloved hand starts to open my mouth. When it's fully open… I scream! And I continue to shriek, until I awaken in my bed with a severe case of the shakes.

Twelve

A SHORT while after composing myself - though my breathing hadn't fully returned to normality yet - I couldn't quite believe my OTT reaction on waking from the peeling-face, VR nightmare. Then again, I meditated, it was the most outlandish and terrifying vision I've ever experienced. But it was only a dream, after all. I glanced at the bedside clock and noted it was just after seven. I got up, a tad unsteadily I felt, and drifted into the kitchen. Virtually lunging for the coffee machine, I turned it on, grabbed a cup and saucer from the nearest cupboard and brewed a triple espresso, no less. I carried it to the dining table, rather than the settee, just in case I fell again into the possibly even more horrendously embracing arms of *Morphia*. I sat down in a reasonably balanced way and reclined against the chair back, still gripping my strong coffee; and maybe aptly remembering some other, less horrific but still dreamily embracing arms of the last night. I savoured some of the refreshingly hot black, authentically crema-topped and full-bodied liquid; and my mind recalled - somewhat lasciviously for that premature phase of the morning, I thought - the taste of another appetisingly hot, but blonde and full-bodied entity. I shook my head a bit too vigorously; doubtless I was seeking to disperse from its shadowy recesses my entangling, night-time cobwebs of shocking incredulity.

Then a peculiar notion, at least for me, crept into my thought network. I felt, quite strongly in fact, that I needed to attend synagogue this Saturday… this Sabbath morning; though I couldn't quite resolve what I meant by *needed*. Anyway, there was plenty of time to get organised, I reassured myself. The service wouldn't commence until around nine-thirty; and the Jewish house of worship was a mere five-minute stroll, if that, from the flat. I relaxed for a while on the sofa, finishing off my comforting tall espresso and trying my level best not to think… about anything. Like my early morning coffee, I found, that was a *tall* order. Anyhow, after my 20-minute R and R effort, or rather failure, I left the crockery in a washing-up basin by the sink. Not really fancying anything to eat, I went immediately to the en suite for a shower, my final wake-up call before dressing in a dark blue suit, white shirt, smartly striped tie and shiny black, pointy brogues. Not everyone, whether permanent resident or student member of the congregation, would be attiring themselves so formally. But that's the way I liked to don myself for my rare annual attendances; and, I supposed, the sartorial choice was influenced by my father's similar custom; and he'd been an infrequent synagogue attendee, too.

I arrived at the synagogue about 15 minutes into the service. The compact, single-storey edifice dates back to 1937, stands away from the narrow road and is fronted by a part-paved, part-planted forecourt. It's quite a close neighbour to old St Clement's Church beside Bridge Street. Yesteryear, its parish extended to Quayside and harboured almost 40 inns, taverns and hostelries, with a large brewery in the beery bargain. Even the synagogue was built on the site of a one-time public house, known as the Nine Pins.

Whenever entering the precinct, the single-storey edifice always reminded me of a large detached bungalow. But the signs affixed to its red-brick façade indicated the nature of the building; one of them noting it served also as a student centre. I parked my coat on a hook in the corridor, put on my *kippah* or skull-cap and entered the orthodox prayer room. There was seating in two sections - one for men, the other for women – with wooden panels stretching the length between them. I picked up a *Siddur*, the relevant daily prayer book, and a *Chumash*, containing the Pentateuch or Five Books of Moses starting with Genesis, from the bookcase close inside the entrance. I selected a white woollen, black-striped and fringed *tallit* or prayer shawl from a nearby box then quietly chose a chair in the rearmost of three rows spread around the men's area. A student was leading prayers from a desk facing the now closed *Aron HaKodesh* or Ark, which contains mantled and accoutred manuscript Torah scrolls bearing the Pentateuch. I placed the *tallit* around my shoulders, whilst reciting the short blessing preceding that action, then sat down. Looking about me briefly before opening my prayer book, I could see that I just made up a *minyan*, the 10-man quorum required for a comprehensive service. The rabbi, a couple of resident stalwarts with the rest students were present currently, together with a few female undergraduates in the women's sector. As the service continued across its various stages, the numbers would increase; as they did that morning to about 40 or so worshippers. During Term-time, as now, services would be organised by the students.

I started perusing my book and, although I could read Hebrew, I hastened through the English translation in an attempt to catch up with the fast-moving, student prayer-leader. When we reached a sort of natural break before the next student took over, I was approached by one of the staunch members of the community. We exchanged a *Shabbat shalom*, to wish each other a peaceful Sabbath, plus the inevitable: *Long-time no see, and how are you?* Then he enquired, serious-faced, whether I had a *Yahrzeit*, the anniversary of the loss of a parent, spouse or other close relative for whom I would wish to recite the special *Kaddish*, a memorial prayer. I shook my head, knowing that he was asking the question because of my rare attendances. Had my answer been positive, he would've passed the information to the current student *gabbai* or warden, who would likely give me an *aliyah*. This would amount to calling me to the *bimah*, the main reading desk facing the Ark, to say or possibly intone the requisite blessings before and after the recitation of a portion from that Shabbat's *sedra*, or weekly Reading of the Law, from the sacred *Sefer Torah* scroll.

As it happened, I was given an *aliyah* in any event; and I was grateful for the enquiring stalwart's doubtless mention to the student *gabbai* that he should afford me one. I believed it was the opportunity I desperately *needed*, recalling fleetingly the word from my thoughts of earlier that morning. Soon the time would come for my call-up. The Ark was opened and a *Sefer* was carried from it to be paraded around the men's section. Then the scroll's mantle and silver adornments were removed; it was laid level on the reading desk, and rolled open by its wooden poles to that week's *sedra*. I was next to be given an *aliyah* after a *Cohen* and a *Levi* - representing the High Priest and the priestly class in the Jerusalem Temple of ancient times - were summoned successively to the *bimah*. After reciting the initial blessing, and as the portion was *leyned* or recited by the student reader, I held tightly to the lower protruding end of the *Sefer's* nearest wooden rod and said silently what I felt *needed* to be said. After that, and having received the customary blessing from the *gabbai*, I waited until the next and final call-up was completed then returned to my seat.

At that moment, I recognised a tall and formally suited, middle-aged man, another normally twice-yearly attendee, who was just entering the room. I knew from past conversations that he lived with his wife in one of Cambridge's satellite villages; and he would've driven to the synagogue that morning. He took a couple of books from the shelf and a *tallit*, looked to see where he might conveniently seat himself, spotted the vacant chair next to me, waved vaguely and sidled his way along the row. After donning the prayer shawl, he sat down. We exchanged a low-voiced *Shabbat shalom* and a few more quiet words that informed me *he* actually had a *Yahrzeit* that day, for his late mother. His tardiness meant he missed receiving an *aliyah*. Towards the end of the service, however, he was asked to open the Ark for the singing - by a congregant's young son - of *Anim Zemirot*, a Song of Glory. At the appropriate junctures during the final stage of the service, we all stood to respond accordingly as he recited the special *Kaddish* in memory of his mother.

After the student society and communal announcements and the shared trilling of *Adon Olam*, a song in praise of the Almighty, all of us shuffled into the synagogue's hall fronting the kitchen area. Here we partook of *Kiddush* refreshments after the traditional blessing over a goblet filled to the brim with the red wine of sanctification. Holding a tot of malt whisky in one hand and a fried fish-ball in the other, I had a few casual words with one or two of the permanent residents I knew reasonably well. The ambience had a chattering buzz to it, emanating especially from the small groups of male and female students. But for reasons I appreciated well enough, I didn't feel quite in the conducive mood to engage fully with the pleasant atmosphere.

I was standing alone when my 'village acquaintance' approached me through the knots of residents and students milling around the food-topped, white paper cloth-covered tables.

"You look a bit down," he said. "I hope everything's alright with you."

I nodded.

"Yes, I'm fine… but thanks for asking," I responded.

"Hope you and your wife are okay, too."

"We're doing well, thanks."

"Oh, and I wish you a Long Life," I added the traditional words said to someone saying *Kaddish* for a departed loved one.

"Thanks… it's now ten years since my mother passed away, may her dear soul rest in eternal peace."

I nodded again.

"*L'Chaim*… To life," I uttered rather than declared.

He reciprocated the toast, looking at me like he was rather concerned at my expression, and we swallowed what little was left of our Scotch.

"Look," he said, "if we would finish here fairly early, as we have done, I was going to have a short coffee break in town before driving back home. Would you care to join me?"

I thought for a moment, looked at my wristwatch, noted it wasn't yet 11:30 and concluded that I didn't have anything better to do than prepare myself for a journey across virtually 800 years to medieval Cambridge very early the next day.

"Okay, let's go get a caffeine injection," I agreed, knowing full well that an orthodox Jewish person wouldn't be doing such on the Sabbath.

We collected our coats from the hallway's row of hooks and exited the building. The coffee route took us past the pubs and restaurants along Bridge Street and across the road at the Romanesque, 12th century and so-called Round Church to St John's Street. We walked at a pace past the college, after which the road is named, and the beautifully restored and refurbished Old Divinity School flanking a small, tree-edged triangle of open land where the church of All Saints in the Jewry once stood. The ancient church, long demolished, was now memorialised by a lofty stone cross; and its erstwhile site used as a regular handicrafts market on Saturdays.

We continued along Trinity Street, hardly saying a word, passing Trinity College and then Gonville and Caius. We slowed down just before the venerable Great St Mary's, the university church facing Senate House and possessing wonderful panoramic views across the city and environs from the top of its tower. Our apparent destination, Caffè Nero, was just a few metres ahead on tourist-cluttered King's Parade and opposite the distinctive, visitor-popular King's College and Chapel.

It was really busy in the coffee shop, with some Chinese customers even sitting at the couple of alfresco tables on the pavement in the cool sunshine. We ordered and paid in coin of the realm for our coffees separately, I for my black Americano and he for his flat white; and which was yet another obvious indicator of our non-orthodox faith-status. Miraculously, and a bit further into the café's bustling interior, we managed to find a couple of available chairs at a table just vacated by more tourists from the People's Republic. We sat down amid the enclosing buzz and babble, and could barely hear ourselves opening a conversation. So mutually acquiescent in saving our voices for the time being, we sat back mutely and took some of our starkly different, hot-beverage fancies.

"Don't think I've seen you for about a year, mm… at least since last *Yom Kippur,*" my fellow infrequent synagogue attendee recollected aloud all of a sudden.

"I think you're probably right, my good friend," I replied, struggling to remember his first name; and thinking he may've been doing likewise, with both of us unwilling to ask embarrassingly for a reminder. I was certain his recall was accurate about my last High Holyday attendance, on the Day of Atonement, the Jewish calendar's most sacred day of praying and fasting.

"So what's news?" he enquired, indulgently licking some frothy white overlap on his cup's brim. "If you don't mind me saying so, you've been looking more than a little preoccupied this morning… I hope everything's alright with you."

Well, there was one particularly mind-blowing piece of news that I was definitely not planning to tell him about. But it did seem like I should say something. So I did, if only to satisfy him and keep the conversation going.

"The other day, my son… I think you may know Michael's based in New York… told me that he's been seeing this woman for a while now, and that it's becoming a serious relationship…"

"Is a good luck wish of *Mazeltov* due yet?" my wide-eyed companion interrupted with emphasis on the congratulatory word.

"Not yet."

"So are you happy about this, and is she Jewish?" he

delved, adding: "Sorry for being nosey, but I understand the inter-marriage rate in the States these days has almost topped fifty percent."

"Yes, as it happens she *is* Jewish… and there's no need to apologise," I replied, swallowing some of my coffee. "And, just like my boy, she's apparently also an atheist…"

He raised his greying, bushy eyebrows

"Is that what's troubling you?" he asked.

"Why should it?" I responded with another question; very Jewish, I thought in the instant, for a not very Jewish individual like me.

"I don't know," he said, a trifle crestfallen. "I just wondered… sorry."

"No need to be," I said sincerely. "I'm a believer, but I've never quite got along with organised religious ritual. So I wasn't really a good Jewish faith exemplar to my son from the beginning. And, of course, my long-standing religious motivation, or rather the lack of it, was the reason my wife and I parted ways a while back now… My spouse told me one day that she'd seen the light, bright and clear. But I could just about perceive it as a kind of tiny and wobbly star."

My acquaintance was nodding slowly, with a sombre look creasing his long face.

"Sorry to have made you dredge up all this…" he said, sounding sorrowful.

I didn't want him to feel bad, especially as he had *Yahrzeit* for his mother that day.

"Don't concern yourself… I'm well over these matters

now," I offered the guy, glad in a strange way that I was being distracted from other, more overwhelming thoughts loitering in my mind. "And my son must do whatever makes him content with his life… if *he's* happy then *I'm* happy, though I'm not at all certain how his mother will be taking the news."

He took a peep at his watch, finished off the remains of his awfully milky coffee and said he had to get back home.

"It was good seeing you again," he said, standing up and smiling. "And there's no need for you to leave, unless you want to… finish your coffee in peace now."

On that final note, I raised a hand in farewell and he left.

I lingered for a while longer, pondering our chat and the conversation that we never could've had. Out of the corner of my eye I saw a couple of young Chinese girls, with their recently acquired coffees, eyeing my half-abandoned little table with some envious and acquisitive glances. I drained the remnant of black liquid in my cup, and got up to go. Virtually quicker than instantaneously, the pair of pretty young ladies seized the two chairs with revolutionary zeal then grinned winningly at me. I kind of saluted them then meandered my way out to the sun-splashed street.

Thirteen

ON getting back to the flat, I made myself another Americano and slumped onto the sofa without spilling it. The weather had turned colder that Saturday afternoon; the city centre areas were thinning out of shoppers; the mostly Chinese, selfie-taking tourists appeared to be a scarcer commodity, at least on the streets as opposed to monopolising the coffee shops; and the rough-sleeping homeless were hardly in evidence in doorways alongside retail outlets and banks. As I grasped the warmth of my coffee cup, I wondered for a moment how freezing it might be when I met with Diva at All Saints Passage the next morning at seven o'clock. Just in case Siberia decided to send one of its 'beasts from the east' blizzards overnight, I proposed to bundle myself into a thick overcoat, woolly hat, multi-wrap scarf, snug leather gloves and manly ankle-boots. Who knew what the local climate had been like in the spring of 1275?

And who knew anything in meticulously detailed fact? I'd read widely about the Jewish community in medieval Cambridge; but the would-be-useful-to-know minutiae of everyday living had been conspicuous by its absence from my source material. I couldn't be certain whether Diva had some kind of brief seminar scheduled in for me before my departure on the morrow. But I needed to assume that, by means of whatever incomprehensibly advanced technological method employed to time transfer me, I wouldn't be catastrophically out of place in my new environment, whether physically or psychologically. And whether in terms of clothing and corporeal appearance, currency matters, plausible explanations for my presence as a stranger in the midst, appropriate back-story and authentic personal nomenclature, communicable language, food and drink acceptability... digestion-wise; as well as comprehension of surroundings and ambience in the broadest possible sense... and whatever the priorities might be.

Yet another tall order, I mused, while taking a sip of my piping caffeine; though there was little, if anything, I myself could do now by way of contingency planning. I was beginning to realise just how critically dependent I would be on Diva and her Alpha Centauri scientists. Though I imagined there could be a need also for much learning on the job, so to speak. The necessity for a fundamental basis of total mental comfort, in my forthcoming and extraordinarily novel milieu, seemed self-evident as a prerequisite for a meaningful sojourn in *Cantabrigia*.

During my many years of journalistic globetrotting, I'd met and had dialogue with people from, as they say, all walks of life... and really dreadful as well as positively marvellous people. I considered my communication skills, including a facility with certain languages such as French and German, often aided my efforts substantially. But I was being forced to accept that what I might be confronting, in raw terms, could be fairly disastrous potentially. Though as something of an adventurer, I had to bear in mind the compelling and, to me at least, more than balancing prospect of accomplishing a gob-smacking objective not yet, if ever, achievable by anyone on Earth. In that connect, there was no contest. Whatever the outcome, there wasn't a superlative I could think of that, even adequately, could've described the remarkable combination of excitement and mind-numbing apprehension that I was feeling.

The fearful part of this highly equivocal mixture compelled me to consider putting in a long-distance call to Michael before my, time-travel-wise, long-distance trip; and despite having spoken to him so recently. But quite startlingly, let alone coincidentally at that very instance, my landline phone rang. It was my son, calling from the Big Apple… and the second time within a couple of days. Absolutely unheard of from him! On quick reflection, however, I would've come out no better in contact terms. I just felt the urgent need to be as close to my boy as I could that Saturday afternoon. My first, and quite exclamatory, words to him were not, "I went to synagogue for the Shabbat morning service today!"… but rather "Great minds think alike, Michael!"

"Why do you say that, Dad?"

It felt really good to hear my son's voice again, and so soon.

"Well, I was right on the point of phoning you, son."

97

"Why, Dad? We spoke only the other day."

I managed a self-inflicted little sneer.

"But I could say the same to you, Michael."

It was a pity we weren't on Skype or video-phone. I might've noticed the look of resignation on his anachronistically bearded face.

"So what is it you want to tell me, Dad?"

"No, son... you go first," I urged. "You rang me, remember?"

"Just about, Dad... anyway, I don't know about yours but mine's good news for you, I think... no, I know so."

What's this all about, I mulled in the instant.

"I'm all ears, Michael," I quipped. "Go ahead."

"Like you, Dad, I'm going to be... a Dad!" my son said effervescently.

"What was that you said?" I asked unnecessarily, adding for foolish good measure: "Our line may be going a bit funny."

"I'm going to be a father!" he declared again, but this time with a disproportionate increase in voice projection.

"That's what I thought you said... So why didn't you mention this when we spoke last?"

There was a slight pause. Maybe a pregnant one, I pondered whimsically. I couldn't help thinking of my recently requested frolic with Diva. Conception seemed to be becoming all the rage these days. But then I couldn't conjure up even the merest of smiles.

"We learned about it only a few hours ago... I phoned you as soon as I could."

"*Mazeltov*, son!" I uttered cheerily.

"Yeah... thanks, Dad. So why were you about to call me?"

"I must be psychic," I replied, yet believing the more apt *bon mot* might've been *psychotic*.

I heard the hint of a chuckle at the New York end. I really couldn't match it.

"No special reason, Michael," I went on. "I just wanted to hear your voice. Guess I was feeling a bit lonely and isolated all of a sudden.

"Really sorry to hear that, Dad," he responded, sounding overtly empathetic. "But I hope my announcement has bucked you up. In fact, I can add that the mother-to-be and I are now planning to get hitched..."

"Wonderful," I commented, again unsure whether I was adopting the most credible adjective and tone of voice. "Do keep me informed."

"Of course, Dad... but I've got to love and leave you now. Bye!"

"Bye, Michael... Take care," I signed off, again not knowing the full and precise import of my corresponding leave-taking; but wondering, in the circumstances, whether I should've been addressing the last couple of words to myself.

I can't recall exactly how I managed to get through the remainder of that waking day. But I do recollect going to bed not that long after a snack supper, around eight o'clock, and setting the bedside alarm for five the next morning. There was nothing more I could've done by way of groundwork, anyway. All would now be in Diva's hopefully expert hands.

Before closing my eyes and drifting off finally, I recalled her important request for me to bring along my smart-phone - which I would charge, probably nonsensically, when awoken - to our now imminent and mind-shattering assignation.

Fourteen

I SET my alarm clock volume at its highest ever level for a wake-up call, so maybe I shouldn't have been so agitatedly startled when I was awakened by the shrieking peal of resounding decibels. I feared it would rouse the entire building's, if not the city's, other slumbering residents that lie-in Sunday's wintry-feel, early morning. I double-checked the timer's digital display, just to assure myself on this personally, and literally, historic day that the numbers coincided accurately with my projected hour of waking. Happily or otherwise, I thought – and perhaps unduly half-pessimistically – they did in fact. I dragged myself from beneath the cosily warm duvet and into the en suite. Ablutions completed in good order, including my customary shower, I was refreshed enough to locate the kitchen space, slide out my machine and brew up a large black Americano - for my "Keep Calm You're In Cambridge" embossed mug - with two 'intense-rated' coffee pods. Doubtless, it would be the last one I would make or drink for however long the duration; although, I believed, a week or so might be sufficient to get the flavour of *Cantabrigia*.

I didn't want anything to eat, other than a chocolate

wafer biscuit; and I was a little surprised to be harbouring an appetite even for that usually favoured, coffee-accompaniment. I drank my steaming mug-full at the table, my mind a helter-skelter of rapidly revolving notions. It would take me little more than five minutes or so to walk to the meeting spot agreed with Diva, so I had a bit of time to spare. But after downing my coffee before it got stewed, I couldn't sit still any longer; so I washed up, put the mug and teaspoon away and repaired to my bedroom to get dressed.

There was no change of intent from my earlier planned, winter attire; and in which I would begin my time travel exploits. I held only the merest suggestion of an idea, from my recall of some medieval English garb illustrations, of what I could be wearing on arrival at my projected destination. Could be that, being spring-time when I landed in the year 1275, I would be togged up in outer-garments comprised basically of a kind of woollen tunic, linen trousers of a sort, hosiery and leather footwear of some sort.

Before leaving the apartment and locking the front door, I made sure that all water taps were turned to neutral, all electrical and other appliances and plugs were switched off and non-operational and the three sets of window curtains were drawn. It was around six-forty, slightly ahead of timing, when I walked past the synagogue and turned left onto Bridge Street. The tower of St John's College chapel loomed up, on the opposite side of the road, against the backcloth of an uncannily silver-blue sky. Being quite early on a Sunday morning, I didn't expect to see many other pedestrians, let alone vehicles of the two or four wheeled kind; and, indeed, I didn't notice any people wandering about. I felt sure that a normally deserted Cambridge on this day, and at this hour, would've motivated Diva to elect such circumstances for our vital rendezvous. I crossed the intersection at the Round Church and continued along St John's Street.

When I reached the open space where All Saints in the Jewry had stood, until its demolition in 1865, my now *intimate* friend didn't appear to have arrived as yet; though, of course, she could've made herself temporarily invisible to my naked eye. Feeling like I was in a city eerily devoid of people, I entered through the open gate in the site's boundary railings, which were partially hung with college, student and commercial notices of upcoming cultural and other events in the town. I walked towards the centred stone cross - atop its loftily slender and four-sided, stepped stone pedestal – ringed by the still wintry, bare-branched trees. One etched face of the plinth informs its readers that the cross not only marks the old medieval church; but also commemorates the literary men, benefactors and other parishioners whose names are inscribed on the other three sides of the monument.

As I moved gradually around the stonework, I perceived that the open ground was bathed in a reflection of the silvery-blue light I first noticed radiating from the heavens above St John's chapel. Peering about, I could see not only its tower rising above the gorgeously elaborate masonry and redbrick façade of the Old Divinity School; but also the substantial, whitish edifice of Trinity College Chapel just across the street. Suddenly, I felt a peculiar and atmospheric sensation that I was steeped in an all-embracing Christianity. Just as I emerged from one side of the dedicatory cross, I spotted Diva; a swiftly snatched glimpse of my wristwatch dial advised me she was right on the button, time-wise. I really couldn't have missed her; yet again, she was favouring the omnipresent red anorak. I was beginning to wonder whether it possessed some extraterrestrial significance. Diva was gazing at me over her shoulder, as she sat on a wooden bench facing the entrance to the Divinity School on one leg of All Saints Passage.

Diva waved welcomingly then beckoned me with the same hand. I hastened to circuit the testimonial monument and sat down beside her. She turned, leaned forward and planted a tender little kiss on my cheek. I smiled, feeling an all-pervading ambiguity of platonic-cum-sexual emotions. She returned my little beam; but an instant later, her expression changed.

"Let me have your mobile phone, David," she said, and quite earnestly. "I need to perform some adjustments to enable you to communicate with me when necessary. Sorry, but you won't be able to use it for any other purpose."

"Okay, Diva," I responded, maybe noting that her seemingly forceful attitude was more in keeping now with what was soon to happen to me. "I understand."

I opened my topcoat, lifted my pullover and undid

a couple of shirt buttons. Finally, I withdrew the smart-phone from a zipped pocket in the security belt fastened around my body, handed it to her and re-wrapped myself quickly before getting chilled to the bone.

Diva turned her back on me; but just a moment or two later was facing me again.

"All done, David... so don't lose it," she advised, her eyes piercing into mine. "Keep it turned off... you'll be in direct contact with me immediately you switch it on. No need to input any numbers, or whatever. And don't worry about it requiring any juice, if you get my drift. All understood, David?"

Inwardly, I ruminated on her words for a few seconds then nodded my confirmation of comprehension. She handed back the gadget that - needless to state, I considered - could literally mean the world to me; and I re-stowed the phone close to my heart.

"I know you've been thinking, and in some commendable detail, about all the necessities of your imminent expedition back to thirteenth century Cambridge," she went on in similar tonal vein. "All I need say, David, is you're fully on the right thinking track, from attire to communication and most things between. Naturally, as you've speculated, there will also be some requisite learning on the job, so far as concerns the people you'll be coming across and various aspects of your new environment. There's no need to worry... everything that needs to be provided for you, will be provided. Needless to say, you'll have to let me know when you wish to return to the twenty-first century. Please be aware that I'm not proposing to initiate any contact with you in any way. If I actually want to do so for any reason, then you'll know about it."

I sighed deeply, the only words then escaping my dry lips being:

"Thanks for everything, Diva."

"No problem, David," she said and I hoped, most sincerely and with a convincing sense of self-preservation, that she was right.

"So what happens now?" I enquired with the bravest face I could muster.

Diva took my hand.

"We'll now go to the spot which you identified as the specific place where you would wish to materialise in the year 1275..." she replied, replete with the self-assurance that my now tremulous nerve fibres were telling me I lacked; unless, of course, they were being affected by the pinching nippiness in the air. It was a real wonder to me that I could still think of a vaguely amusing line.

"I've done something else to your smart-phone, David," Diva continued. "It's important regarding your return trip in, I believe, a week or thereabouts. But, again, my adjustments would be inexplicable to you."

With that, Diva stood up and brought me to an upright position, too. I glanced rapidly at my time-piece – which I guessed would vanish before I attained *Cantabrigia* - and saw, with some amazement, that we'd been conversing for only a couple of minutes. I supposed the subject-matter just made it seem like hours. Still holding my hand, she led me across the park-like area and through the gateway. Close together we turned right; then, after a few metres, right again into All Saints Passage.

Soon after passing the stone-arched entrance doors to the Old Divinity School, we stopped in front of its lofty, decoratively fashioned and gated iron railings. Through these tall bars could be seen an open area progressing between the buildings comprising the School. In gold lettering above the ornate, lock-secured gateway and below a fixed crest were the words: "St John's College 1511 – 2011". Immediately underneath them was etched the name, "Quincentennial Gate".

Diva dropped my hand lightly then proceeded to physically face me towards the gate. Next, she walked resolutely behind me.

"Close your eyes, David," she whispered into my right ear. "Place your arms straight down at your sides and keep them there…"

Immediately, I did as I was told.

"I'm now going to place an index finger on each of your temples," she said, again very quietly. "I'm telling you so you won't be surprised and open your eyes. Okay, David?"

"Okay, Diva," I responded, matching her low volume level.

My almost final thought was how spectacularly astounding and incredibly mind-boggling it was for me to be standing where I was; and for the journeying motivation

I was there. In the final analysis, it was all so hugely stunning to be *in situ* because of the most unbelievable, so far half-implemented arrangement of all time.

The last things I felt and heard was a velvety fingertip, soothingly tactile, on each side of my forehead, and a silky voice caressingly close to my right ear.

"Bon voyage, David…"

Fifteen

WHEN I opened my eyes, I was surprised not to be seeing what I was half-expecting to see. Directly ahead of me was the sky… bright, light blue and daubed with billowing white clouds. It took quite a while to distract myself from a virtually hypnotic gazing towards the heavens; and to begin thinking straight about where I was actually situated. Naturally, I'd hoped to be somewhere around *Cantabrigia's* or medieval Cambridge's old Jewry location; and at an edge of the so-called St John's Triangle where I'd been standing, eyes tight shut, when Diva sent me packing back to the year 1275. Had something gone wrong with her Alpha Centauri, time-travel navigation system, whether regarding place or even time or possibly both? Am I not where I was supposed to be? I asked myself. I was becoming more than a little perturbed about my current space-time warp, or whatever, destination. And Einstein wasn't around to help me. I did begin to shiver a tad, despite noting on my arrival that the air around me felt comfortably warm and definitely spring-like.

As an avid reader of books about the Second World War, I only understood partially why the notion of wartime parachute drops entered my head suddenly. The rationale was doubtless the fact that, not infrequently, the airborne troops were despatched unintentionally from their aircraft to land dangerously close to, and sometimes well behind, enemy lines and miles from the planned drop zones. So I couldn't help but reflect, for a moment or two, on whether something akin to that kind of perilous fiasco had just happened to me. And in spite of the advanced technology available to Diva and, I supposed, my senior partner in space-time.

Somehow I extracted myself from this bemused state of mesmerism, and looked around in a more consciously focused manner. Lowering my eyes to a new field of vision at once assisted in broadly verifying my physical location. The panoramic vista clearly dictated that I was situated on a hill overlooking an oval-shaped town displaying many greenswards and ringed by fields, with some woodland, to the horizon. There was also a sun-dappled river, curving gently around the town and fairly proximate to my end of the relatively built-up locale. I couldn't identify, anywhere near perfectly, the nature and make-up of all the buildings spreading before and below me. The comparatively compact, urbanised area - at least from my present height above the surrounding land level - appeared to be dotted with several church spires, which alone were indicative of a reasonably sizeable, quite well-to-do and religion-inclined population.

Then waves of reverberating sounds, of what undoubtedly were the peals of church bells, rose up to me from several belfry towers. Accordingly, I became alerted evidentially to the fact that I was present on a Sunday morning; and that I was hearing the town's campanologists summoning its Christian faithful to Mass. Now I was beginning to realise for certain - knowing 21st century Cambridge well, and having studied conjectured diagrammatic plans of the city's medieval layout and architectural content – that I was, indeed, at my intended target. Though not quite precisely, I was thinking. I could even name some of the churches observable from my elevated position. On my side of the river was St Giles and St Peter's... on the far side, St Clements and St Sepulchre's, that would become known as the Round Church, also the one I knew as All Saints in the Jewry and, not that far beyond it, Great St Mary's and others.

That thought process awakened me at last to my immediate locality. I turned and registered the round battlement towers and defensive curtain walls of a castle. Fairly quickly, I concluded this was the Norman motte-and-bailey designed fortress erected by William the Conqueror in 1068, a couple of years after his successful invasion of Anglo-Saxon England. That citadel was a largely wood-constructed palisade of a stronghold in this countryside-commanding position. At an even earlier time, the Romans had built a walled and ditched fort and settlement on and around the heights of what, much later, became known as Castle Mound or Castle Hill. And long before the time of post-modern Cambridge, from whence I'd journeyed, evidence of all these military bastions had disappeared, save for some earthworks exposed by teams of archaeologists.

My rapid review of this historic structure – that now and quite literally towered, almost menacingly, above me – firmly fixed my geographic location. And without any GPS assistance, I pondered with maybe a touch of whimsicality but perhaps more of an apprehensive tremble. Now that the ecclesiastical bells had fallen silent, my immediate vicinity was utterly and opportunely calm and quiet. Peculiarly, the quirky GPS thought compelled me to tap my chest; around which, I trusted, the cloth and zip-pouched security belt still held my smart-phone. I was more than heartened to have the tangible reassurance of its continued presence close to my body. And I considered – momentarily, but with a surprising internalised grin – contacting Diva to ask why I'd been landed, though without a parachute, about a quarter of a mile from the agreed drop zone. But my inner smirk wasn't all that amazed me.

First, my tapping fingers were sensing some clothing material other than that of the overcoat I was attired in as I stood in front of the Old Divinity School's Quincentennial Gate. Fortunately, I jested to myself, there hadn't been a full-length mirror facing me when I was touching down close by the motte a short while back. Had there been one present, my reflection probably would've caused me to plummet in shock from the hilltop with possibly disastrous consequences; and even before my sojourn had properly commenced. I looked down, and nearly jumped out of whatever I was sporting on my feet; though, at first, concentration was glued to my medieval clothing. I appeared to be wearing a longish, not overly loose tunic of indeterminate hue, which hemmed a few inches below my knees; but which, to the touch, felt like it was made from some good quality wool. But in a prominent position on my tunic was sewn the discriminatory badge generally worn by Jews over a certain young age at that time. I knew this symbol was termed the *Tabula*; and that it supposedly depicted the Tablets of the Law brought down by Moses from Mount Sinai, as described in the Old Testament.

I leaned forward to peer at my longish legs which, to the naked eye, apparently emerged from the tunic-top encased in a sort of skin-tight and likely beige-coloured pantaloon-hosiery of some sort. On my lower extremities was a pair of what looked like something out of the 'Arabian Nights' tales: elongated, seemingly fashioned in leather, laced ankle-shoes with my enwrapped feet noticeably behind the lengthy, upwardly curving and pointy-toed footwear. I just about recalled they were known as *poulaines*. I took a couple of unbalanced steps but - although the novel lace-ups felt and looked very odd, awkward and un-me – I didn't trip over my feet and fall headfirst onto the spiky grass.

I was on the brink of lifting my tunic to discover whether I was wearing any form of underwear, when I noticed a grey cloth bundle tied to the end of a long walking stick and lying on the ground nearby. I went down on my haunches and loosened the top of the bulging, sack-like holder. Peeking inside, I saw what looked like more clothing; but there was also a strange-looking article that appeared to be headgear of some kind. I lifted out the grey woollen item, and left the bag on the grass. I knew almost instinctively that it was the typical, floppy-pointed hood customarily, if not requisitely, worn by Jewish males at that time. Earlier in 13th century England, and pursuant to the strong papal influence there, a 'Jew hat' had been introduced. The obligatory headwear was well put together, roughly conical and knob-pointed; and of the identity genre that men of my religion were compelled to put on in public. Wealthier members of the faith were said to have purchased the benefit of being excused wearing the hat; even some communities apparently paid for this privilege, though many individuals just ignored the rule. I was aware of that - as well as of the types of civilian clothing worn variously by noblemen and ladies, the middle classes and peasants – from drawings, paintings and other images of contemporary illustration. But this knowledge, stemming from my casual researches, was far from meaning that I wouldn't be totally flummoxed by actually wearing the gear, including the hoodie, as I was. But that would seem to be, inevitably if harrowingly, part and parcel of my proposed contact with the Jewish community in the town... my raison d'être for being in medieval Cambridge.

It appeared that Diva had thought of everything; but then I wondered about the important subject of money... from a survival viewpoint. Surely she wouldn't have missed out on supplying me with the indispensable coinage of the realm to make my fated way in this new world. So now I did raise my tunic; not to seek for underclothes, but to detect the existence of some hard and valuable cash or currency. And there it was, a broad belt with buttoned pockets strapped below the security wrap-around containing my smart-phone. I opened its three purse-like holders. One was full of smallish silver coins; another held other coinage, and the third had a number of small gold pieces. It was a real wonder I hadn't felt them earlier; but now in the know, I did sense their tangible but fairly marginal substance. I would check on values later, I speculated. Meanwhile, I felt fairly confident that I was reasonably well set up by Diva for my own proposed, relatively short stay. I moved to glance at my watch; but, as I'd foreseen, it no longer graced my wrist. Now I wouldn't know the exact hour of the day or night; and Diva had ensured my mobile phone - which, I supposed, she could've enabled to give me the time - was disabled for anything other than the permitted purpose.

Continuing to hold the 'Jew-hood' in my hand, I shielded my eyes and gazed skywards, reckoning it was somewhere between eleven and noon. I was now thinking about descending from the castle mound; and, to that end, I could make out a rough path circling the looming round tower and moat-circled walls ahead of me. Hopefully, I considered, it would lead also in a downwards direction to what I knew, in my own time, as Castle Street. I could then make my way southwards across the river bridge, on the site of the ancient Roman ford, and towards the main part of town. Though from sketches I'd perused of the medieval stronghold, I was cautiously aware that its gatehouse stood on the blind side of the tower to me.

Apparently, I 'spoke' too soon. All of a sudden, I heard nearby sounds of raucous laughter. Moments later, on the pathway circuiting the base of the lofty battlement, and from the gated entrance side of the castle, two brawny male figures emerged. It was obvious to me, and instantly, that they were pike-carrying soldiers, maybe on a guard patrol of the castle's outer limits. They spotted me at once and approached this lone and frightened individual, their now extremely sour expressions and aggressive postures much in evidence. Before they reached me, I noted with my journalistic eye that both were wearing identical army uniforms: a black and silver, coned helmet; and a breastplate over a whitish, short-sleeved chemise covering a long-sleeved, brown-hued tunic. That item of clothing hid much of what looked to me like short brown trousers, with emergent blue hose and dark boots of some hardwearing variety. Hanging sinisterly from their broad leather waist-belts was a red-handled, short sword housed in its scabbard.

"Get your bloody hood back on, Jew!" one of the well-armed sentinels screamed at me, whilst pointing to the headwear gripped in my hand; and as his similarly garbed colleague moved swiftly around to my rearward side. "Or else… you know what!"

I didn't quite know whether the anti-Semite was addressing me in Norman-French, Anglo-Norman-French or Middle-English. I didn't think that Latin - the language of the law, the church and the learned – would be a real possibility for the warrior. But language differences didn't seem to matter because, quite miraculously it felt, I was actually receiving within my brain a kind of instant and neutrally-spoken translation in the modern English idiom I understood. I conjectured it was like someone sitting in, say, the United Nations General Assembly and listening, with full comprehension, to a speech in an unknown foreign tongue, but minus a translation through headphones. Without a further word, I obeyed the order at once, fitting the flaccid headwear firmly over my head; but bearing an ache in my guts because of the starkly unprecedented, personal threat.

"Now get the hell out of here, you bloody Christ-killer! And if we see you anywhere near this place again, your life is forfeit!"

Next, and with a grimace that wouldn't have shamed a rampaging ogre, the militiaman came right up to my face and shrieked into it:

"Got it, you Jew idiot?"

I nodded meekly, eyes downcast subserviently and submissively, as I believed the not only verbally hostile guardsman might wish to have me respond.

I was a little surprised that the guy was acting in this way, and also by his adoption of the old chestnut trope. My general belief had been that a Royal castle in this era would be held out as a sanctuary in times of mob rioting and other troubles involving a closely neighbouring Jewish community. Perhaps, I pondered, it was a personal thing for these particular sentries out on a limb below the fort's walls. I was aware, however, that times were a-changing during this period, for one reason or another, and inexorably

117

affecting England's Jewish population. Nevertheless, I hoped that not all non-Jews in medieval Cambridge would be reacting to Jewish people residing or present in their midst in the same despairingly anti-Semitic, insulting and derogatory, if not physically antagonistic manner. Sighing with relief, I considered myself lucky that the intimidating military duo hadn't seen fit to search, or even to rob me. But I wasn't best pleased with Diva for putting me, doubtless inadvertently, in this hazardous situation. Possibly even in the Alpha Centauri system they weren't as perfect, scientifically and technologically, as she might've led me to believe.

"Pick up your bag of rubbish, you filthy Jew, and bugger off... now!" the soldier standing vigilantly close behind me shouted in my right ear, giving me a robust push in the process.

That's all I needed in my new shoes, I thought quickly, while just managing to save myself from falling headlong onto the coarse grass.

The two sentries cackled with laughter at my stumbling antics. I stooped to pick up the long stick and its attached, lumpy sack; though not before receiving a painful kick in the backside from one of the guardsmen. I staggered with my baggage onto the narrow pathway and headed in the direction, with any luck, of a safe and secure route into the town and towards the Jewry neighbourhood.

Sixteen

FORTUNATELY, I made it to the level roadway without further problems of any kind, the walking stick - even with its attached bundle - assisting on sections of the more steeply inclined route downwards. When I reached Castle Street and turned onto the gentler sloping gradient to the river crossing, a few hundred metres away, I reflected transiently on whether what looked like a dirt-track of a thoroughfare hadn't fared so well over the 1,000 years or so since its existence as the Via Devana of Roman times. My course into *Cantabrigia* appeared quite deserted; though as I passed St Peter's on my right, the smallish church virtually opposite the rather bulkier St Giles, I caught the emerging sounds of hymnal singing and was reminded of the Christian Sabbath that day. Of course the Mass would be led in Latin, a language not otherwise familiar to the vast majority of worshippers. I continued heading for the river, passing an intersection then entered the constricted end of what I knew as Bridge Street. The roadway was flanked by variably designed but picturesque, at most three-storey, domestic houses - including a few, presently closed shops of whatever sort - constructed largely of wood, wattle and daub, some with sharply slanting, thatched roofs. I knew that several of the properties, some with overhanging upper floors and wood-shuttered window-openings – to be fitted later with glass panes, not generally affordable by home-owners in these medieval times – would survive into my future day after inevitable re-building, refurbishment and restoration over the intervening centuries.

As I walked along this narrower part of Bridge Street, I thought of the vehicle-passing problems sometimes faced frustratingly by buses and other traffic in my 21st century Cambridge. This little musing nonetheless distracted me, and I was nearly knocked over by a cantering horse ridden by a man in a splendid hat and cape. Luckily, the sound of the animal's approaching hooves must've re-sparked my concentration, and I managed to jump out of its path just in time. Fleetingly, I wondered whether the conspicuous *Tabula* on my tunic had anything to do with the near impact. I stared back at the horse and rider, who was glaring over his shoulder at me with an uncompromising expression. To avoid further potential calamity, I decided to continue on my way hugging as near to the houses and shops as practicable.

Then I came up to the arched stone bridge, and gazed over the left-hand balustrade towards what I knew as Quayside. In the modern world, lines of flat-bottomed, pleasure craft would be moored there, while awaiting tourist passengers gathered in by competitive young punt touts, some sporting straw boaters in fine weather. Now I could see a few other types of larger and rudderless vessels, with a single mast, anchored beside the river bank;

these, I reckoned, were cargo-carriers of different kinds. I considered that at least one of the few wooden structures close to the riverside area, many centuries later to be the site of popular bars and restaurants, could've been a warehouse or other storage facility. Looking up and down the then gently flowing watercourse, I could make out the expanses of fertile alluvium deposits left, and gradually built up, by periodic flood waters over the years.

I moved off the bridge and continued my saunter, now along a broader stretch of Bridge Street with buildings of various heights and make-up lining the thoroughfare, including a few relatively imposing stone structures. There appeared to be numerous criss-crossing ruts and grooves in the surface of the highway, doubtless caused by the constant weekday movement of horse-drawn, or peasant-towed, wagons and carts. I strolled past St Clements Church, rising to my left, and could see the distinctively domed architecture of St Sepulchre's a little way ahead. I noticed what appeared to be some retail premises, of whatever sort; and also what I thought might be a hostelry, inn or ale-house. That particular assessment jerked me into confirming I needed, and fairly soon, to find a place to stay. But as a conspicuous Jewish individual, I felt there could be difficulties involved in seeking accommodation other than at a hostel specifically established for Jewish merchants, travellers and other visitors. I knew that at least one such temporary quarters existed somewhere in the Jewry area, at that point in my hike just a short distance away.

My last notion, about me being a person labelled as of the Jewish faith, was affirmed very soon after I noted people starting to come onto the street as church services ended. As the loyal and faithful, church-going men and women passed by me donned in their Sunday best tunics - with the female variants waist-belted and covering long gowns or dresses – I seemed, self-consciously, to be receiving an assortment of reactions. These included sneers, frowns and other pulled faces, as well as a couple of moderately waved fists. But mostly, I was completely ignored; as if, perhaps, I didn't exist or was invisible or too minute to be seen by the naked eye. Though it's possible that many of these people were otherwise occupied mindfully with their own concerns; or, indeed, they weren't anti-Semitic and held a benign attitude towards, and had no problem with residing alongside, their Jewish neighbours.

In a few further strides, and seeking not to attract too much adverse attention, I reached the spot close to St Sepulchre's where the main roadway divided. Bridge Street continued straight ahead; whilst veering off to my right was a road – then known as the High Street, later St John's Street - which led more directly to the commercial and civic heart of *Cantabrigia*. I decided to proceed rightwards, and ambled the quite short distance to the Church of All Saints in the Jewry, passing on my right-hand side the Hospital of St John the Evangelist. The cemetery associated with the hospital stood to my left, as I moved forward some more; and, on that same side, I came to the church which was circuited by a passageway, known then as *Vims*

Judeorum. I turned left into the so-called Jew's Lane, with the tower of All Saints rising above me. People were exiting the church but appeared not to be overly concerned with me - a Jewish man strangely, if not imprudently, going walkabout alone on the Christian Sabbath, I postulated on their behalves. Maybe my being largely side-lined was down to the fact that I was positioned adjacent to the Jewry, the *Vicus Judeorum* or Jews' Village, where the town's Jewish community - descended principally from French Jews who'd followed William the Conqueror to England, I pondered again - resided in the main.

Surveying my environs, I endeavoured to calculate - just for the quirky fun of it, I thought oddly - exactly where I'd been located before Diva transported me to my slightly off-centre, landing place on Castle Hill. When I accepted the last of my ranging estimations as being reasonably accurate, I strolled towards it and loitered on the spot where I'd stood, eyes shut, however long ago now. Standing stock still and grasping my faithful and uncomplaining companions, the stick and bag, I shut my lids again and thought of England... well, the country I knew from another time. In the now silent locality and in the dark — in more ways than one — it actually felt like I could be anywhere at any time, maybe even somewhere in Diva's Alpha Centauri star system.

Perhaps it was a foolish thing to do - not feeling as if I could've been wherever and whenever, but rather having my eyes closed. For in the next instant, I was feeling something else entirely... something physical, and actually happening then and there. The vicious tug on my long walking stick at once prompted a return to full but startling visuals. A short and skinny, dark-hooded and rough-bearded man in a filthy tunic was trying very hard to pull the rod and bundle from my grip. I increased the power of my one-handed hold on these possessions; and with the other hand, my weaker left, sought ineffectively to fend off the ruffian. For his height and build, or rather the lack of these attributes, this unspeaking and unspeakable male of indeterminate age, but with a frightful and menacing grimace, seemed to pack a disproportionate strength, possibly due to desperation; though, could be, with an anti-Semitic twist to it.

The tug-o-war went on, my concern growing exponentially, until suddenly the wild man released his overly hairy-handed grip. In a literal flash, he pulled a long-bladed and glinting knife from beneath his ragged and heavily stained outer-garment then brandished the terrible weapon at my body. At the same time, he held out his free hand, palm rigidly upward, doubtless as an indicative demand for my stick and bag... or else! Next I heard someone screaming, and almost failed to credit that it was me. I've never howled like that in my life, save maybe when I was a babe-in-arms. So was I acting like a baby now? Somehow, I didn't think this was the case in my unprecedented, let alone petrifying position.

I was tremblingly on the brink of turning and making a run for it, but probably was very lucky I didn't do that. I would've been helplessly vulnerable; and the savage-faced beast – whether professional robber or violent vagrant and beggar – confronting me could've rapidly and easily stabbed me in the back and made off with my belongings, such as they were. All my shrill yelps, panicky notions and crazed antics were occurring within a mere few eye-blinks. But all at once, the horrendous state of affairs changed dramatically. As my armed, and thus superior, adversary looked primed to lunge at me, possibly fatally and with unknown consequences, I heard a noise coming from behind my knife-wielding foe. The sound - of what turned out to be a heavy door opening in one of the substantial stone houses adjoining the alleyway – had the effect, and thankfully, of distracting my terrifying assailant. He hunched up and quickly peered over his shoulder. Simultaneously, two men in smart white, loose-hanging, buttoned and short-sleeved blousons over leg-wear tucked into hose – presumably, I thought, home-lounging clothes – leapt out of the building onto the lane. They looked swiftly in my direction, but only after mistakenly looking up the deserted end of the church-side path.

These two individuals must've heard my panicked hollering, apparently loud enough to penetrate the thick stone walls of the property from which they emerged hurriedly. Now it was clear they were espying the Tabula affixed to my tunic; and doubtless comprehending immediately the potentially tricky, if not hazardous circumstances in which I was situated. Without more, the unarmed duo of apparently single-minded rescuers dashed boldly along the several metres of passageway. Or were they rescuers? I wondered such unwillingly, and with the instant and unwanted outcome of an enhanced angst. Could it be that the wicked aim of these fit-looking men was to join in the assault on me? Happily, my fearful speculations were way off the mark. Even the incipient thief seemed to be acutely aware of that. Despite his ostensible knife advantage, and without more, he took flight and hurtled himself past me. In his desperate getaway efforts, and deliberately or otherwise, I received a glancing blow from his fleeing and accelerating body. It threw me to the stony ground, my stick and bundle falling alongside.

I looked up, more than a trifle dazed, at my two heroes of the day as they arrived immediately on the scene and lowered themselves sympathetically to my aching side.

"We heard your screams… are you alright?" one of the men, who looked to be some years younger than me, enquired with what sounded like a kindly and compassionate voice.

I nodded then heard unfamiliar words leaving my mouth, the first spoken words – though not the first emitted sounds – since my arrival in *Cantabrigia* that day. Now I knew for certain, and very reassuringly, that the English I was hearing in my mind would be emerging through my lips in a language readily understood by my present, good-hearted listeners.

"Y-Yes, I think so… and thank you for saving me from that atrocious assailant," I said, more or less evenly.

The fallen baggage was moved away from my legs.

"My brother and I are very glad to have been of assistance to you," the man's hovering and sympathetic face told me. "These random and vicious acts against Jews appear to have increased to a worrying extent over recent times."

The speaker, having taken hold of my left arm, then turned to his close relative.

"Come, Aaron, help me raise this gentleman from the ground."

"Yes of course, Joseph," was the instant reply from the evidently younger brother.

The names sounded Jewish to me, I pondered as Aaron gently but firmly grasped my right arm. Very efficiently and not uncomfortably, I was lifted to a vertical position. But in all likelihood they could perceive my features were displaying shock, as well as shades of wooziness.

"Would you like to come into our house for a rest?" Joseph asked me, adding: "It looks very much like you could use it."

I tried to create a little smile on my indubitably pale cheeks.

"Thank you so much for that very thoughtful offer," I said. "I believe sitting down for a short while would be very helpful to me."

Aaron picked up my walking staff and bundle; then he and his older brother physically assisted, rather than escorted me along the lane. The still open, thick and wooden, iron framed and hinged portal gave entry to the roof-tiled, gabled and stone-constructed house. As we

127

entered the building I noticed, without any doubt on my part, what was a *Mezuzah*. Within its wooden case, affixed at an angle to the doorpost on my right, would be a small scroll of hand-written prayer dedicated to the Almighty. Its presence confirmed that I was being taken into an observant Jewish household.

Seventeen

ON entering what appeared to be a lobby area, with light spraying down from a window above the hefty door, I was beginning to calm down and feel a distinct physical and mental recovery. Perhaps, I reflected, this was down to my being taken into a safe Jewish environment; and I was pleased to be thinking fairly sensibly again. As Aaron locked the door behind us with a large iron key and pushed home resoundingly the lengthy and sturdy bolts, top and bottom, I noted another closed door directly ahead, with a centred lock and down a few steps. But we didn't proceed in that direction. Instead, Joseph led the way up a stone stairway to our right with me following him and Aaron, doubtless satisfied that the building was appropriately secured, bringing up the rear. On reaching the first floor, I noted not only that the staircase continued upwards but also that we were entering a spacious hall through an archway bearing another, rather decorative *Mezuzah*. I couldn't help noticing a long, dark wood table with chairs; and that the expansive room was well-illuminated by sunlight bursting in through elevated windows with panes of glass. I could see that, affixed to the windowless wall on the archway side of the living space, were a number of ornate, wrought-iron torch and candle holders; there were also some branched candelabras spread along the table-top. Between the windows and at the far end of the hall – above a closed door beside another, matching archway – hung what looked to be tapestries of idyllic pastoral scenes. All very impressive so far, I thought; so it went without saying – and, naturally, I didn't say it – that this was a quite valuable property.

I followed Joseph beneath the beamed ceiling and along the polished wood floor beside the lengthy table while passing a couple of leather-padded benches and a round-topped, wooden chest. At the end of the hall – where I could see, beyond the archway, a flight of steps leading only downwards – the three of us came to a halt between the long table and a considerably smaller one sited against the wall. Joseph sat down on the highest backed chair at the head of the table and beckoned me to sit to his left, below a window from which the sun streamed down. Aaron placed my stick and bundle beside the little table then sat himself beside his brother and opposite me.

The older brother turned to face me.

"As you've possibly gathered... or maybe not, due to recent events, my name is Joseph and my brother's name is Aaron," he said, with the hint of a twinkle in his eyes. "What's yours?"

"It's David," I replied, unable to resist a little grin; and even after what I'd just experienced outside in Jews' Lane. "And may I thank you most sincerely for your timely intervention before? Your prompt action could well have saved my life."

"I'll not say it was a pleasure for us to do so, David," he responded, "because the words don't ring true, but you'll understand what I mean…"

I nodded and Aaron dipped his head a couple of times, too.

"My brother and I are very relieved we were able to help you, David," Joseph continued. "Where do you hail from? Don't think we've seen you in these parts previously."

"I arrived earlier today from London, Joseph" I replied instantly but, sadly, untruthfully. "I haven't visited this city before now."

The two brothers stared at me in a funny-serious kind of way. Perhaps they were pondering whether I was a spy; that the recent confrontation was a con; that my tunic was bearing the *Tabula* as a feint; and that I wasn't actually Jewish. Certainly I could've proved I was, if they wished. Then their expressions appeared to change; and as if - though not quite like Diva, I mused - they had read my thoughts.

"So why have you come here, David?" Aaron asked. "What do you do?"

"Before David answers your question, my brother," Joseph interjected, "I think we should tell Miriam to get him a special hot drink… I can see that you're recovering well from what must've been a frightening episode for you. But one of our customary medicinal and herbal beverages could be of real benefit. What do you say?"

"It couldn't do me any harm, and I'm obliged for the kind thought," I said, adding: "And yes, I'm feeling much better now… thanks to both of you."

"No, the drink can't do you any harm, David," Joseph confirmed, I thought with a bit of a cheeky grin. "And if you might be thinking about water quality, our local source isn't the filthy river down the road, but rather the well we share with a number of brethren."

I was a bit startled when Aaron suddenly called out: "Miriam!"

A young slim girl, in a kind of off-white smock and cap, and looking no more than ten or eleven years of age, appeared instantaneously at the nearby archway and as if by magic. Knowing, for sure, that my new Jewish friends wouldn't be practising the occult arts, I suspected she must've been waiting patiently within earshot in case needed for any reason.

"Ah, Miriam," Aaron said. "Tell your mother to make a big cup of the hot barley and honey drink for our guest, please."

The bright-eyed youngster nodded, at once turned on her wooden heels and hastened down the stairs.

"May I ask… who is Miriam to you?" I enquired.

"Of course," Joseph said. "Her mother, Rebecca, is a widowed Jewess. After her husband, a loyal messenger for our business over several years, passed away, she fell on very hard times. We took her in… she's an excellent cook and very well looks after our kitchen, which is annexed in the courtyard at the rear of the house. There's also a smallish, adjoining room there where she and Miriam live. After our beloved father and patriarch of the family, Joshua, may his soul rest in eternal peace, passed away some years ago now, his then long-employed and hard-working cook felt she couldn't stay here any longer. Rebecca was her replacement."

I nodded my thanks for the information supplied, and Joseph said:

"So… how about answering my brother's questions now?"

Surprisingly but happily, my recall of them was on the button; and, maybe pathetically if not shamefully, it was time to use my prepared script.

"I'm a teacher, actually a private tutor, in London. As I mentioned, I've never been to this town before, so I decided to spend some time here…"

"Sorry for asking, David, but are you married?" Joseph interrupted politely; though I wondered about the motive behind this personal enquiry.

"No, I'm not," I responded, hoping he wouldn't go on to delve into any previous marital status; and, fortunately, he didn't.

"Please go on," he said.

I couldn't decide whether to relate my horrible experience on Castle Mound that morning, but then I did.

"Why did you climb up there?" Aaron asked.

"Well, I arrived quite early by wagon after a long journey in a cramped and uncomfortable position," I replied or, rather, lied. "I needed to stretch my legs, so took a walk up the hill to observe the view from the summit. I didn't expect to be subjected to a not insignificant, anti-Semitic verbal and physical assault. After all, and although we're tantamount to the King's possessions, aren't the monarch's citadels supposed to provide sanctuary for his outlandishly taxed Jews in times when they need such protection?"

Joseph smiled and somewhat resignedly, I felt.

"I guess the response 'Yes and No' is a fitting one nowadays, David, as you would probably agree on further reflection," he observed. "As undoubtedly you know from your own knowledge and experience, much has gone downhill for the Jews of England over the last decades… and for all sorts of nefarious, practical and other reasons. But we mustn't forget that underlying, if not overriding, what has been happening in material ways to affect the inevitably declining Jewish population in this country, is the blatant and sometimes fatal anti-Semitism to which we're continually subjected."

I nodded with deliberation then supplemented my head movement.

"You're right, of course, Joseph," I said, "and there's little I can add for now."

Joseph and Aaron nodded in turn.

At that moment, Miriam re-appeared with a steaming, bowl-like vessel containing my hot drink and atop a tray. She set it down on the table, gave me a little bow then disappeared hastily through the archway. Joseph held out his palm.

"Do drink, David, but not quite yet," he warned. "Allow it to cool down a bit, and we hope you like it… it contains also some beneficial herbs."

I followed his advice then, from time to time over the ensuing period of time, I held and sipped from the bowl whilst indicating, by my expressions, that I was enjoying the very soothing concoction.

"So where were you intending to stay during your sojourn here?" the older brother asked before I took my first sip.

I thought for a moment or two.

"Well, I was proposing to stay in the Jewish hostel set up, I believe, for itinerant merchants and other travellers like me… and that I understand exists somewhere in the Jewry area," I offered. "I was about to search out the place when I was attacked by that evil-looking vagabond."

"Indeed it does exist, David…" Joseph remarked, "but it's not very comfortable or restful. The lodgings are in a dormitory format, and I've been told it's difficult for guests to get a good night's sleep… and even apart from the cacophony of snoring noises. Look, I'll tell you what. We seem to be getting along very well, David, and I would like to make up for your so recent and terrible experiences here. This will be a privilege for us, and someone new with whom we can share some interesting conversation. There's a spare room or two on the floor above us, and where our sleeping accommodation is to be found. You're welcome to stay with us for the duration of your visit to the town. What do you think?"

I was almost rendered speechless, but not quite in light of the advantageous offer.

"Y-You've been so caring and benevolent to me, Joseph… and, of course, Aaron," I uttered, feeling a tad emotional. "I-I really don't know what to say. But many thanks… I would be so pleased, and feel so safe and protected, staying here with you and your family."

"Ah yes, my family…" Joseph said, with a sudden look of recollection. "Well, you've met my brother Aaron, who has a lovely smile, as you can see. He now lives with his family and the Jewish community in the not far distant town of Huntingdon. He has just come here for some business discussions with me. We also have a sister, Ruth, who lives with her husband and children in Norwich, which I'm sure you know possesses the largest Jewish population in East Anglia. My mother, Sarah, and older sister, Naomi, are currently in the chamber beyond that door over here… they're quietly engaged in some elaborate embroidery work. It will be a gift for a very close, family friend, who will soon reach the grand old age of fifty. Currently, my wife Deborah and our three children are staying with her close relatives in London."

There was a lot to think about already, and my pensiveness may well have incited Aaron's question about his sister.

"Perhaps you're wondering, David, why our sister Naomi, the eldest child of our mother and late father, isn't married…"

I shook my head.

"Not really," I responded slowly, various odd notions now flitting through my head.

"We don't mind being frank about the reason for her spinsterhood, David," Aaron went on. "Wretchedly, during her childhood she developed a serious medical condition, now thankfully long cured but which our doctor cousin advised had nevertheless, as a side effect, made her infertile. In consequence, of course, our father was unable to arrange a betrothal and husband for her…"

"Aaron's right," Joseph added, "it has been very distressing, for everyone… and our parents were truly heartbroken when they heard of the unexpected result of Naomi's illness."

I must've appeared quite taken aback by the poignant story being related to me.

"I'm so sorry to hear of this melancholy outcome for your sister," I commented with as much compassion as I could muster. "I do hope that Naomi has been keeping well…"

Joseph continued.

"Yes, thank the Almighty, she is very well… and thank you for asking after her. If you wish, Aaron will fetch our mother and sister so that we can introduce you. Would that be conducive to you, David?"

"Absolutely," I responded keenly.

Aaron rose from his seat and approached the proximate chamber. Before going in, he rapped on the door and closed it behind him on entering. I carried on a brief conversation with Joseph about the very tasty and apparently healthy drink I was imbibing. It was some little while after his temporary departure that Aaron came back to the hall followed by his mother and older sister. The seemingly delayed return was likely due, I mused, to a fairly detailed explanation by him about my presence in the house; and perhaps also to some time spent stowing away the women's handiwork. I stood up and nodded smilingly in their direction. Dressed in the most attractive belted tunics and under-gowns, mother and daughter reciprocated similarly then sat down opposite me. Naomi took the chair next to Aaron, when he resumed his original place, the mother sitting beside her. Then Joseph introduced me formally.

"At our request, Aaron has told us all about you," Sarah said, a beam creasing her sympathetic round face. "We hope you'll not mind about that precursor to our meeting with you, David… and we're delighted that Joseph has asked you to stay with us during your visit to the town, and that you've accepted."

She's so endearing and welcoming, I thought as she spoke. But my eyes did drift momentarily in Naomi's direction, I hoped not too noticeably. Although her oval-shaped face possessed a certain pallid quality, she was quite beautiful to behold. My hope for inconspicuousness may've fallen short; out of the corner of my eye, and when Sarah finished speaking, I kind of perceived Joseph glancing at his brother with raised eyebrows.

"Thank you so much for that," I said, and straight from the heart. "What you and your sons have said means a lot to me. It's so good being within the enveloping warmth of a Jewish family here... it was rather more than I'd anticipated might happen here, and so soon. I really do appreciate your very kind and generous spirit... and I'm really enjoying the honey drink that was so considerately made for me."

Naomi remained silent, but sent me a coy little grin; and it could be that, in my earlier quick look at her, our eyes met fleetingly. Now she lowered her appealing blue eyes. I couldn't help but look down the hall again, to admire its affluent décor and ponder the well-heeled status of the handsome stone house's residents. The older son had seemed fairly on the ball in his interpretation of some earlier, contemplative expressions of mine; and he didn't fall short on this occasion.

"I can see you're taking in the detail, David... and possibly you're wondering how all this came about..."

I was about to say something, but he stopped me with a very slight lift of a hand and went on.

"My late father built up a strong and influential, money-lending business over many years. And with initial financial help from his father, my paternal grandfather. Later, he took me and Aaron into the very successful enterprise and, of course, we benefited greatly from the income... and despite the increasingly heavy *tallage*, taxation as you know. You may be aware also that, when King Edward came to the throne not that long ago, pressure on businesses of our kind began to take us even further in the wrong direction. And, naturally, my brother and I are considering and discussing this situation and all possible implications..."

Everyone around the table was nodding, including me. Joseph rose from his chair, and appeared to sigh deeply; then we all got up from our seats.

"Perhaps we'll talk about this some more at another time," he said finally. "Meanwhile, I think David might like to have a quiet rest in his room. Aaron, perhaps you could please escort our guest to the chamber."

The younger brother nodded, picked up my baggage and handed it to me.

"This is very good of you," I said, thinking I was being overly repetitive.

Sarah and Naomi smiled at me, the daughter maybe with slightly more emphasis – I imagined, for whatever reason – then returned to the private chamber and shut the door. Aaron beckoned me to follow him back down the length of the hall to the stairway leading to the upper floor.

Just before I started off after him, Joseph took my arm.

"Do excuse me for saying this," he began, "but when you're inside your room you don't have to prove to Aaron that you're Jewish. I suspected earlier that you might be thinking about the question of trust which, of course, is a two-way thing. We didn't know you from Adam... and, theoretically at least, you could've harboured miscreant motives. But from our conversations and other considerations, we know, and probably have known since coming upon you in circumstances that were assuredly not staged, that you're definitely Jewish... *Baruch Hashem,* Blessed be the Almighty, and we wish you well."

Despite having an age beyond adolescence, I do believe that I may've reddened a tad, especially near the start of my host's fine speech. Now we faced each other, both of us smiling with a seeming element of affection, then shook hands very cordially.

"Go now," he added, "and I hope you like your private room."

Eighteen

I FOLLOWED Aaron up the staircase to the next, and what looked to be the uppermost floor and the family's solar or private living and sleeping quarters. Just ahead of us lay a relatively compact, carpeted and bench-seating area between two windows. Beyond this cosy space ran a centred and wood-floored corridor separating two rows of chambers; no doubt these included a few relatively large rooms as indicated by the distance between their clearly lockable, carved-wood doors. Aaron led me to what must've been the smallest of the chambers – each had a Mezuzah affixed to its right doorpost - positioned to the right at the far end of the passageway. Its door was a metre or so from another facing inwards to the aisle.

There was a key in the lock of my door, which Aaron turned then withdrew and handed to me. He pushed open the slightly creaky portal, and beckoned for me to enter first. The room wasn't that diminutive, really. Against one wall of the fairly high-ceilinged and square-shaped chamber stood a blanketed bed beside which, on the polished wood floor, lay a small, grey-woollen rug. High on the wall ahead of me was a smallish glass window, through which the day's sunshine squeezed to light the room; and quite adequately, too. Below it was a desk-size table, on which rested a candle in a holder with a handle, plus a stool. To one side of my temporary accommodation, opposite the bed, was a quaint little fireplace.

I absorbed the chamber's adequate dimensions, simple décor and unfussy ambience quite speedily, of course; then I turned to face my guide who was standing just inside the doorway.

"It's very nice, indeed... please thank your brother again for me, and my thanks to you for conducting me here," I said earnestly.

Aaron smiled.

"Thank you, and you're very welcome... I will certainly do as you ask, David," he responded. "My brother will be glad this room is suitable for you."

I placed the door-key on the table and my bundle on the floor alongside the cute old mini-hearth. I was content with my lot, though there was something playing on my mind.

"I hope you'll not mind my raising a particular matter, Aaron," I said, with appreciable hesitance. "But when your brother spoke of his and your late father, it seemed to me there was more than a natural sadness around the table regarding his passing. I could be wrong, of course, and the emotional feelings on his loss could, understandably, still run deep... please forgive me for raising this."

Aaron nodded slowly and his face adopted a sombre expression.

"You are right in a way, David," he said, a little more sensitively than his usual speaking voice. "Our father died in, we believe, absolutely dreadful circumstances. It happened about eight years ago... during, as I'm sure you know about, the time of the Baronial War of the sixties. And, especially, the wild protests and anti-Semitic rampages of the so-called Disinherited in the middle years of that terrible decade..."

I was nodding my awareness of that dangerous period, as Aaron continued.

"... Whilst, as you must know, the mobs killed numerous Jews, including money-lenders, commodity dealers and other affluent and prominent brethren in this country, the Jewish community in Cambridge fortunately suffered few casualties. Only Saulot Motun, the patriarch of one of England's wealthiest Jewish dynasties, was known for certain to have been slaughtered here. His eldest son and heir Josce, who deals in wool, corn and other commodities, is a close friend of ours. He owns some properties in Bridge Street. Anyway, during that fraught if not violent and terrorising era, our father was found dead one evening near the main river crossing here, the one that was built over the ancient Roman ford..."

As he spoke, almost biting his lips in the process, I nodded my knowledge of the location.

"... When we reached the horrible scene, some people in the area said our father had fallen and hit his head on the stonework of the bridge. His face was covered with blood, and parts of his brain were oozing onto the ground from his smashed skull. W-We knew the alleged witnesses couldn't be trusted, and speedily concluded that the appalling injuries to our father's head couldn't have been caused by a mere fall and a glancing hit on the bridge structure. H-He'd been brutally and cruelly attacked, without doubt by a gang of anti-Semitic louts who had no compunction about, literally, beating our helpless and elderly father's brains out!"

Aaron rubbed his face with both hands; and I felt really bad.

"I'm so sorry to have raised the matter," I said, eyes downcast. "It was really unnecessary, and quite wrong of me."

"N-No, that's alright, David… it's good that you know about this," Aaron remarked benignly, and with a restoring calmness. "I'm sure my brother, or some other close family member, would've mentioned it to you even without an enquiry."

I made a gesture of acceptance with my hands, and fleetingly touched his arm.

"Thank you, Aaron, and now I mustn't keep you any longer," I said with a sad sigh. "I'm sure you've got lots to talk about with Joseph."

"Yes, you're right, we do have much to discuss about our family's future."

As he turned to leave, with me pondering his last few enigmatic words, I asked one more question, which I thought was quite important to me.

"Sorry to have to ask, but could you tell me where the toilet is, please?"

Aaron grinned, and I was glad he did… though not for the obvious reason.

"Our *garderobe* is right next door to you," he said, pointing to the door facing the walkway while stressing the toilet term.

I might've guessed, I thought; and whilst musing drolly that this was a real convenience.

"And if you would like to bathe at any time," Aaron added, "we can arrange for a wooden tub and buckets of hot water to be brought to your bedchamber."

I gave him my thanks again, and he walked back down the hallway.

As soon as he disappeared, I went to the loo… and rather urgently, too. It must've been the barley, honey and herb potion I was ingesting recently, or so I wondered. I opened the tightly-framed door, and secured it inside with the centrally fitted bolt; but I couldn't claim that the air within was particularly fragrant to my nose. The restricted space was dimly illuminated via a tiny overhead window. Had it been night-time, I would've needed to bring a lit candle in the handled holder on the table in my room. But I couldn't recall having seen anything handy with which to kindle it. Right in front of me, stretching from wall to wall, was a low and wood-encased seat - with a hole in the middle - more than sufficient for sitting, and almost comfortably. I noticed what looked like a pile of plain cloth scraps propped against the wall at the rear of the seat. All in all, the totality wasn't quite of the luxury standard of the en suite back at my apartment. Nonetheless, and having no requirement on this occasion to be seated or to use one of the rags so thoughtfully made available, the facility appeared to serve its purpose well; and for which, I was relieved. For medieval times, however, I knew this level of amenity was of pure extravagance, comparatively. Generally, the peasants and other poverty-stricken folk had to make do with a dirty cavity in the ground or, if to hand, an obviously soiled river, stream, ditch or hole in the ground.

Naturally, I was conditioned to activate a flushing mechanism and to hear its cleansing gushiness. But, from my reading, I was aware that any end product would, in the present context, find its way down through an enclosed wooden shaft - affixed to the outside wall of the building - into a below ground-level, stone-lined cesspit. From my researches, I'd learned also that these trenches were cleared and cleaned out regularly by a fairly well-paid, so-called 'gong-farmer', a job title based on the fact that a lavatory or latrine was often spoken of as a 'gong'. After completing my business, and as normally, I would wash my hands. In the present context, I asked myself: Where the hell was I going to meet my hygiene needs? The frustrating, if not exasperating, thought lingered unredeemed. I pulled back the bolt, exited then sealed the pong in the gong.

But I felt my face colouring again when I saw, approaching me along the hallway, the pale-faced yet exceedingly fair sister of Joseph and Aaron... Naomi. As the woman got nearer, she smiled at me; and I half-smiled back, largely due to being conscious that my hands remained unwashed. Just ahead of me, she halted. I think she was aware of where I may've been of late; and that could've amounted to *her* current destination, though she didn't appear to be in any great hurry. In a way, I may've been blocking her route; but it was what came out of my mouth that caused me more embarrassment.

"Ah, Naomi... I'm glad I bumped into you," I said with a related silly grin. "Could you tell me where I might wash my hands, please?"

"Do you not have a bowl of water and a cloth towel in your room?" she enquired politely.

I shook my head.

"I'll go fetch the necessary items for you, immediately... and I'll bring them to your room," she said.

"How very kind," I commented with an expression maybe revealing more than my sincere gratitude.

At the same time, however, I was wondering whether she should be coming to my chamber without a chaperone; and even though, I surmised on the protocol, her personal circumstances were such that she might've been considered other than a maiden, so that the normal rules didn't apply necessarily. I returned to my room, leaving the door ajar, as Naomi walked back down the corridor.

Nineteen

I SAT on my bed after Naomi had gone off to get me some water to wash my hands after using the lavatory. I supposed my crib could be described as a large single, and it was quite comfy. Lifting the nearest edge of blanket, I exposed – as I hoped, and actually expected – a spotless sheet. I pressed down on the linen and it felt like a fairly firm sort of mattress, possibly packed tightly with feathers, lay beneath on the wooden framework. A large pillow rested against the bedstead's curved headboard. It seemed like I was sitting on the bedclothes for some while, and I recall drifting into a snooze, when suddenly I was sparked out of my doze by a tap-tapping on the door. I jumped up and went to open it. Directly in front of me was Naomi clasping some articles close to her upper body in case, I assumed, they should fall. Next, I was surprised to see Miriam standing alongside her holding, by its handle, an ewer, which I presumed was full of water, and a hand bowl.

"Sorry, we've taken a bit longer than I imagined," Naomi apologised as she entered my room, closely pursued by what, I contemplated, might be termed the servant girl or kitchen-and-chamber maid, and quickly placed the items she was clutching on the small table. "Miriam hadn't been told that you'll be staying in the house for the time being, else she would've ensured your room was fully prepared…"

Then Naomi waved Miriam towards the table, where the nodding young lass deposited the jug and smallish basin.

"You can go now," Naomi instructed her, and the girl departed niftily with the hint of a bow in my direction.

At once, I picked up the pottery pitcher and poured some water, which gave off a pleasantly scented aroma, into the smooth pottery receptacle. Naomi reached around me and grabbed what appeared to be a cloth package, one of the bits and pieces she'd brought with her. She unpeeled the square of material, removed from within it what looked like a bar of soap and gave it to me.

"Thank you," I said. "Looks like you've thought of everything."

"You're very welcome, David," she responded, watching me soaping and scrubbing my fingers and palms thoroughly then rinsing digits and hands in the fragrant water.

After that, she handed me the square of cloth. I left the lump of soap in the bowl and dried myself with what, clearly, was to serve me as a towel. Naomi reached into the basin and managed, wonderfully adroitly, to grasp the slippery slab between thumb and forefinger, lifted it out of the sudsy liquid and let it drop onto the towel now lying on the table. It was quite apparent she'd developed a knack of performing this routine.

"Thanks, Naomi," I said and, I trusted, meaningfully. "I should've been thinking about conserving the soap chunk."

The dark-haired woman smiled; and again, in a way that I was starting to find really attractive. It was evident to me that she was a very kind, thoughtful and, all in all, naturally sympathetic and sensitive person. With that thought flitting through my head, I couldn't help but feel for Naomi's miserable incapacity which, seemingly, had stymied the possibility of her being betrothed, thus preventing her from having a husband and family.

"Okay, so let me show you what else I've brought for you," she began, moving the jug, bowl and soap-topped hand-cloth out of the way then picking up two other objects from the table. "Doubtless you know that this is a tinderbox with a flint, a fire-steel and some brimstone-tipped, little sticks to enable you to light the candle... when you would wish to do so at night."

It was quite an elaborate tinderbox, examples of which I'd seen in history museums. But, of course, I'd never before used this kind of paraphernalia in my life. Throwing a switch for illumination was so much easier. But I doubted whether I could perform the obligatory procedure efficiently, or at all, in a pitch-black room.

I could tell that Naomi was noting my quizzical expression.

"I'm getting the message," she said, "that, when at home in London, you prefer either to keep a fat candle or an oil-holder burning all night at your bedside... or to have some flaming embers going in a nearby fireplace, even in the warm weather, and from which you can light a candle. Am I on the right lines, David?"

Ah, I thought, here's a useful escape clause.

"Yes, I would have a bit of a fire going in a small hearth overnight," I fibbed and, I thought, with increasing skill; but also with some internal chastisement for having to lie so brazenly. "And I don't feel that hot in here, to tell you the truth."

Naomi sent me another of her appealing beams.

"Not a problem, David," she reacted. "When Miriam calls you to join us for supper this evening, she'll light your fire at the same time."

Swiftly, I stifled a chuckle at her last, unsuspecting words; and to which she added:

"I'll tell her to come prepared to do so. We want you to feel at home here."

"Thanks so much, Naomi," I said. "Your empathy is much appreciated. And I'm really grateful for the wonderful hospitality being shown to me by the family… truly, it's beyond words."

"It's important to us, David," she said in a heartfelt manner. "But I think that I need to be off now. My brothers wish to speak to me about something. Perhaps we can talk some more at another time."

For a few moments, I marvelled at the post-modern, English idiomatic translation of her medieval language that I was receiving loud and clear. And I felt that I wanted to converse more with her. Though, of course, the prevailing circumstances were seeking to induce a hesitative diffidence in my rational mind. As she moved to the still open doorway I fought, but unsuccessfully, to comply with that cerebral pressure.

"And I would like to talk again with you, Naomi…" I stated finally, and honestly, "if that would be alright with everyone."

"Of course, David," she responded, to my delight, and with another of her enchanting smiles. "If the weather's fine tomorrow, maybe we'll be able to go for a pleasant walk along the river. And contrary to what you may be thinking, I'll not need a minder to accompany us…"

For a few moments I wondered, maybe unkindly or inappropriately, about whether she would've felt able to say that if her patriarchal father had been alive still. In any event, my features must've displayed elements of a fraudulent and soon to be regretted mystification.

"Thanks for the respectful expression of ignorance, David," she said with a strange glint in her eyes, "but I know that you've been told all about me."

Fortunately, she couldn't have observed my momentary facial flash of mortification as she turned, entered the corridor and moved off towards the staircase at its far end. I went to the doorway and peeked out. Halfway along it, Naomi stopped and glanced over her shoulder. She must've sensed my eyes following her.

"See you later," she called to me.

With that, she continued to the archway.

Twenty

I MANAGED to light the candle on the table when it began to grow dark in my room, having – by, blissfully private, trial and error - taught myself to use the stylish tinder box, and the other flame-creating gadgets left for me. And all before Miriam arrived to alert me to supper-time and also, in Naomi's literal words, to "light my fire". I'd been lying flat on the bed for a few hours, just drowsing spasmodically or reflecting restively on the morning's wild experiences. These had culminated in my unbelievably serendipitous status as a guest in a relatively affluent, Jewish home. After a while, what little section of the sky I could perceive through my chamber's little window turned as black as night which, of course, it was. I washed my hands and, this time, also my face with the supplied water and dried off on the towel. In the circumstances, it was the best that I could achieve in refreshing myself.

I rummaged in my bag, and was relieved to find a small, contemporary mirror and a comb, a new tunic, some other attire and sets of fresh under-garments, which I was glad to change into for the family's evening meal. On doing so, I was reminded of the belts around my upper body containing the mobile phone and a variety of coinage.

Unsurprisingly perhaps, I was tempted to call Diva and tell her of my safe, no - unsafe and slightly off-target arrival in *Cantabrigia*, and my adventures in the town so far. But I knew this was prohibited. As I threw my discarded clothing on the bed, my heart skipped a beat on hearing someone knocking on my door.

I should've remembered it would likely be Miriam, come to alert me for supper-time. I turned the key, which I'd left jutting from the lock, and opened up to the young girl, who was carrying a dark-hued sack with a bulge in it. She bowed a smidgeon, as now becoming customary, and I invited her into my room.

"You should go to the main hall, sir," she said softly. "They're all waiting for you, and my mother will be serving supper soon... I'll be down shortly to help her, after I've made and lit your fire."

"Thank you, Miriam," I said to the extremely efficient Jill of all trades. "And I'm going to join the family right now."

She placed her bag on the floor and, as I was about to leave the room, she mentioned something, again quietly.

"I'll leave the sack for you, sir."

"Why's that, Miriam?" I enquired.

"So you can put in it any clothes that you would like to be washed, sir," she replied prudently, her head at a slight angle. "You can leave the bag outside in the hallway before breakfast, please. I'll collect it during the morning, and return the cleaned and dried apparel later the same day... I hope that will be suitable for you."

I nodded my delighted approval.

"That will be absolutely enormously helpful, Miriam… thank you."

With that, I left the girl to set up a useful fire in my pint-sized hearth, deciding it wasn't vital to ask her to lock up and bring the key to me. How could I possibly even think of doing that, I mused while hurrying along the corridor to the stairwell? On my arrival in the main hall I was, indeed, the last man standing. I noted at once that, as earlier, Joseph was seated aptly at the head of the table, with Aaron immediately to his right. Next to Aaron sat a man, whom I considered be of similar age to Joseph, that I hadn't seen before. There was a vacant chair on the head man's left, which I assumed was intended for me; and its adjacent two seats were occupied by Naomi then Sarah, the mother nearest to the ornate but unlit hearth. I was uncertain about whether to be surprised or not that the sister had been placed – most likely, she hadn't been given the option – beside my chair. Though perhaps I shouldn't have been so naive, I thought – though quite oddly - in the instant. The other thing I noticed – and despite the room being dimmer by candle-light than when sunlit earlier - was that the diners were clad immaculately in fine tunics, with whatever accessories befitted male and female. I felt more than a tad under-dressed. But at least, I reflected for a moment, Diva had seen fit to provide me with a change of moderately good quality clothing; even if it didn't quite reach the modish degree of the gentrified Jewish individuals now sitting around the table.

Joseph smiled and beckoned me to sit down. Of course, he wasn't the only one to smile at me; but, despite the gap between chairs, I felt as if Naomi's grin was tangibly glossing my face. Then her older brother addressed me.

"You've met everyone here, except for the gentleman seated next to my brother. So David… this is Josce, a close and dear family friend here in Cambridge. Unfortunately, his dear wife couldn't be with us this evening. And Josce… this is David, our esteemed guest from London."

Josce rose slightly from his chair, to lean diagonally across the table, and held out an arm. I got up smartly, and met the amicably proffered right hand half-way with my own.

"Very pleased to meet you, David," he said with a really genuine smile.

"Likewise from me, Josce," I responded accordingly.

As we shook hands firmly but warmly, I recalled the mention earlier that day by Aaron of a Josce who was "a close friend of the family". This must be he, I thought. Though, if I was right about his identity, I recollected also that he was the son and heir of a Saulot Motun, former patriarch of one of the apparently wealthiest dynasties in the country, who'd been killed tragically in the mid-sixties by anti-Jewish rioters from a group of the so-called Disinherited. We released our extended grips and sat back down again, with me possibly looking a touch sombre.

"I do trust your wife is well, Josce" I said in the process of re-seating myself comfortably. I felt obliged to make the enquiry due to her absence. But also, because it may've distracted him from thinking I'd been told something about his family by a third party.

"Yes, she's very well," he reacted. "And thank you very much for asking after her."

My nod was accompanied by a relieved smile.

Miriam was now in the hall helping Rebecca - who must've just brought up the steaming first course from the kitchen - at the table next to the wall. I had to acknowledge that, in spite of her young age, the girl was most adept at whatever task was engaging her. She struck me as being intelligent, and with a lot of common sense; as well as having some very useful practical skills, even though she may've had little if any formal schooling or training. Before the food was served, my focus returned to the table; this was spread with a white tablecloth and well illuminated by candelabras. Each diner had a fine wooden bowl atop a metal platter, beside which was a linen napkin, an ample silver goblet and some cutlery comprising a wood-handled knife and a silver spoon. There was also a large, handled pitcher centred between us, but I couldn't see its contents; and a rectangular salver was piled with chunks of bread. I was noting with interest the absence of forks when Miriam collected our bowls; and in one journey, she carried all half dozen in a stack to the side table and set them out individually. Once her mother had ladled from a tureen into each container, the lass returned them one-by-one to us. We placed the napkins on our laps, picked up the spoons and began eating, whilst Rebecca and her capable daughter disappeared down the stairs with the round, metal container.

I was finding what appeared, and tasted, to be a thick vegetable soup quite delicious. Joseph, who must've spotted the look of appreciative pleasure on my face, gave me his attention.

"Glad you're enjoying this delectable potage, David," he commented with a grin. "We're so lucky to have such a wonderful cook like Rebecca, as you'll hopefully rediscover as we progress through tonight's courses. It's good to consume such culinary excellence... really cheering in the unpredictable and depressing times our Jewish communities have to live now. Would you like some wine, David? It's French, of course, and even more uplifting than the lovely food of which we're partaking."

Everyone around the table, including me, chuckled over their soup, Sarah actually coughing a few times before recovering.

"Yes... I'd love some," I said after composing myself.

The host got up, grabbed the handle of the jug, took on the role of wine waiter, circulated and filled all the goblets with some red liquid. When he took his seat again, after pouring for himself and setting down the jug, he raised his goblet.

"*L'Chaim!* To Life!" he toasted then all joined him in taking a draught.

After the traditional Jewish declaration before imbibing, and somewhat surprisingly to me, my fellow diners concentrated on eating rather than speaking. Naturally I followed suit, not wishing to break with norms of social behaviour; and if such was the case in this or any similar household. The ethos of silence continued throughout the three courses, so ably dished up and served by the deservedly praised cook and her proficient helper, respectively. The tasty soup was followed by a scrumptious entrée of fish, which seemed to have the flavour of perch to me, and finally a choice of dessert between a lovely fruit tart and an ample wedge of inviting almond cake. Joseph was vigilant in refilling or topping up our wine vessels, as necessary. Especially during consumption of the main course, I emulated my fellow diners' use of their fingers in eating the pieces they were slicing off the fish with their knives. Certainly, this didn't make me feel so uneasy as compared to the want of supper-time conversation around the table.

When the meal had been completed – noticeably to everyone's satisfaction, including mine – the family and Josce got up from their chairs, rather unexpectedly, and I raised myself too. I understood from some words, now being exchanged, that the women would be retiring to their own rooms upstairs; and that the men, including me, would be secluding themselves in the hall's private chamber. I noted also that we would repair to the hideaway with our goblets and a fresh jug of wine, which Miriam had just brought from the kitchen on a metal tray.

The girl then proceeded to clear the table while the two brothers and Josce disappeared into the chamber, which I could see was candle-lit. I was about to tag along with them – on Joseph's kind invitation – when Naomi, who was eyeing her mother strolling back along the hall, spoke quickly to me.

"Just a few things to mention, David," she started. "In case you were unduly worried, I've double-checked with Joseph… and it's quite alright for us to go walking together, that's just the two of us, tomorrow morning. I'll get Rebecca to prepare some food to take along. We can have a mid-morning picnic, so no need for breakfast or to get up too early. Miriam will knock on your door when I'm ready to leave. Is all that alright with you?"

I hadn't heard as many words spoken in the previous hour or so, and was glad to hear also my own voice at last.

"Thank you for that, Naomi," I said, nodding smilingly. "Absolutely fine, and I'm really looking forward to our excursion along the river."

"Goodnight, David," she said, turning to head for the stairs.

"Goodnight, Naomi," I reciprocated, watching her lithe figure glide away in the gorgeous, belted blue tunic overlaying a long, dark blue gown.

As I swivelled to follow the men-folk, doubtless now installed at their ease in the restricted-entry compartment, I deliberated for a moment or two on how old Naomi might be. Maybe upper 20s into her 30s or so, I speculated hazily; and well beyond normal marriageable age for the era in which, more than astonishingly, I now found myself. I could've been virtually double her possible years. But when I registered that notion, thoughts of Diva instantly entered my mind; though her transiently intimate contact with me was based, undoubtedly, less on the physical or intellectual and more on the motivational.

Besides, I was aware that longevity generally wasn't that extensive in medieval times. In my own time, I'd happened across some statistics stating the average life expectancy for a man was a little over 30 years; though I also recalled reading that, if he made three decades or so in fairly decent nick, the chances were good for attaining his 50s or even beyond. I estimated that Joseph was somewhere approaching his mid-30s; but as the mirror so considerately provided by Diva had confirmed very recently, I didn't look that much older than he appeared to be.

"Sorry for the slight delay," I said on entering the side chamber.

"That's alright," Joseph reacted with a kind smile. "Please close the door, come sit down with us and pour yourself some wine."

I did just that, joining the three men sitting on well-padded, bench-type seats at the polished wood table and drinking from their goblets. On it stood a sturdy and powerfully glowing candle in a classy holder, the pitcher of wine and my own goblet. There was what I assumed to be a window behind now drawn drapes, and some smallish items of tapestry work on two of the other walls. As soon as I sat down on the firm upholstery, I did two things right away. I poured myself some wine, as requested to do, and noted that I must remember not to lean backwards.

Twenty One

EARLIER during the afternoon, when I was stretched out on my bed thinking rather than snoozing, I meditated on how I might enhance the trust that seemed to be growing between the brothers and me. We seemed to be hitting it off; and, thankfully, there seemed to be no doubt in their minds that I was Jewish. Indeed, Joseph had stated as much when, jokingly or otherwise, he waived any implicit need for proof of circumcision. I wondered, quite foolishly really, whether anyone had been quietly lingering outside my bedroom door in order to spy on me through the keyhole. If so, he - definitely a male - would've been thwarted in observing the changing of underwear by my key being put in the lock. However, I felt a strong compulsion to do all I could to demonstrate authenticity; and even though this time traveller was telling white lie after white lie in certain instances.

So, once in the private chamber and to start the conversation that was inevitable in the context, I started the ball rolling by mentioning something I formulated tentatively in my mind when I was resting on the bed.

"I've mentioned already that I'm a private tutor," I began. "My client-parents are generally quite well-heeled, and a few of them actually have notable contacts in high society, including the aristocracy. By way of illustration, one of them is a member of a team of doctors that serve the Royal family…"

Each of my companions in the room stared expectantly at me, and I continued.

"A few months ago, and quite by chance, I overheard a private conversation between the medical professional and a Westminster official who was visiting him. They were speaking of the Jewish communities in England, and mentioned something they believed King Edward was planning to do. This was maybe reason enough for my coming to Cambridge… in the hope of being able to inform some people prominent in the community here."

"What is it you have to tell us?" Joseph enquired with serious curiosity.

"Well, as I understood the tête-à-tête," I went on, "Edward had apparently agreed to implement the request of his Queen Mother, Eleanor of Provence, to expel all Jews from the dower towns she'd been given on her marriage to King Henry the Third. One of these towns, as you doubtless know, is Cambridge… and it seemed the plan was to deport its Jews, under supervision of the County Sheriff and his officers, to Norwich some time during this year. Is this yet public knowledge in the Jewry here?"

"No, it isn't, David," Joseph replied. "Only some of us have been aware of the King's firm proposal, but subject to knowing from our reliable sources that the originally intended destination of exile, Norwich, has been amended to Huntingdon. That market town, which has its own Jewish community, is just fifteen miles from here. This is one of the reasons why Aaron, I and others agreed he should move with his family from Cambridge to Huntingdon a couple of months ago, in part to sound out things there and make some preparations. But I think Josce can say some more on this, as he has regular trade dealings with certain merchants in the town and some farmers in its surrounding area."

We all turned our attention to the close family friend, who was nodding.

"Of course, David, this isn't the first time the three of us have spoken about this together... and also with some others in our community here," Josce started to explain. "Needless to say, we're very concerned, although hardly ever surprised these days, by anti-Semitic actions, designs and proposals from the Royal government or any other Jew haters for that matter. On the whole, the Kehilla... the community here in Cambridge may've experienced fewer fatal and other calamities than our brethren have sadly suffered in other provincial towns, as well as in the capital city. We've got many Christian neighbours in the Jewry and, although we're not bosom friends as such, we do tolerate and respect each other as human beings, if not as people with religious differences. The very recent execution of the Cambridge Jew Bonnenfant for coin-clipping offences, which he'd roundly denied, might be regarded as an exception. And I believe you now know, David, that my father was slaughtered by anti-Semitic thugs some ten years ago now..."

I nodded with as compassionate an expression as I could produce. Coincidentally, all of us took a swallow of our wine at precisely the same time then Josce went on with his narrative.

"What worries us also, David, and to say the least, are the long-term and wider, as well as the immediate, implications of our relatively new monarch's present decision on expulsion. Without question, the Queen Mother is a stern adherent to the Christian faith, if you know what I mean... and, undeniably, she's antagonistic towards England's let alone her dower towns' still not insubstantial Jewish populations. Her late husband's increasingly heavy and onerous taxation of the Jews, as you're doubtless aware, David, even in your role as an educator, has had the effect of not insignificantly diminishing their financial status as well as their demographics, economic usefulness, general morale and capabilities. Could be that she can't resist making further hostile inroads regarding these important matters. But we can't be absolutely sure that her regal son is acting at *her* behest in the proposed deportations. It's also possible that Edward, having relatively recently ascended to the throne, wishes to exert his newly acquired power as sovereign and, at the same time, do some deeds that would be bound to please his Christian subjects in addition to his mother."

Josce paused to take some more wine from his goblet; and Aaron seized an opportunity to speak.

"My feeling, Josce," he said, "is that the Queen Mother is pressuring her son to do what she wants. But how would

I know what the truth is? It just seems to me that the King may be sacrificing more than he has bargained for, and not merely by way of his mounting *tallages*... including those to help pay for his crusading ventures in the Holy Land, and other military exploits. Although these taxes have inevitably decreased in value commensurate with the reduction, across previous decades of this century, in profit-making activities and opportunities open to us Jews..."

"I can't disagree with you, Aaron," Josce interjected magnanimously. "None of us can know the veritable motivation or cause, though I don't think any of us can deny it's all underwritten fundamentally by anti-Semitism."

Everyone, including Josce, nodded after that statement was made. But I had something to contribute to the debate, too.

"I know no more than all of you," I remarked somewhat untruthfully, "but I'm just wondering whether Edward's plans, whether they're down to him or his mother, are a kind of experiment."

Of course, my initial words amounted to a downright lie. I did know more than them, much more. The three men gazed at me, mouths poised to open, but Joseph was the first to speak.

"What do you mean, David?" he asked pointedly.

"I'm not sure really," I was fibbing again, and continued to feel very bad about doing that. "But I'm seriously wondering whether it's reaching a point in the history of Jewish people in Christian England where the consensus is that we're not wanted here any more. And that a day will come, in the not too distant future, of a solution to what King and country might refer to as the Jewish problem…"

"What do you mean by 'a solution', David?" Joseph enquired with interest, as Josce and Aaron looked on with similarly intrigued expressions.

"I don't mean our complete destruction," I replied, with the word 'Holocaust' searing into my brain, "but rather a comprehensive expulsion from England."

"That could never happen, David," Joseph reacted steadfastly. "I know, and you know, that things in general haven't been consistently wonderful for the Jewish population here… and that we may not now be as useful to the King as once we were. But, in my view as a moneylender, we're still of significant usefulness to the nation and, therefore, the monarchy. We're not finished here yet…"

"Hear, hear!" exclaimed Josce, and Aaron followed suit.

There was virtually no reason for me to look crestfallen.

"All I can say is," I said, "what do I know?"

Joseph pointed to his brother.

"From the viewpoint of his fresh habitat, and our new branch, in Huntingdon," he explained, "Aaron will give you an example of how useful we can still be to our Christian neighbours, and in the widest sense."

Aaron nodded a confirmation.

"That would be good," I said, but I didn't really need to add: "Concentrating on my kind of work, I don't get to know too much about the bigger picture, or the smaller ones for that matter… though, of course, I do see or note the abysmal effects of some of the statutes, edicts, decrees or whatever."

After my brief defensive intervention, Aaron began speaking:

"Well, David, it may be helpful to you then if I widened my brother's terms of reference a little… For a long time now, over many decades in fact, Jewish moneylenders based here in Cambridge and elsewhere made substantial loans to significant members of the nobility and others of high ranking in the upper and knightly classes of society, and also to the church hierarchy. They would hold us in contempt, of course… but were more than content to receive our financial assistance. Nevertheless, for a really lengthy period, but especially since the baronial conflicts of the sixties, business hasn't been quite what it was… which has been noted earlier. As a compensatory consequence, lending has focused on clients such as minor landowners, some lesser urban notables and the lower gentry in local villages and rural farming areas as well as other, smaller-scale borrowers. And this financial pattern has developed and applied to Cambridge moneylenders, like our family…"

Aaron stopped speaking and, like the rest of us, drank some more of the fine red wine.

"By way of a Cambridge town illustration," he went on, "our business and others here have, for a long time, been lending comparatively small sums to local government officials, such as the Sheriff and even the Mayor. This kind of loan has been reasonably lucrative, though profits now are no way near as good as previously. Although we here in Cambridge are more than merely surviving, also having several still operating landlords amongst our brethren like Josce's family, the ever-increasing levels of taxation and other pressures on us have been seriously affecting the wellbeing of the community…"

The speaker paused again for another, manifestly pleasing swallow of the French alcohol, and I took the opportunity to ask a question:

"Sorry, Aaron, but to what other pressures are you referring?"

I so enquired because I remembered reading something possibly relevant to what he was saying. The Hospital of St John the Evangelist had been established near the beginning of the 13th century and, perhaps intentionally, directly opposite the Jewry area on a site later to be occupied by St John's College. Aside from its physical care activities, it was postulated in the text, the Hospital was possibly also making charitable and maybe other loans. Moreover, it was noted, the aim could've been to compete with, and therefore deliberately lessen, the Jewish financial influence in the town and its environs. As it turned out, Aaron didn't mention the Hospital at all.

"Well, David," he began to respond to my query, "several Christian Orders, and for many decades now, have been establishing houses within and close around Cambridge. And they've expanded their properties as well as their religious impact and preaching, including against our faith, so very close to the Jewry and other nearby places where there yet exist some Jewish residents."

"Who are these, so to speak, encroaching Orders?" was my supplementary.

Aaron replied in detail; and very promptly, I thought.

"Directly across the road to the west of us, we have the Augustinians... and immediately to the east, the Franciscans or Grey Friars, with the Benedictine Nuns of the Convent of St Radegund just beyond the King's Ditch. Across the Ditch, to the south-west of the town centre, there are the Dominicans or Black Friars. Whilst a bit further to the south are the so-called Friars of the Sack. So you can readily see, David, that these religious houses are making some significant encroachments on town land and, especially, quite proximate to our Jewry neighbourhood."

I nodded and, I supposed, understood why this knowledge might be at the forefront of his and other Cambridge Jewish residents' minds. Then another but unrelated notion occurred to me.

"S-Sorry to change the subject," I said hesitantly, "but could I ask a question about the *Tabula*, please?"

"Go ahead," Joseph replied.

"It's about identification," I began, knowing that I was speaking other than merely from recent, first-hand experience. "In London, you don't see that much of the one-time requisite, knob-pointed Jewish hat being worn by men these days... it seems to have fallen into desuetude. I know the discriminatory headgear was introduced in consequence of a Lateran Council recommendation earlier this century. Some males in London do still sport them, for whatever reason. But the authorities don't seem to be implementing any general enforcement action in that connection. And that seems to be the case, I might add, also in relation to the Tabula, the badge that distinguishes us from our Christian fellow countrymen. Although many Jewish people, of both genders, do wear it prominently as obligated by Henry III's confirmatory Statute of Jewry almost twenty years back. I've got a couple of tunics with me. The one I'm now wearing doesn't have the Tabula sewn onto it... the other, in my room, does. That's the one I was wearing this morning and which, as Joseph and Aaron know well, caused me some malevolent anti-Semitic aggression, verbal and physical, on my arrival in Cambridge..."

Joseph very quickly summarised what had happened to me for his friend's sake; and Josce shook his head a few times during the telling.

"Sorry you had to go through all that, David," he said sympathetically.

"Thank you, Josce," I responded. "My bad experience here earlier today suggests I need to know what the current local situation is regarding the *Tabula*. If there's no compulsion to wear it in public here at the present time, then I probably won't."

Joseph leaned slightly across the table, with an earnest expression.

"I don't know whether you know this, David," he said, "but before the late King Henry III made his annoyance with non-compliance into a Royal command, many who had the money to do so, and even some entire communities, paid to be let off wearing the Tabula. Nowadays, we have a mixed bag of submission, disobedience, enforcement and payment… much depends on the prevailing atmosphere locally, if you know what I mean. The decision whether to wear the badge or not is yours alone, David, I'm afraid to say… though perhaps relevant to your choice is the fact that your face isn't well known in Cantabrigia."

I nodded, despite thinking that my host's analysis wasn't particularly helpful to me.

"Alright," I said, "I'll bear in mind what you've told me, Joseph… thank you."

He made to top up our drinks again, but I placed a hand atop my goblet.

"Sorry, Joseph, but my head tells me I should probably refrain," I announced, a bit wearily. "Think I've had enough wine for this evening, but thank you. In fact, my head tells me also that I should be off to bed now… I'm really quite tired, and it has been a very long, rather extraordinary and, earlier on, somewhat painful day for me."

"Say no more, David… we understand entirely," Joseph said, with both brother and close friend nodding agreement with his benign words.

"You've been so good to me," I added. "But maybe there's just one more piece of information that I've gathered inadvertently, aside from the projected expulsion to Huntingdon, and which may or may not prove to be reliable…"

"Please…" Joseph said, holding out his open palm towards me. "You have the floor again, David."

"Sorry… I was going to mention it earlier, but it slipped my mind," I remarked. "Our discussion about the Tabula and the extent of its enforcement has reminded me, thankfully…"

Three pairs of eyes focused unwaveringly on my face, and I carried on:

"It's another conversation I was definitely not supposed to hear… though I should mention, at once, that the subject-matter wasn't specifically related to the Cambridge Jewish community. Unfortunately, I didn't hear the entire exchange but what I did take in gave me serious pause for thought. As far as I could make out, it would seem that Edward wishes to promulgate another Statute of Jewry, this time rather more dogmatically than his father…"

"My apologies for interrupting you, David," Josce stated anxiously, "but we have heard rumours on our own special grapevine… but little in the way of hard detail or confirmation. If you were able to assist to any degree, we and indeed many others here would be extremely grateful."

Joseph and Aaron were nodding as I went on with my scripted, but hopefully, beneficial account.

"Well, one of the major potential provisions of the proposed legislation was to utterly ban usury. Another was to relieve certain debtors from their Jewish loans. There was also said to be a proposal for banning Jews from residing outside specified urban areas. And what reminded me about these planned statutory provisions is the Jewish badge. Apparently, Edward is fed up with disobedience in that connect, and intends to ensure that Jewish people wear

174

in public a larger and yellow-coloured Tabula on their outer garments. I'm not sure about this, but I believe it was noted also that Christians are to be barred from residing alongside Jews…"

Joseph's features took on an image of unrestrained horror.

"Even though we can't be absolutely certain, at present," he interjected, "if what you've overheard and we know vaguely is likely to happen, it could spell disaster for all of us. What, if anything, did you also eavesdrop that might offer us some salvation… in the way of our making a living to survive?"

"There *was* something else mentioned, though it wasn't very comprehensible to me. I believe it related to Jews being allowed to continue as traders or to become small farmers. But please don't rely on my possibly faulty reportage."

"Traders or farmers, eh…? That's really a big deal!" Joseph exclaimed. "Seems clear to me that the King and, for that matter, his mother are determined to destroy us financially… if not otherwise!"

I emitted one hell of an unexpected yawn, not raising a hand to my gaping mouth in time.

"Why don't you retire now, David," my host advised. "You're obviously very fatigued, probably exhausted by your trials and tribulations earlier on."

"I will and I am, Joseph," I concurred, thinking also of my wine consumption as I rose slowly from the bench-seat. "Thanks again for all your help and hospitality. I'll go to my bedroom now, if I may."

Everyone nodded their empathetic consent.

I was on the point of departing, when Joseph said:

"It's a pleasure having you with us, David. Although we met in dire circumstances, it was the Almighty's will that brought us together... And our thanks are due also for your useful contribution to our knowledge of what may be in the wind for England's Jewish communities."

As I reached the door and turned to send a goodnight wave, Joseph called:

"Oh David, do enjoy your riverside walk with Naomi tomorrow morning."

I smiled, and exited the chamber. I began closing it behind me, but not before spotting Joseph winking grinningly at his brother...

Twenty Two

SO I left the three men to their further debate concerning the future and, it doubtless went without saying, some nattering about me. It was really more than sad for me to know, and not to be able to tell them, that their King would definitely be expelling all Jews from England 15 years hence.

Unsurprisingly, and even though my mind was awhirl, I fell asleep almost as soon as my head hit the pillow. A short time back, I found myself lighting the fat candle - rooted firmly into its handled holder - from the small fire Miriam had kindly kindled for me. I repaired to the *garderobe*, necessarily after all that wine, put one set of underwear and my dirty tunic in the wash-sack she'd supplied, left it outside the door then cleaned myself as best I could. As I washed, awkwardly and superficially, I felt my end-of-day and fairly modest growth of prickly stubble on cheeks, chin and neck. Like Joseph, Aaron and Josce, I was a clean-shaven guy; though, to compensate seemingly, the four of us did possess more than enough hair on top. That morning, I noticed that a number of the men leaving church were sporting eclectic beards, with or without moustaches of various shapes and sizes. So before falling into the all-embracing arms of *Morpheus*, my last thought of the day was whether I should lazily allow myself to become hirsute; or maybe ask Joseph if I could borrow, or where I might acquire, some shaving equipment. At that fading moment of consciousness, my inclination was to let matters follow their natural course, whatever that might be.

I awakened with a start from a dreamless slumber, my eyes springing open. In that instant, I accepted my sudden waking could've been due to a flash of light in the chamber from the window above my head. I swivelled in the bed and saw the lit candle on the table, and the dying embers in the fireplace. As my brain began to function again, I tried to calculate how far into the morning it might be. I knew there existed types of aptly marked clock-candles in these medieval times, but mine wasn't one of them. I couldn't assess how high the sun was in the sky; but - thank heavens - there hadn't been a solid rapping on the door by Miriam, to inform me Naomi was ready and waiting to leave the house for our proposed walk along the river. At least, I hoped Miriam hadn't yet called.

I got up hurriedly, straightened the bedclothes, carried out some ablutions — noting, happily, the bag of clothes for washing was still where I'd left it in the corridor — and dressed myself. I recalled Naomi telling me there was no need to rise early or to go down to breakfast; though I would've murdered an Americano, had one been available. On an impulse, however, I left my room and moved into the quietude of the house. Possibly I was its only inhabitant to be awake, I pondered. There was no one around when

I arrived in the now naturally illuminated, main hall; and I ambled along the length of it to the archway at its far end. On reaching the staircase, both to the kitchen and courtyard, I took some steps down and summoned up some *chutzpah*.

"Miriam!" I called out, albeit with circumspection and a certain volume restraint.

But I wasn't at all amazed at her appearance, as if magically, a few steps below me and within moments of my calling her name; though the young girl herself did reveal some surprise in her enquiring eyes.

"Can I help you, sir?" she asked softly, virtually in a whisper. "I would've knocked on your door, as arranged, at the right time."

"Yes, Miriam, I know…and I'm sorry to disturb you," I responded, a smidgen guiltily but perhaps incongruously in relation to a housemaid.

"Please don't apologise to *me*, sir," she stressed, lowering her head for a moment. "It could've been some time before I called on you, sir… it's still very early in the morning."

Now I knew the timing score, I asked the helpful lass whether I would have time for a bath.

"Most certainly, sir," she said, nodding confidently. "If you would kindly return to your bedchamber, the tub and hot water together with drying cloths will be brought up to you as soon as possible."

As it turned out, Miriam arrived with the necessities sooner than I would've thought practicable. She was ably assisted, in what I imagined to be a problematic task, by an equally young but sturdier female unknown to me.

Two trips were required to be undertaken by the pair of girls. After they left me to my own bathing devices, and having completed them, I felt brilliantly refreshed when re-donning my outdoor garments. But I still needed to wait until Miriam returned to inform me that Naomi was ready for me in the main hall. I found her seated in the non-dining section close to the archway and steps leading down to the lobby. We exchanged a smiley "Good morning". Then she got up – I could now see fully her attractive, belted tunic and its underlying longer dress, a leather shoulder bag hanging diagonally across her upper body – and grabbed a sort of cloth holdall from another chair then glanced through the nearby window.

"Let's go then," she said cheerily, "looks like another fine sunny day."

I nodded and, with a chivalrous gesture, motioned her to lead the way. In any case, I mused, Naomi was far better aware than I of the anticipated route. We departed the house - with me a step or so behind her comely figure – and proceeded along Jews' Lane beside All Saints. Next, we turned right into the High Street to pass the Hospital of St John then, shortly afterwards, left into the broader Bridge Street heading for the river. We endeavoured to keep close to one side of the roadway with other pedestrians, in a cautious effort to avoid the noisy-wheeled traffic. This comprised horse-drawn wagons and manually-towed carts, juddering and clanking on the mucky, rutted highway with their drivers and haulers screaming sporadic obscenities, for one reason or another.

We walked at a judicious pace, and almost level-pegging, in total silence; and I tried to identify some of the shops that I'd noticed the previous day. The possibility of an inn was corroborated when we needed to move around a couple of heavily built men, garbed in leather overalls and rolling barrels - presumably brewer's men delivering beer or ale - from a parked wagon with its strong and fine-looking, grey cart-horse standing still and calm. Then I spotted a shop that appeared to stock a variety of wearing apparel, including tunics for men and women. I vowed to pop along there the next day to supplement my meagre wardrobe.

With that thought, and almost instinctively now, I touched a hand to my chest; and felt the comforting little bundle of valuable coinage, and my vital smart-phone, bound and concealed protectively beneath my shirt and tunic. As we approached the quayside area bordering the Cam, I noted also what looked like a barber's shop. I knew that many of the proprietors of such premises were also dentists, of a sort, largely capable only of extracting diseased and rotten teeth. Some of the owners were in the clinical business of blood-letting, too; sometimes, I reflected pseudo-wittily, unintentionally after cutting a client when shaving him with the straight, sharp knives customarily employed for the purpose.

After turning into the location set aside for the loading and unloading of cargo-carrying river-craft, Naomi glanced over her shoulder to attract my attention.

"And now we'll begin our stroll along the riverside path," she said, a little glint in her eyes.

Twenty Three

AS Naomi and I began to cross the quayside towards the Cam pathway, and at the same time coincidentally, we pushed back our hoods to feel the growing warmth of the sun on our faces. It was only then that we both noted Josce mounted on a handsome brown steed. Dressed in some rather neat attire, and a swanky wide-brimmed hat, he appeared to be talking to a robust man in work overalls. From his demeanour, the guy on foot appeared to be in charge of the loading, by a couple of huge dock-men, of a number of hefty sacks from a nearby cart onto one of the flat-bottomed, single-mast riverboats moored at a short wooden pier. As we passed close by the family friend, he espied us smiling in his direction, acknowledged with a little hand-wave then continued his conversation. Of course, I knew from my reading about this personality that Josce would – and in the not too distant future – be exiled to Huntingdon alongside all other members of the Cambridge Jewish community. I supposed he was preparing for that expulsion. But I did wonder whether he was aware of one or two other factors connected with the transfer. I wondered, rather than knew, because he might've been knowledgeable about more than I might've expected, due to his and his family's status in society.

I was also apprised of the fact that, shortly after arriving in the destination town, he would be appointed one of the four – two Christian, two Jewish – chirographers or keepers of the newly conjoined Cambridge and Huntingdon *archa*. I knew that an *archa* was constituted by a large chest in which were retained deeds and other legal documents pertaining to financial transactions entered into, generally, by Jewish moneylenders, bankers and pawnbrokers. I was aware also that Jews would be permitted to live only in those 20 or so English towns possessing such a depository, the contents of which were subject to periodic scrutiny by the Exchequer of the Jews in Westminster, and thus by the King. My reading had revealed that Josce would be the only deported Jew authorised to return periodically to Cambridge - where he would be able to reside in the nearby village of Chesterton - in order to maintain his properties in Bridge Street. So as Naomi and I took to the riverside path, I imagined that his family's wealth and influence may've had something to do with such especially advantageous treatment by those in power, centrally and locally.

"We start here," Naomi remarked suddenly, and maybe superfluously; though her voice effectively drew me out of my Josce musings.

I noted the hint of a slight breeze rustling overhanging leaves in the lines of willow trees flanking the sun-sprayed and gently flowing river. I couldn't help but be conscious of the old castle on its high mound, strategically commanding the town and its surrounding landscape. In my own time, I wouldn't have been in a position to even see the hill – absent the citadel, of course – because of the then intervening and impressive buildings of Magdalene College on the opposite bank of the Cam.

"Fine," I responded laconically, largely because of not knowing what more to say.

Initially on our ambling ramble, and in fairly close succession, we passed a number of people heading towards town, many of them quite poorly clad and a few noticeably without footwear of any kind. Several of them were carrying heavy-looking bundles on their backs or pulling smallish, wheelbarrow-type containers. As we progressed further along the edge of an expansive grassy area – which in my day would be a park, long-known as Jesus Green, with some tennis courts, a bowling green and an enclosed summer lido – the number of other pedestrians reduced considerably. On both sides of the river – which in the 21st century would've seen anchored houseboats below the occasional stylish apartment development, rows of upmarket residences, university boathouses and the occasional public house – there was tree-studded, open country and farmland. I could just about make out some flocks of grazing sheep. Back a little way, I was conscious of passing the geographical point at the riverside from where the so-called King's Ditch began its circumnavigation of the medieval town and close environs, to terminate upstream. I knew that the extensive feature had served mainly as a rubbish tip before Henry III reinforced the defensive trench during the baronial wars of the 1260s. Now, and only a few years after that long and murderous struggle, it was reverting to its erstwhile usefulness as an elongated, garbage disposal pit. You could tell by its odorous whiff.

But what I was noticing most of all - as we strolled beside the gently curving Cam at the edge of a spacious green area, later to be named Midsummer Common – was that Naomi and I hadn't exchanged a single word for some while now. As I was, to her, a newcomer to Cambridge, maybe she was thinking I would prefer to concentrate on discovering and absorbing my surroundings. Or perhaps she felt in some way inhibited or deterred from speaking to me in case, I inferred, the discourse might become embarrassingly personal. But if she was so sensitive about her sad circumstances, I thought, why had she invited me to walk with her in the first place? Possibly, as I sought oddly to answer my own question, Naomi had meant her words to be taken literally and exclusively - our excursion was intended as a walk, not a talk. Next, I pondered about what motive I might have for not myself initiating some sociable chit-chat. After all, I mused, a dialogue is a two-way affair.

All of a sudden, I was stopped in my tracks – and in all senses – when my mute companion halted, gazed across the river and pointed.

"The village of Chesterton is over that way," she said like an amateur tour guide.

As the woman turned to face me, I nodded at the somewhat banal information; and she said, with an expression of earnestness marking her features:

"How old do you think I am, David?"

Her very delicate question stunned me into continuing my speechless state by its unbelievable inaptness. When, after some indefinable passage of time, I recovered the use of my vocal cords, I still wasn't sure if or how I should reply. But in a short while more, I was and did; and in the traditional Jewish way, with yet another question.

"Why do you ask me this, Naomi?" I enquired fairly neutrally.

Then I saw her pallid yet beautiful face start to crumple, and her eyes fill with tear-pearls that began to trail down her cheeks.

"I'm an old woman, and I look like one!" she exclaimed sobbingly. "I'm twenty-eight years of age."

In that more than uneasy instant for me, I thought she was jesting; though I realised rapidly that such was the complete converse of the case. Bearing in mind her own situation and also medieval life expectancy, even amongst the well-to-do sections of the social order, I could maybe grasp where she was coming from in her emotional outburst. For certain, Naomi didn't appear anywhere near "old" – in the generally accepted sense - and, of course, looked rather younger than me. Perhaps I was verging on the naïve, and her real intention was to fish for compliments, genuine or otherwise. But I dismissed that notion swiftly, and with the contempt it deserved. She looked to be in considerable and authentic, psychological pain. I reached out tentatively and touched her arm empathetically. She dipped her head slightly, and teardrops plummeted onto her very feminine tunic.

"Naomi," I said softly, "you're not an *old* woman… and you most assuredly do not look like one. In fact, and if I may say so, you're a most attractive lady."

She looked up, and stared directly into eyes that hopefully mirrored my sincerity.

"Y-You're j-just saying that to make me feel better," she opined with emotion.

I shook my head.

"I meant every word I said, Naomi," I added. "Please believe me."

I removed my hand from her arm. She placed the bundle she was holding on the grass verge, and removed a small square of linen cloth from her shoulder bag to wipe her face and eyes.

"I-I'm really sorry for asking you the question… and for my childlike behaviour," she uttered, but now with a more tranquil voice. "Sometimes, I get quite emotive about my circumstances… circumstances that I know you're aware of. Please forgive me, David."

At that moment, I felt quite anxious about her knowing that I knew of her barrenness. But I tried to put on a brave face.

"There's absolutely nothing for you to apologise to me for, Naomi," I said, trying hard to offer a kindly smile.

"I'm very grateful for that, David," she said, trying hard to reflect my expression. "And I don't want you to feel ill at ease about knowing of my infertility… everyone knows about it."

"Thank you," I offered briefly.

"And again my thanks to you, David… you're a good person, and I like you."

As I contemplated Naomi's last few words, she put away the damp cloth and said:

"Let's continue our walk now… we'll soon stop to eat and drink our picnic package prepared by Rebecca."

I nodded my agreement, glad to see that the woman - at least on the surface – had apparently emerged from her melancholic but comprehensible display of feelings. Then I said something which, immediately afterwards, I seriously questioned why I had done.

"And I like you, too, Naomi."

She received my words with an endearing beam.

Shortly we were passed by a few more people, including a bruiser of a man with a huge dog that my companion and I flinched away from as it snarled menacingly at the two of us. Then Naomi pointed to what undoubtedly she considered to be a convenient spot, under the graciously spreading, foliage canopy of an old oak tree, where we could rest and have a bite of food and a drink. The household's first-rate chef had provided us with sharing hunks of rustic-style bread, chunks of cheddar-like cheese and some apples, together with a couple of water flasks. Basic fare really, and which Naomi placed atop the supplied large square of cloth to cover our grassy table. The rations were more than adequate and tasty enough to satisfy our peckish palates, and to sate our modest thirsts. The image of an intense black Americano percolated into my mind. Unfortunately, the nearest coffee shop was not far off 800

188

years away. For a while, we ate and drank wrapt in our separate thoughts. Naomi's life, I reflected, could've been so different had she been born into my future world. Postmodern medical diagnostics and revolutionary treatments might've allowed her, at least a chance, to have the child or children she doubtless though forlornly and desperately desired. I really didn't think she would've encountered any problems attracting a husband; and so much would've been available to try for a family of her own. I needed to assume that, in the medieval Jewish milieu, adoption would be out of the question, even on the basis a spouse could've been arranged for her. I felt so sorry for her sorrowful predicament. Naomi was far from being - as she sadly expressed herself to be - an "old woman". But I could understand, readily enough, her hopeless state of mind. Chronologically, she was still under the age of 30 - well within marriageable age in my century. Though, I supposed, it was to be borne in mind that girls in her time were not unusually married off by their first teen year.

"Are you enjoying our, albeit plain but tasty, spread, David?" Naomi enquired, her voice again plucking me from my miles-away daydream.

"Very much so," I replied, after quickly swallowing some well-chewed dairy product and reaching for one of the two flasks to wash it down. "It's hitting the mark, for sure."

She gave me a winning smile, and said:

"I know what you mean, David…"

I grinned, and she continued.

189

"And it's so pleasing being out in the lovely warm sunshine, rather than cooped up in my chamber because there's nobody available to walk any distance with me. Sometimes I feel so lonely, and even when working on some embroidery with my mother, that I can think only of…"

She stopped there for a moment or two, not finishing the sentence, so that I was unable to construe her meaning or intent.

"And it's very nice for me to be with you here," she went on.

I sent her, what must've appeared as, an equivocally coy smile.

"Nice of you to say so, Naomi, and I'm very pleased to be able to escort you."

I took some more of the very acceptable bread and cheese, as we sat on the dry ground a few metres from the river. I glanced around us, and all seemed deserted and quiet now; apart, that is, from the cries of some birds swooping above us towards the water. Then it was still and calm again; and it just seemed to me like the two of us were all alone in the world.

"What was that?" Naomi said suddenly.

"What do you mean?" I asked a trifle confused.

"I just felt something small hitting the back of my tunic," she replied, an edge of concern in her voice.

I looked up and about us.

"I hope it wasn't a bird… you know what I mean," I said. "Please turn round and I'll search for any evidence."

Naomi did so, but I couldn't detect any sign of a bird strike.

Then I took a stinging hit on my shoulder, but this time I knew what caused it. A small stone rolled down my tunic to land on the grass. Next, a small shower of pebbles flew over the two of us and rebounded off the ancient oak. I could see from Naomi's expression that she was quite scared, as we both now focused our attention on the relatively narrow river. All was revealed when we perceived – at one and the same time - three bearded, poorly-clothed and bedraggled men on the opposite bank. They were stooping to grab handfuls of small rocks then hurling the missiles in our direction, accompanied by throaty guffaws of rough laughter. Somehow, I couldn't see the joke. But like my increasingly nervous-looking companion, I was beginning to feel - and probably appeared - more than a little panicky.

"See… see, David!" Naomi uttered loudly. "It's those oafish men on the other side of the river. They're throwing stones at us. And can you hear the anti-Semitic abuse the loutish good-for-nothings are screaming at us now? True Anglo-Saxon expletives… and they know we're Jewish!"

"B-But how could they possibly know that?" I enquired with edgy surprise. "We're not displaying the *Tabula* on our tunics."

"They know," she replied scornfully. "Believe me, David, they know… Ouch! That one hit me on the head. We used to be able to walk around here in peace… things have deteriorated so much for us. We'd better get out of here, David, and right now!"

"Alright, Naomi… let's go!" I said worriedly, and with added decibels. "Leave all this stuff where it is, we've no time to clear up… Quick now, before those foul-mouthed hooligans find some bigger stones and knock one or both of us senseless… their aim seems to be on target!"

We stood up quickly and hurried, at a tactical angle, across the grass to the pathway, now concentrated determinedly on heading back to the comparative safety of town.

"Oh, no… please, no!" Naomi shrieked suddenly - her shoulder bag bouncing at her side – and sending a stark shiver along my spine.

"What is it?" I called out, as we reached the track and moved hastily along the pathway.

"Didn't you hear the splashes, David?"

"What splashes?" I queried, glancing over my bobbing shoulder at the Cam as Naomi then I further quickened the pace.

She didn't need to reply to my question because I could see the three aggressive delinquents had jumped into the river and were swimming towards our bank.

"Run… run for your life, David!" she yelled with terror. "We've just got to dash as fast as we can… this is a really dangerous situation we're in!"

I began to sprint somewhat, but not as fast as I might've done if alone. Naomi probably wouldn't have been able to keep up with me, maybe largely due to the length of her tunic and dress.

"I-I'm so s-sorry, David," she said, panting out her words. "I-I should've known better than to bring us out here, s–so far from town... and p–particularly in these unpredictable times for the J–Jewish community. W–Who can tell... c–can tell what will happen if they catch us... and there's n–nobody around at this lunchtime hour to help us, even if they c–could or w–would."

I grabbed Naomi's hand in an effort to assist her more fluid movement alongside me, her distressing comments having drilled a sense of real urgency, if not fear into my own head. I couldn't shake off some horribly vivid thoughts of rape, mutilation and death for her and a painful end for me, too. Having made, I estimated, reasonable progress along the trail, I took another rapid glimpse back. And I noted that the river-current, at a point parallel to our ill-chosen picnic spot, may've been indirectly assisting us fugitives from imminent violence. I believed it was taking longer, more time than the bank-to-bank distance might've suggested, for the three vicious, dog-crawling landlubbers – rather than expert swimmers, thankfully – to reach our side of the Cam. We ran and ran, Naomi doing well to keep up. I continued to yell encouragement, even if she didn't need to be urged on in this harrowing situation.

"Keep going, Naomi!" I pressed her. "We're increasing the gap, and our pursuers haven't begun to chase us along the path yet."

I was just a bit out on that one. A moment later, when I peered back again, the potentially rapist and murderous rogues were clambering out of the river. Luckily, they were still some way behind us; though, scarily, not a million miles away. But, frighteningly, they would certainly be more agile and speedy on land than in water.

"Do try to run faster, Naomi," I pleaded. "They're climbing out of the water now!"

Even though physically inhibited by her clothing, she was definitely striving to keep up; and doubtless incited by some fatal notions invading her terrified mind. Auspiciously, as we attained the parkland area sprinkled with trees, I was struck by a possible brainwave rather than a big rock.

"T-This way, Naomi," I advised, almost out of breath and with a less than gentle pull on her hand. "I've just got an idea how to lose them."

"I-I really do hope so, David," she reacted, equally breathlessly, "and very soon, please God... I-I can feel my body weakening."

I led her away from the riverside and between the scattered trees. Then I stopped, Naomi halting alongside me and both of us virtually winded and breathless. Our noses told us well before our eyes that we were hovering at the edge of the stinking King's Ditch.

"I-I know you're not going to like, to say the very least, what we're about to do, Naomi," I said quickly. "B-But I really do believe it's our only chance of survival now."

With a sense, if not the stench of horror masking her features, she gazed down into a trench filled – as far as the eye could see, and almost to the brim – with rotting rubbish of every possible variety. We were aware also, and with a sickening revulsion from the foul smell, that it included a considerable amount of human and animal excrement. At that perilously dithering moment, we understood clearly there was no other option. So after staring at each other, like through a glass darkly, we closed our eyes and mouths tight shut then lowered ourselves into the hellish pit.

"Bury yourself at once!" I said incredibly, as we lifted our eyelids momentarily. "Let's get as much of this shit, excuse my French, over our heads… and straightaway!"

I was soon sure that Naomi and I were out of sight of anyone surveying the trench from its rim. Being a 21st century guy from a civilised culture, it was impossible for me to believe our present situation. But, somehow, I had to find the psychological clue to seeing both of us through this mess. I didn't suppose that Naomi felt any differently, even as a 13th century girl. As I strived and grappled to create some breathing space for us - in the incredibly obnoxious clutches of the tightly-packed, and not necessarily motionless, ooze and filth — the woman seemed to find the, albeit perverted, rationale quicker than me.

"I guess it's better for us to be buried alive than dead," Naomi whispered in my close ear. "And, incidentally, the Jewish cemetery isn't that far from here."

Beyond that, we waited in dreadful silence, our hearts beating wildly.

An accurate calculation of passing time was, of course, unachievable. After an indefinable period, we heard some vague noises that could've been voices calling to each other, and not that distant. I was assuming the three men, with their patently evil intent, had been searching around for us, perhaps mystified by our sudden and inexplicable disappearance. Possibly, their eyes had scanned the river and far bank in case we'd swum to the other side to make our surreptitious escape. Maybe they were probing around, and up into every tree, within a certain radius of the water's edge. And whilst blocking their noses, they now could be peering into our disgusting place of concealment yet sanctuary... the King's Ditch.

Then I heard some revolting, anti-Semitic language being screamed and, with much angst, relatively nearby. Naomi must've picked it up, too, because I felt her hand first touch then grip my arm. Although trembling in our boots and aghast in our minds, we had the good sense not to utter a word and not to move unduly. The voices were yelling again; but this time it seemed the thugs were giving up the hunt, and even swearing at themselves for their failure to locate us. I could swear to have heard a couple of sentences, loudly exclaimed: "Let's be off to the flipping pub!" then "I could drink a whole barrel of flipping ale!" It could've been a feint, and I realised that. So I reached out, grasping Naomi's arm, to convey a silent message to remain quiet and as rigid as possible. The swine could've been out there waiting for us; and time, I felt, was definitely on their side.

So we waited... and waited. But there came a point when I thought we would die in the ditch anyway, and for obvious reasons. But I was really concerned about Naomi; understandably, she wasn't feeling at all well – to put it very mildly. It seemed to me that the last sentence

I heard called, by one of the gang of three, was plausible. Holding Naomi's cold gooey hand, I felt there was no alternative now; but I didn't want her to start moaning loudly. I felt the strong need to gamble with our lives, because remaining in this horrific abyss would've soon spelled the end of them in any event. I detached my hand from hers, and slowly raised myself out of the putrid bog of refuse holding us prisoner. I reached up, gripped the brink of the trench and peered cautiously over the top. I gazed around, a complete 360 degrees, but couldn't see another soul. The sun suggested it was about mid-afternoon. I slithered back down into the hellish pit, rooted about for Naomi and found her. I explained quickly why we were leaving now. As speedily as possible, but with much difficulty, I manoeuvred her ultra-slippery and muck-strewn body upwards and into a level position on the grass.

We rested there for a short while; and it's nigh on impossible to describe definitively how we must've appeared. Other than that we were covered, from tip to toe, in a clinging and appalling array of malodorous filth, waste and grime. With the shoulder bag amazingly still attached to Naomi, I managed to open it, took out a small cloth that remained within and wiped her face then mine as best I could. But the head-spinning vapours from the black hole dictated we had to leave, and immediately. I lifted Naomi to an almost upright posture, and helped her walk slowly to the riverside footpath. Needless to say, I wasn't feeling that good myself. But I needed to summon the will to get us back to the Jewry safely, and as fast as possible, so that a physician could examine Naomi and maybe me as well. After a short while, some people – fortunately, of the non-violent sort - began to pass by; though they gave us an understandably wide berth, and really distasteful if not repugnant looks. At last we were approaching the quayside, still busy with the loading and unloading of cargo. As soon as anyone could smell us coming, they moved rapidly out of our way; and, by doing so, a usefully unimpeded passage was afforded to Naomi and me.

Quite astonishingly, I heard our names being called; and I think Naomi heard this, too, because she raised her lowered head a little at the familiar sounds. My surprise included the disbelief that anyone would be able to recognise us in our present abominable state. But Josce must've done, and for whatever reason. We were so amazingly glad when he hurried between the piles of boxes, sacks and barrels to our sides, his face a picture of full-blown incredulity. Very succinctly, and to his utter shock and dismay, I sought to relate what had befallen us that afternoon. Without more and readily noting our horrendous condition, especially that of Naomi, he quickly located one of the horse-drawn, commodity carts that belonged to him. We got her onto the back of it; and I climbed up to sit beside the severely anguished woman. Her head, eyes closed, and body were propped against mine for necessary support, as Josce took the driver's seat, grabbed the reins and headed off towards the Jewry area.

As the horse cantered and the cart clanked along, Naomi opened her eyes then turned her face slightly, but clearly achingly, to look into mine.

"T-Thank you for saving my life… and my v-virginity, David," she said slowly and quietly; and seemingly, I thought, with a glimmer of hope rather than despair.

Twenty Four

WHEN we entered the house, there was a fraught blend of horrified immediate reaction by the brothers – who emerged quickly from the ground-floor doorway, drawn by noises outside the main entrance – at our unspeakable state, then extreme anger on hearing of our dreadful ordeal followed by emotional expressions of eternal gratitude for my actions in protecting their sister. Next and in rapid response, further assistance was provided by everyone else in the household to get Naomi and me to our respective chambers. Before we were helped up the first staircase, an irate Josce offered loudly, generously but perhaps too impulsively to round up and lead some horsemen along the river to hunt down the miscreants and give them what they deserved. While Joseph succeeded in persuading him of his proposal's likely impracticality, and its potential for adverse though unforeseeable consequences, Aaron rushed off to summon the family's physician. Josce needed to return to the dock area, but again expressed his profound dismay at what had happened to us. I thanked him profusely for his helpful and timely assistance then he departed.

It was manifestly clear to all that Naomi required a medic's attention rather more than me. Joseph and his mother agreed that we shouldn't be washed and cleaned, even though we stunk to high heaven, until the doctor had seen and assessed our condition. When at last I lay down shattered on my bed, it wasn't long to wait for Jonathan to appear, examine and give me his diagnosis. Before his arrival, I was informed by Joseph – who stayed with me while Sarah, with Miriam's help, comforted Naomi in her room – that the Jewish physician lived with his wife and children, and had his consulting room and surgery, in a house not precisely within the Jewry area but just off Bridge Street and near to St Sepulchre's Church. Apparently, he was requested to take a quick look at me first because I seemed to be reasonably alright physically; though, naturally, I was still in a state of shock. Literally within seconds, Jonathan – who appeared to be of similar age to Joseph – gave me the swift okay for a scrub-up, advised bed rest for a day or so then hastened along the hallway to Naomi's room, pursued by her brother.

All was arranged hurriedly but efficiently for my cleansing procedures including, it was said, some health-enhancing and fragrant oils. After washing and bathing myself - in private - more thoroughly than ever in the long history of my personal hygiene routine, I was becoming something like a new man, at least appearance-wise. But also, and understandably, I was deeply weary. Lingering in my head were tremors from the nauseating outcome of our day's walkabout. As I rested under the bedclothes, Miriam fetched me from the kitchen something nourishing to eat in a bowl and a special drink in a glass vessel, a remedial amalgam of herbs and spices the doctor had recommended, ostensibly to aid my recovery. Gingerly but admirably, the proficient youngster took away with her the pile of my foul-smelling clothes in a sack. Shortly afterwards, the girl brought back a fresh outfit that Joseph had donated thoughtfully; and knowing that I wasn't that much taller than him. Alongside the attire, he gave me a wide leather belt which, I noted welcomingly, held a useful dangling purse attached by short cords. Of course I hid my smart-phone, and placed my body-belt with its valuable currency, in the original clothes bag Diva had sought fit to supply for my sojourn in *Cantabrigia*. Now I could transfer my coinage into a more compact, accessible money bag.

From the moment the family's physician left my chamber to attend on Naomi, I couldn't stop thinking about her; and hoping that there wouldn't be any seriously unfavourable, medical prognosis. Impatiently, I waited to learn the results of Jonathan's visit; and, though maybe not that strangely, I felt the distressing events Naomi and I had shared that day served to create a kind of bond between us, at least for my part. Prior to Miriam finally closing my door behind her, I enquired whether she was hearing anything yet about Naomi. But she wasn't. Not long after I dressed, consumed the food and beverage left on my table and sat myself down on the bed to mull over matters that there came a knock on the door. It was Joseph, and I was gladdened at once to see the glowing expression of relief on his face.

Standing in the doorway, and to doubly confirm the message his eyes conveyed, he announced:

"Thank the Almighty... Jonathan has declared Naomi completely free from physical injury or incapacity. But, David, I'm sure you won't be surprised to hear that she's really suffering the after-effects of her trauma, and likely to a greater extent than yourself... though I don't belittle your current state of mind for one moment. My sister can be very sensitive at times, as I do believe you may understand. But having said that, I don't think anyone facing the terrifying ordeal that both of you experienced this afternoon would come away from it without any post-traumatic reverberations..."

I nodded compassionately.

"May she be fully recovered very soon," I added.

"Thank you for your kind words, David," Joseph said. "And I thank you again, on behalf of our entire family, for what you did today. How can we ever repay you?"

"I'm repaid already by having Naomi confirmed to be in no danger physically," I responded. "And you and the family have been so helpful, welcoming and benevolent to me since my almost fatal arrival in Cambridge that I'm so pleased to have been able to repay you, albeit in awful and alarming circumstances."

Joseph approached the bed and shook my hand warmly in his firm grip.

"Our esteemed doctor has prescribed my sister a special tonic," he said, "and definitely some bed-rest for her, too. She's now being sensitively cleaned and delicately bathed in the most comforting scented water before being put to bed. Jonathan estimates that it will take a few days for her, and I believe you also, to return fully to your normal selves again… though, unfortunately, it's unlikely you'll both be able to forget this terrible episode soon."

I pursed my lips and nodded resignedly, while Joseph made to leave.

"My parting words to you, David, are not to worry about anything… we'll take good care of you, as requisite, and with the same amount of attention as will be given to our dear Naomi."

As matters turned out, and quite extraordinarily really, the family's doctor was a little out in his estimation of recovery times; though maybe he wished to err on the side of medical caution. Subsequent to some really beneficial sleep sessions, I felt quite myself again by the evening of the following day; though I decided it might be best for me, and other members of the household, to remain in my room at least for a further day. That was no real problem for me; but it meant I was waited on virtually hand and foot for all my living requirements, and I felt rather guilty about that state of affairs.

Constantly, I was asking Miriam, Joseph and Aaron - when they brought provisions and supplies of one sort or another, or just visited me for a chat, during my waking hours of rest and recuperation – about Naomi's progress. Each time they replied to my anxious enquiries, I was more delighted than previously to hear of her increasing normality, even liveliness. So much so, that I got the notion

– if not the urge – to pop along to her chamber and have a chat with her. But, on reflection, I was glad that common sense prevailed; and certainly with regard to any customary aspects of social protocol, on which I wasn't the medieval Jewish world's premier maven.

Early on the Thursday afternoon, however, Joseph came to visit me with information on two matters. The first item on his agenda was to tell me Aaron had returned that morning to Huntingdon, that his brother had sent me his very best wishes and a hope that we might meet again before I went back to London. The second piece of news, which Joseph relayed to me with a smile verging on a broad grin, was that Naomi was now feeling one hundred percent better. He added that his sister was proposing to leave her room and sit in the casual space at the end of the corridor; and that she would be happy if I could join her there in, say, an hour or so for some light conversation. I readily consented to the invitation, and thanked Joseph for now passing my message of acceptance back to her.

Twenty Five

I SETTLED myself in the social area of the solar, on a comfortably upholstered seat below a window, before Naomi arrived on the scene. When she did, I stood up smartly to graciously greet her smiling face with equal joy on mine; and I believe that both of us were quite astounded at the difference a few days can make. I felt sure that, like me probably, she considered our distressing and ghastly experience to have been a bad dream or, rather, an incredibly frightening and gruesome nightmare. I beckoned her to sit opposite me, hoping that didn't give an impression I owned the place. Somewhat chivalrously, I reckoned, I waited for Naomi to sit down before I followed suit.

I was so delighted that she appeared to have recovered her usual demeanour; and relatively speedily, despite the abysmal occurrence that had given rise to her dire condition. In fact, she looked really lovely, both facially and in her blue tunic and charcoal-grey under-dress, with her long dark tresses splaying over her shoulders. I just hoped she considered I was scrubbed up and rehabilitated to the standard she'd accomplished. When Naomi spoke, and she was the first to vocalise a thought, I could've kicked myself for not being alert enough to beat her to it. I could tell from her flowing and confident delivery that, thankfully, all was well with her mind, too; at least in the instant context.

"You look fine, David, I'm very glad to say... and I hope you're feeling likewise."

I was elated to receive her initial words, but still felt slightly culpable for not myself launching the conversation in a similar manner.

"I'm all-round good now, Naomi... but I need to know about you," I stated with an earnest anxiousness. "I'm delighted to see you're looking fit, too. But I understand, and can well appreciate, that the awful incident we unhappily shared took, unfortunately, a much greater toll on you."

The woman smiled winsomely; and I received the distinct impression she desired to extend a hand and touch mine. But it was probably a little out of reach for her.

"Thanks for the compliment, David," she said with an enchanting coyness, and perhaps even the hint of a sparkle in her eyes. "After all the wonderful attention lavished on me, and the very useful bed-rest and excellent remedial tonic prescribed by Jonathan, I should've expected this auspicious outcome..."

I nodded, and she continued.

"But additionally, though not everyone accepts this, I do possess a firm will-power and fortitude to get through problems in my life. And it goes without saying that I've needed to develop such a personal support system over the years."

Again I nodded with empathy, mentioned how grateful I was for the generous help and care afforded to me by her family, and added:

"From what I've now been able to observe, Naomi, I can't help but acknowledge, respect and comprehend what you're so trustingly telling me… after all, I'm a virtual stranger here."

She shook her head – I assumed, assuredly, at my latter words – and quite vigorously.

"Not any more, David," she said with a gentle resolve in her voice. "But let's change the subject, please… and not refer to our joint misadventure ever again. I hope that's alright with you."

My expression conveyed a complete concurrence with her sensible sentiment.

"Very good," Naomi said laconically, but with an adorable little grin.

Before she could pre-empt me again – this time with a novel topic of conversation – I raised the urgent need for me to purchase some new clothes, and mentioned how indebted I was to Joseph for providing me with a set of his own for the time being.

"I was thinking of dropping into that shop in Bridge Street tomorrow… hmm, Friday… hmm, I think it will be Friday morning," I said, a little vague about days of the week now. "Do you know if they would stock something suitable for me?"

Naomi propped her fingers up against her pretty lips and pondered for a moment or two. Then she shook her head slightly; but did affirm that the next day was, indeed, Friday.

"I believe you might like to go to the market here in Cambridge, especially as you haven't visited the town previously," she suggested. "It's a lively, boisterous and often raucous place with loads of atmosphere, colourful stalls and kiosks, including a couple of small outlets vending menswear. And, in certain allotted areas, there are animals from surrounding farmlands and many different goods and provisions... even some exotic foreign items brought here on riverboats from the coast..."

I smiled while listening to Naomi's pleasingly clear, descriptive details.

"Though I should add," she continued, "and despite my urging just before not to allude in any way to our very recent torment, that particular sectors of the spread-out bazaar can be more than a bit smelly. Would you be alright with that, David?"

"Yes, no problem," I responded. "But only if you would feel able to accompany me around the marketplace as my guide."

"Absolutely," she agreed. "I wouldn't have mentioned the option otherwise."

Then the two of us were quite startled by the sudden and silent appearance of Miriam at the archway by the stairs. After a neat little nod, the lass announced softly that she had a message for Naomi to join her mother in the private chamber. The daughter excused herself, apologising for the rather premature conclusion of our more pleasantly developing discourse, and followed the girl down to the main hall. But before vanishing, she turned in my direction.

"Looking forward to seeing you for supper this evening," she called with an appealingly sweet smile. "It will certainly make a nice change from eating and drinking confined to our solitary rooms, eh David?"

I agreed with an apt nod.

At my request, Joseph provided me with an iron key to the main door of the house, and that I could conveniently store in the larger purse at my belt. He agreed it would give me some more freedom. He came up to my room, not long after Naomi's departure to join her mother, to so kindly check on how I was doing. He was pleased to note I was feeling well, and that his sister and I met as arranged for a nice talk. It was then I asked – a bit reluctantly, bearing in mind my status – about the possibility of obtaining a key to the house. Joseph insisted I should have one. He added, of course, that it would be of use only if nobody was at home. Otherwise the door would be bolted and secured from the inside, and I would need to bang on it for entry. He added that I must let him know at once if there was anything else I required, or with which he could assist. He went on to say that what I'd done for his sister would never be forgotten; and that he held no doubt I would've given my own life to safeguard hers. I was almost overcome with emotion by his generosity of spirit; and which he referred to as a *mitzvah*, or a good deed performed to repay another.

I was intrigued when he asked me to follow him down to the ground-floor hall, where he would hand over the key.

When he unlocked, then secured behind us, the sturdy door of the large chamber – which, in dimensions, appeared not too dissimilar from the main hall – I could see a number of hefty wooden chests occupying positions next to the plain and windowless walls. There were also several, floor-standing cupboards with drawers in their lower halves. And I noticed, at the far end to me, a large bookcase with what looked like many manuscript scrolls piled onto its shelves. Along the centre of the lengthy, rectangular and slightly vaulted room were a few tables of varying sizes; one of them had presently a couple of chairs and another, a short bench. All the tables had, atop them currently, what appeared to be metal boxes.

Joseph led me to the first in line of the tables, opened one of the boxes, took out a key and presented it to me. I thanked him heartily for treating me almost like a member of the family.

"You *are* now an honorary member of our family," he said, and it was clear from his tone of voice that he really meant it.

I thanked him yet again for his thoughtfulness.

Then he took my arm.

"I'm sorry, David, but I have some work to do here now," he said. "We'll meet up again tonight."

"Of course," I responded. "I'm thinking about going for a short walk around the Jewry area… just to stretch my legs for a while."

"Take care," Joseph said, with a tinge of concern. "There are Jewish people here who may pressure you into entering their homes for a meal!"

I got the jest instantly, and we both erupted into unrestrained laughter. It felt great, I think for both of us, to be able to do that now.

"But before you go, David, I would just like to show you something," he said, and a little mysteriously I thought. "This way, please."

I trailed Joseph to the end of the hall, where the bookcase stood tall; and I could see I was right about the rolled and tied scrolls that covered the shelves. They may well have related, I speculated, to the family's banking and money-lending business which, as I was led to understand earlier, wasn't quite what it once had been in the way of a highly profitable enterprise. Next, he moved to one side of the not insignificant piece of furniture and, to my utter surprise, began to push against it with both hands. I couldn't imagine that the heavy-looking, wooden structure would've budged an inch; but I stared, in utter amazement, when it appeared to slide quite easily for a metre or so. I was even more flabbergasted when I saw what this movement revealed to me. A couple of stone steps led down to what appeared to be the start of a tunnel!

Joseph was doubtless taking in my trance-like expression.

"I assume you haven't seen one of these in a house before, David?" he enquired, with a wry frown.

I was peering with such a mesmerised focus into the darkness of the subterranean passageway that the stark distraction meant my observer had to repeat himself.

"Y-you're t-too r-right," I stuttered then mentally shook myself into full awareness of the situation. "W-What is it, Joseph? Where does it go?"

"It's not that uncommon with regard to a few of the big stone houses in the Jewry, David," he began. "There are underground passageways that have been excavated, and have existed for quite a while now, between some of our Jewish homes here. The original intention was for them to be safeguards in times of seriously bad trouble for us, and that has proven to be the case... at least, to an extent."

"I understand," I said. "But where does your subterranean channel lead, if I may ask?"

"You may, David. In fact, it leads to the home of a great friend of our family, Solomon... known here as Solomon the Wise..."

I nodded but somewhat too soon maybe, because Joseph hadn't finished.

"Solomon's house has a synagogue within it," he continued. "It's where we go for Shabbat and festival services... and, hopefully, you may wish to accompany us there on Saturday morning."

When - after some moments - I absorbed what Joseph was telling me, I nodded quickly while reflecting on making my way to the house of worship through the tunnel.

"Yes, I would very much wish to attend the Shabbat service," I said keenly, and even though synagogue attendance wasn't really my forte. But I was swiftly disabused of my notion about a fascinating adventure.

"If you're thinking our route to the synagogue is generally via this passage, David," Joseph added with a faint grin, "I'm afraid it isn't… we normally walk the very short distance to Solomon's house."

I nodded again, with a matching small smile, when I realised my thinking was wishful.

After my host had returned the bookcase to its standard position, I took my leave of him with a warm, firm handshake and left the house. I didn't know where Solomon's house was situated, though I would've liked to look at it. I ambled briefly around the Jewry in a lackadaisical way that wouldn't have helped my lower limbs as much as a longer and more athletic walk. But it was good to take in the ambience of the area; and a number of Jewish men stopped me and asked after my health and that of Naomi's. Clearly, this was an exceedingly small Jewish world that I was living in temporarily; and, undoubtedly, any news or information travelled really fast around it. I shouldn't have been bewildered that people here knew of my existence. However, I was somewhat amazed then gladdened to be approached by a couple of non-Jewish inhabitants of the neighbourhood, an elderly man with his wife, who enquired after Naomi as well as me. I soon acknowledged that Joseph wasn't joking about my being invited by his brethren to enter their homes for refreshment. However, I declined their kind offers most politely, explaining there was a need for my return to the house. That wasn't too inaccurate an excuse, because I wished urgently to attend the *garderobe*; and, fortunately, it wasn't too far away.

Twenty Six

WE convened for supper in the hall early evening... Joseph,
Naomi and their mother in attendance. A lamb stew was
served as the main course; and we all thanked Rebecca for
the delicious meal. I knew the animal would've been killed,
in accordance with Jewish ritual, at a slaughterhouse in the
Jewry itself; and I recalled from my reading that animal
bones with kosher marks had been discovered during
archaeological digs in the area. In fact, I recollected passing
the local Jewish abattoir during my stroll that afternoon. As
we ate, Naomi – who was sitting opposite me alongside her
mother – and I exchanged glances but few words. I asked
Joseph how his wife and children were getting along in
London, and when they might be returning to Cambridge.
I was glad to hear they were well but at his request, he
told me, they were prolonging their stay in the capital.
Then he gave me the reason. Although there had been no
official public promulgation, as yet, of the proposed Royal
Edict banishing the Jewish population in *Cantabrigia* to
Huntingdon, Joseph mentioned that it was anticipated to
happen fairly soon.

He and other leading members of the Cambridge
community had been discussing at length, Joseph said, the

procedures, consequences and implications of what would be a problematic situation after well over a century of Jewish presence in the town. He noted that Aaron, as a current resident of Huntingdon for good reason, was very much involved in consultations with the principals of that town's Jewry; some relevant meetings being held in its synagogue and library. He told me that questions concerning real estate in Cambridge - where not involving rented premises - and sale transactions were uppermost in Jewish property owners' minds; as well as the accommodation available to be occupied in Huntingdon for the arriving Jewish exiles. It was foreshadowed, Joseph added, that where property sales in Cambridge were necessary, prices likely to be obtained would inevitably be below market value in the prevailing circumstances.

It was a depressing conversation at the table that evening; and not only for me, as someone exclusively aware of the ultimate fate of England's Jews. And especially whilst consuming a scrumptious repast, and imbibing some very palatable French red wine. In a metaphorical kind of way, this pointed up for me the relative highs and lows of Jewish life and survival within an undulating, anti-Semitic environment; though, contemporarily, there did appear to be rather more lows. Contingency planning was vital for the community, Joseph urged; and I couldn't have agreed more. Particularly, he advanced, because the precise date or period for the implementation, presumably by the town's Sheriff, of their projected expulsion from *Cantabrigia* was unknown at that time;

and a formal, comprehensive announcement was awaited with increasing apprehension.

Cook had baked a tempting parve fruit cake, one made without milk to meet Jewish Law after eating meat, to round off our supper very tastily. As we finished eating, and Miriam started clearing up, Joseph mentioned that he and his mother would now be retiring to the private chamber in order to go through a number of important household matters. Also Naomi excused herself, she said for only a moment or two, and hastened down the stairs with a gratifyingly noticeable vim and vigour. She returned in next to no time at all, as promised; her mother and brother were still with me at the table.

"I've just stuck my head into the courtyard to check on the weather, David," she reported to me. "It's beautifully tranquil and mild out there."

"Good," I responded, only guessing where she was heading with the current forecast.

"Would you like to sit outside for a while?" she asked expectantly.

From the corner of my eye, I more than imagined detecting a smidgeon of surreptitious, smiley nods being exchanged between Joseph and his mother before they rose from their chairs, wished us a good night and repaired to the private chamber.

"Yes," I answered, pensively. "That would be a congenial way to end the evening."

I followed Naomi to the bottom of the steps, passed the kitchen and servants' sleeping quarters then entered the reasonably compact, square-shaped, largely flag-stoned and high-walled yard. One tree – I could only guess at an elm – occupied a corner of the enclosed area away from where we stood beside the house. There was a wooden bench against its stone wall behind which, I estimated, would be the kitchen. The glow from a candle within cast a soft light through a small, usefully-positioned window above the convenient two-seater. The clear sky was growing dark, but Naomi's weather report was quite accurate. She sat herself on the bench, and invited me to sit beside her.

"It's very agreeable out here, Naomi," I said.

"Yes, David… and in the summer time, it's even better," she commented with a little chortle.

I could've been wrong – I'd drunk my fair share of the very drinkable supper wine – but I would've sworn the woman was edging closer to me. Then she turned and, to my complete disbelief and astonishment, planted a peck on my cheek. Bearing in mind my expected mores of this era, I was virtually stunned by what just transpired. I swivelled to face my companion head-on.

"W-What did… W-Why did you do that, Naomi?" I stammered like an innocent.

"I'll tell you why," she said, with one of her almost trade-mark coy but engaging grins. "But please don't mention to anyone what I'm going to say now… Promise, David?"

"You don't have to tell me anything," I countered. "But if you do, for whatever reason, I give you my word it remains with me."

"Thank you," she said. "It's only that I've needed to tell someone for a long time… and now I feel that I can, and want, to tell *you*."

I nodded with a sympathetic acceptance of her feelings; while, at the same time, anxiously wondering what she wanted to tell me but nobody else. I pondered, ineffectually, whether she might think I was some sophisticated Londoner open to hearing anything without raising an eyebrow… little did I know.

"I mentioned summer just before, and it reminded me of something that occurred during that season last year," Naomi began. "I was feeling a bit lonely and down one afternoon, as I took a rest in my room after returning from the market. I'd taken off all my clothes, and lay under a cool sheet on my bed. There was a knock on my door. Before going to my chamber, I'd asked Miriam to bring up some drinking water for me. The girl entered bearing a pitcher, nudged the door closed behind her, poured some of the liquid into a glass and handed it to me. Unthinkingly, I raised myself to grasp the vessel and the sheet fell away from my bosom…"

"Sorry, Naomi," I interrupted, "but do you *really* want to tell me all this… it sounds quite private and personal?"

"Yes, I do," she replied resolutely. "Please allow me to continue, David."

I nodded an okay, and threw out an open palm.

"Anyway," she went on, "I grasped the water-glass safely, and just as the shy youngster averted her eyes from my upper body. 'I'll set down the jug here on your table, in case you want some more,' she said with her back to me, as she turned towards the door. At that moment, I felt so solitary and friendless that I couldn't have been genuinely responsible for my uncharacteristic actions… it was just that I needed someone to be close to me…"

Naomi paused, either to reflect for a moment or to take a breather. I was giving her my undivided and intrigued attention.

"I called to the girl, 'Please don't leave me, Miriam…' as I put the glass on the bedside table and slid back beneath the sheet, with only my head exposed now. 'I need you to stay.' She looked round and, with some relief in her eyes, noted that I was covered up again. Then the youngster asked how she could help me further. Her words struck a sensitively material, though atypical chord with me. 'I would like you to join me in the bed, Miriam… I feel very lonesome and forlorn, and wish for someone, you Miriam here and now, to be close to me.' The girl appeared totally incredulous and, obviously, extremely inhibited…"

"Sorry, but are you absolutely certain you want to tell me this, Naomi?" I interjected, becoming somewhat bemused by the subject-matter.

"Yes, David, I *do*," Naomi confirmed before going on. "I wasn't aware that Miriam and her mother were noticeably religious. Clearly, the lass couldn't accept what I just asked of her… for that matter, nor could I. But the point I want to make firmly is that this wasn't and isn't the real me, in the sense that I don't desire other women… and I'm sure you know what I mean, David. I just feel that I need to get this lingering memory out of my head for good. I can talk to you very easily and I like you, so maybe that's the motive behind my disclosure. I hope you can understand what I'm trying to say, David…"

"I'm not sure that I do comprehend fully, Naomi," I interrupted again, this time absent an apology. "But do go on, if you feel you have to…"

"Thank you," she said. "Anyway, I'll merely summarise what happened next. Eventually, I did persuade a burdened Miriam, but I can't recall how exactly, that she would be performing a great service for me by removing her clothes and coming into the bed alongside me, which she did though hesitantly. At first, and quite naturally, she flinched and pulled back when I first attempted to put my arms around her. But then she seemed to soften her approach to what was happening, and surrendered willingly to my warm embrace. As you may've noted, David, the girl's shorter, a bit slimmer and therefore somewhat lighter in weight than me, so I needed gently to bring her up to where her head rested beside mine on the pillow. I held Miriam's body, I suppose caressingly, against my own as we gazed at each other… but there wasn't any more to it than that, if that wasn't enough. In fact, and after a very short time, both of us fell asleep…"

Naomi paused briefly from, I mused, her mildly erotic narrative… and without me being the cause this time.

"When we awakened," she carried on, "and more or less coincidentally because of the movement, Miriam left the bed hurriedly and dressed herself. Before she departed my chamber, I told her that she was to say nothing of what had occurred to anyone. She agreed readily… no less than I would've expected of her in the circumstances."

That appeared to be the end of the fascinating story Naomi was telling me. She was still looking directly but now silently into my eyes, when I considered the woman might well have wanted to lower her gaze. I was yet unsure of the intent behind the relaying of this slightly ambivalent encounter of last summer, so I tried my hand on the discernment curve again.

"But Naomi, could you explain to me more precisely the motivation of which you spoke a little while back?"

She remained unspeaking for some moments then turned her gaze upwards to the heavens.

"It's quite dark now," she said. "But it's wonderfully clear… you can see so many of the beautiful shining stars in the firmament."

I followed her eyes, and both of us seemed to become virtually hypnotised by the starry vista. Then I realised she was probably trying to distract me, in an effort not to reply to my significant query. Before I could repeat it, Naomi spoke first.

"I think we should retire now, David," she said, with an edge of finality in her voice. "It's getting rather late."

I didn't think the night hour was that advanced. But I knew for sure she wasn't going to answer my question, at least not on that occasion. Her last words to me after leaving the backyard, climbing the stairs, negotiating the main hall and taking the second flight of steps to our bedchambers were not to forget our proposed excursion to the town centre market the following morning. As I left Naomi at her door, she reminded me that Miriam would let me know when to come to the social area. But after I nodded my assent, we smiled in a sort of mutual recognition of what earlier had been said and, maybe, not said. We wished each other a goodnight and, before I walked onward along the hallway to my own room, I couldn't help thinking that another little kiss on my cheek was conspicuous by its absence.

Twenty Seven

IT TOOK me a while to get to sleep that night. My mind was clearly preoccupied wall-to-wall. The initial part of my wakefulness was virtually monopolised by ambiguous thoughts of Naomi; and especially the sudden but delightful little press of her soft lips on my undoubtedly prickly cheek. However, the following section of my restive insomnia - although interrupted throughout with similar and not unpleasant musings – seemed to be fixed mainly on the looming plight of the Cambridge Jewish community. My sympathetic feelings for them, in any case, were enhanced since my clandestine arrival from the future. Not all members were property owners, by a long chalk; but several would sustain, and inescapably, severe financial losses. They would suffer accordingly, after many decades of hard work building up their now not so successful enterprises; and against an oftentimes grave, anti-Semitic background. Furthermore, I reflected sadly but realistically as I lay sighing on my bed, nothing much had changed in persecutory terms across the centuries and into modern times.

I knew, of course, that Joseph, Josce and, now, Abraham owned their own substantial stone houses and, possibly, other premises as landlords. And not necessarily within the boundaries of the triangular area of land beside All Saints, then known as All Hallows, in the Jewry. I'd read somewhere, in my own day and age, that Jewish property ownership had extended to the edges of the medieval town; the Trumpington Gate locale, towards its southern outskirts, certainly rang a bell with me. Perhaps my head was becoming so grid-locked - with a build-up of queuing thoughts - that my overloaded sub-conscious decided to call it a day.

Slumber then took the initiative, and with a tangle of dreams that I couldn't unravel – and really didn't yearn to recall – on waking. When I did open my eyes again, some light was entering the chamber; but I didn't know the exact time, of course. From the amount of illumination available, I guessed it was still quite early in the morning; though I couldn't be certain of that. I did miss my readily accessible, bedside clock; and nearly as much as my black Americano, wake-up shot.

Being a fairly buoyant sleeper, I knew almost for certain that Miriam hadn't knocked on my door as yet, to advise of Naomi's readiness for my market outing. I decided to get up and dressed, and carry out my ablutions. When washing my face, I couldn't help but feel the growing rough stubble. I didn't care for being hairy in that kind of way; and had always been clean shaven, thanks to my trusty electric razor. I checked my emergent beard and moustache in the small mirror kindly provided by Diva, of now almost blessed memory. Although the thought of her, when looking at

225

my reflection, impelled me to wonder for precisely how much longer I would wish to stay in medieval Cambridge. Possibly just another few days, I reckoned; though that proposition was overtaken by a loathing of my facial appearance. I could've enquired of Joseph about acquiring some cut-throat shaving equipment. But I resolved to attend the barber's shop I'd noticed on Bridge Street. If it was still closed at this hour, I would wait outside until opening time, no problem.

I went down to the kitchen where, and I was quite sure, Miriam would already be in evidence with her mum. I told the girl of my intention, but perhaps perceiving her momentarily with a modified focus. She confirmed the hairdressing salon would be open at this time today, because Friday was an important market day in the town and business would be good. She offered solicitously to bring me some breakfast in the main hall before I went for a shave; and added helpfully that, if I were to be late in returning, she would inform Naomi of my whereabouts. I thanked the able young girl, who encouraged me to linger for a fast-food bite and a hot drink before I left the house.

Even at that apparently premature hour – though, with Miriam's market information, it shouldn't have been so unexpected – I passed lots of trundling wagons and carts, horse-drawn or otherwise, driven farm animals such as cattle and goats and numerous pedestrians, some carrying heavy back-packs, including traders and peasants… all heading towards town from the river crossing then along the forking High Street or Bridge Street. The barber's shop was open for business – the hair but not the dental section, so far as I was aware. The youngish hairdresser who shaved me, garbed in his crisp working outfit, was an amiable and, maybe universally for his line of work, talkative guy. I was his first client that day, and I was very pleased with the result of his expert workmanship. As I sat in the chair, it occurred to me that this would be my initial expenditure of money in the medieval epoch. I was gratified to have been instilled, by Diva's Alpha Centauri magic, with the valuable capacity to identify the denominations of coinage she'd also aptly and amply supplied. I thanked the barber for a job well done, and paid the not unreasonable price for his professional services. I told him I was a visitor from London; and that I might well drop in again before returning home in a few days or so. He smiled and opened the street door for me, as another customer was about to enter.

When I got back to the house, Miriam opened the door for me with the aid of a kind of step-ladder to reach the upper bolt. On reaching the main hall archway, and as the girl informed me, I could see Naomi having breakfast with her mother. After exchanging the usual pleasantries, I mentioned in passing my trip to the barber's salon. Before I left them to continue gossiping and enjoying their primary meal of the day, Naomi remarked: "We could tell you've been for a proper shave… you look really good."

I departed with a grin, and headed for my room.

While awaiting Miriam's call, I sat on my bed and thought about the neighbourhood at the town centre, around which Naomi and I would be perambulating. In my future, I'd researched the area in several books on the wider medieval history of Cambridge; and I was familiar with the names of many of the cobbled streets and alleyways in the market zone. In my time, the earliest extant map or chart of the town dated from the latter part of the 16th century. But I'd studied some sketches, plans and diagrams produced centuries later that sought to convey a projection of *Cantabrigia's* 13th century extent, together with contemporary architectural and other content. Naturally, I was excited to soon be able to see for myself the living sights; as well as to hear the many different sounds of an animated, open-air marketplace and undoubtedly smell its varying aromas, both good and bad. That was all part of my unrestrained enthusiasm to be where I was. And, I supposed - with perhaps a crazy acceptance of the possible risks involved in my time travel adventure - thanks to Diva. Though I retained, and believed that I would continue to hold, a sense of shame and guilt at the means by which I'd achieved my dream.

I didn't have to sit around for too long before Miriam knocked on my door. Naomi was waiting patiently for me in the usual spot, looking beautifully turned out as usual. We left the house and, in just a few moments, joined the now stream of people moving along the High Street and heading for the multifarious sectors of the Friday market. As we approached the busy, narrow thoroughfares leading to the heart of the main trading areas, and unsurprisingly, a sensation of smell was the first of our senses to become pointedly operational. Naomi took my arm, leading me away from the mainstream flow of market-goers and on a detour through a stony alleyway that opened up to reveal the corn, then the poultry and, finally, the butter market. I pondered whether the butter vendors might've been more relevantly setting out their dairy wares on the southern side of the main merchandising square, along a street known as Butter Row. But then I thought to myself: What do I know? Next, we were transiting the principal trading square named Garden Market, replete with its colourfully canopied stalls offering a wide range of fruit and vegetables from the surrounding farmlands and beyond. The tower of Great St Mary's Church loomed majestically to our right, with the distinctive steeple of St Edward's Church a bit further on.

There was a mounting cacophony in the general vicinity; and due not only to the sales-pitch cries of the official stallholders and other, mostly itinerant, merchants. The central market area, as I appreciated, needed to be acknowledged also as a point of contact and communication, the hub of public social intercourse in the town; and, from time to time, the launch-pad for formal announcements, whether national, provincial or borough-based. As Naomi guided me around the busy and noisy stalls, barrows and huts – both of us taking reasonable care to avoid impact with hurrying customers, peripatetic hawkers, the occasional early-day drunkards and several beggars – our nostrils were still being assailed by pungent odours emanating from the meat market behind us. Or possibly that stink was merging with those spiralling from platters of meat pies and other carnivore concoctions, carried ubiquitously on platters by some brawny young lads or farmhands.

Naomi held tight to my arm as we steered a gradual passage slightly farther south, beyond the fruits and vegetables, to take in the dubious aromas of Butcher Row. Then we half-circled round, turning northwards into the equally whiffy fish market in Peas Hill - an area flanked by a number of large, two and three storey, stone-built houses - near to St Edward's. Being more a fish than meat eater, I invited my guide to ease up on her pace so that I could linger briefly to inspect the occasionally still slithering harvest of sea creatures on display. The range of fish and crustaceans from river, coastal waters and open sea appeared tellingly extensive. I recognised some of the fishy offerings spread out on the many, well-subscribed stalls. In an instant, the maybe odd thought of *gefilte* fish, a poached mix of ground carp so beloved of many Jewish people centuries later, entered my mind. Only then - possibly strangely in the context, but perhaps provoked by the distractingly active environment - did I remember there was a particular building in the locale that I was extremely keen to see.

I asked my companion whether we could now go look at the nearby Tolbooth, which I knew would've been responsible for operating the highly successful market and collecting requisite payments from licensed stallholders. Naturally, I supposed, Naomi asked about my rationale. But as soon as I mentioned my understanding that there had once been a synagogue on its site, she nodded her head a few times and confirmed, in outline, her awareness of the building's history over recent decades. I couldn't match Naomi's personal knowledge and experience, of course. Though from my own delving into library archives, and some on-line research into contemporary documentation, I knew the structure housing the Tolbooth - which served also as a kind of Town Hall – had once been owned by a 'Master Benjamin the Jew'. I'd learned he was one of the wealthiest businessmen in the town. By all accounts, he was known also to be a very pious man, an exegete and also an expert on the *Halachah* or Jewish Law.

But Benjamin's house, I'd read, had been confiscated by Royal order, for an alleged misdemeanour; and its ownership was transferred to Cambridge burgesses, for the purposes of a gaol, in the 1220s. The original records indicated that there had existed a smallish synagogue annexed to the house; and that the space it occupied was given to the Franciscans when they arrived in *Cantabrigia* at that time. Despite the generous donation of these albeit restrictive premises, the Grey Friars – as they were also known – found it insufferable to share the building's entrance with a prison. It wasn't until some decades later, however, that the town jail was transferred elsewhere; and the monastic Order was given the entire edifice. Additionally, I was aware the religious group were allocated - and moved to - a much larger area of land, situated some hundreds of metres to the north-east. By my own future time, this was a site long in the possession of Sidney Sussex College. I knew that, in or about the year 1270, the entire house once owned by Benjamin was converted into the Tolbooth. Now Naomi was leading me to the building - via the milk market, and past the main marketplace's stone cross – which with other substantial houses, in its terraced position, overlooked the northern entrance to Butter Row.

Amid the continuing shindig ambience, we managed to find a fairly safe spot to stand; and for me to contemplate the handsome stone building rising opposite us. A continual flow of people, some obviously officials and others evidently merchants or traders, were entering or leaving through the front door of the Tolbooth. It was enthralling to observe the range of expressions on their faces; and I couldn't help speculating on the possible causes, whether beneficial or disadvantageous. But I needed to express to Naomi my sadness that the old synagogue no longer existed; and her pale, though pleasing, features conveyed her own corresponding feelings.

"So… where would you like to go now, David?" she asked, gazing around us at the constant hither and thither of market-goers and other participants in the gathering and milling throng that Friday morning.

Personally, I noted amongst the crowds - and with a certain inexplicable fascination - the better-off and thus better-attired, as well as the fairly poor and thus poorly-garbed, citizenry passing alongside us. I felt that, even though they were worlds apart in their separate lives, these individuals both of wealth or poverty – and all categories betwixt and between - were actually sharing, though doubtless in different proportions of quality and quantity, what the central Cambridge market had to offer.

"Maybe I can get some new clothes, Naomi," I replied, adding: "I really think I've got to do that… and as a matter of priority."

"Alright," she said, "follow me and we'll get you sorted out."

And she did just that, escorting me to an aptly sheltered kiosk in a rather quieter and calmer sector of the market. Here I was able to select, with the skilled and useful advice of the affable clothes merchant, some sets of really fine items. Even Naomi approved of my choices. After completing my purchases to the satisfaction of all concerned - and I knew that bargaining was customary - we left the smiling trader and agreed to head back to the house. On our return, and while making our way up to our chambers, I thanked Naomi copiously for the very interesting, if not beguiling jaunt that morning. She said I was very welcome, and looked forward to seeing me at supper that night, which would be of course – she added - a Sabbath eve meal. When I left her, I needed to confess to myself that it had been some considerable time since I last sat down to such a repast at the start of the Jewish day of rest. Little did Naomi and I know that Joseph, who knew we were going to the market together that morning, would mention that our return to the house must've been shortly before a certain public, and importantly material, announcement was made from the steps of the Town Hall; and which had led to some spiteful consequences in the locality.

Twenty Eight

NAOMI was the last to join Joseph, his mother and me for the Friday night meal. She apologised for her tardiness, but was informed by her brother we'd only just arrived. Still standing, the siblings and I watched as Sarah placed a linen square on her head and, after reciting the appropriate sanctification in Hebrew and striking a flame from a nearby tinderbox, lit two Sabbath candles in their silver holder placed on the table. We all declared 'Shabbat shalom', wishing each other a peaceful Sabbath, then followed Joseph - his head covered and mine, too - to the serving table. Here, one by one and after saying the necessary blessing in the ancient language of the Jewish people, we washed our hands using a double-handled vessel to scoop water out of a basin. Then we sat down successively, with Joseph at the head of the table and Sarah to his right opposite me. Finally, Naomi took her seat but, I was amazed to note, immediately next to me. Nobody seemed to raise an eyebrow, except me, at her choice of chair which, I thought, should've been the usual one beside her mother. I didn't say a word, of course; if everyone was happy with the seating arrangements, so was I.

We remained silent as Joseph took the two large loaves of *challah*, or Sabbath bread, from the silver platter directly in front of him, held them together and recited the relevant blessing over them. Then, from one of the loaves, he broke off four chunks and dipped each of them into a small dish filled with salt. He bit into his own piece and began chewing, whilst distributing the other three portions to each of his fellow diners. Right on cue, Rebecca and her daughter came through the archway to set some steaming fare, in a kind of tureen, on the small table together with four bowls. The three-course supper that evening was as delicious as seemed to be the norm in a household with, what would be considered in my day, a top chef in its kitchen. But our capacity to enjoy the tasty repast, with its entrée of mutton and vegetable stew, was marred alas by the more than depressing news that Joseph felt it vitally imperative to inform us about.

I got some inkling of what he was on the point of telling us after he used similar words to introduce his subject. He adopted an even more serious expression than any I'd observed creasing his face during my time in the house. Little did he know I was aware of much relating to the topic, and its consequences, on which he was going to speak.

"David… Naomi," he began, "you were very lucky returning to the house from the market when you did…"

"Why's that, Joseph?" I enquired intently.

He looked over his shoulder and acknowledged cook working at the side table; and, in turn and having doubtless overheard his words, she nodded at him. Together with Naomi, I couldn't help but notice the silent connect.

"We have a first-hand witness of the events that took place there… Rebecca, who was at the market to buy some vegetables, saw and heard everything that happened, before hastily returning home…"

"What did we miss, brother," Naomi enquired earnestly, "such that we were fortunate to do so?"

Joseph poured some red wine from a pitcher into our goblets, made a blessing then we drank some. Sarah had been silent throughout so far; though her demeanour and puckered brow said everything.

"Tell them, Joseph," she said, but in a tellingly solemn tone of voice.

"I'm just about to, mother," he responded with a slight nod. "Perhaps I should start by saying something that David, with respect and being a Londoner, may not have heard about in detail…"

I pricked my ears, and my host continued.

"Well, David… in January of this year, King Edward issued a proclamation to the effect that, and I can quote its exact words you won't be surprised to hear, 'No Jew shall dwell or stay in any towns which the Queen Mother holds in dower'. Cantabrigia is one of several dower towns, given to Queen Eleanor on her marriage to Edward's late father… as you know, Henry the Third. Not long afterwards, for example, the Jewish community of Marlborough was exiled to Devizes, that of Gloucester to Bristol and of Worcester to Hereford…"

"And Cambridge is one of the dower towns…" I said.

"Yes, David, as we may've mentioned to you before in this general connection…"

I nodded a couple of times, and Joseph went on.

"So the proclamation applied to the Jewish community here… and its original provision was that Cambridge Jewry should be deported to Norwich, the largest centre of Jewish population in East Anglia, but with somewhere between one hundred and two hundred brethren nowadays. Of course we knew of the declaration, but nothing happened here. And we might've been forgiven for thinking, even hoping, that for some reason unknown to us we were to be made an exception from the general rule of dower town expulsions…"

"I can understand that, Joseph," I broke in, not really knowing why – save maybe to suggest, hopefully benignly, that we were having a conversation rather than a lecture. "Sorry, Joseph, please go on."

He did, after Miriam had cleared away the first course dishes, and prepared our place settings for the second.

"Even as moneylenders," he said, and surprisingly whimsically, "we couldn't bank on our thoughts and hopes, though contingency arrangements were obviously a prerequisite in the unprecedented situation. And we were soon disabused, on hearing through our essential grapevine that the Royal government had been debating whether the Cambridge community would be better, for them and not us, pushed out to nearby Huntingdon, rather than the more distant Norwich. So this was the cause of a delay in our expulsion…"

After Miriam had been allowed to conveniently serve the next course, Joseph topped up our goblets and carried on with his compelling though gloomy and disheartening narrative.

"And so we come to events at the market this morning… Apparently, and the news is now known to all brethren here, the liveried Town Crier came out of the Town Hall or Tolbooth to make a public pronouncement. He rang his loudly clanging bell several times, until all in the crowded central market area and beyond, by passing word of mouth if necessary, were alerted and giving their focused attention to his imminent declaration. Then reading from a parchment notice that afterwards would be posted nearby, he barked out the decision made by the Royal authorities that all Jews residing in Cambridge would be evicted from the town, and must go to Huntingdon, by the conclusion of the next ten days…"

"Ten days!" Naomi exclaimed. "Is that possible for us… for the entire community?"

"It is possible for *us*," Joseph said with a gentle reassurance. "And whether it is or it isn't for our fellow Jews here, no Jew can remain here after the ten days are up… on pain of very serious punishment."

Sarah raised her hands to hide her face; even though, and undoubtedly, she was given this information earlier. Naomi - to whom her brother's report was new, of course - acted likewise. It was really dismal for me to observe. Joseph moved closer to his mother's chair then extended an arm and placed it around her shoulders. She dipped her head in thanks for the comfort it brought. My host looked at me, and nodded in Naomi's direction. I took the hint, edged my seat nearer to Naomi's and put my arm about her shoulders. She peeked through the fingers concealing her face and nodded a smidgeon; and I may've detected the sound of some low sobbing. Joseph re-adjusted the position of his chair and I followed suit, then both of us released our arms from their target shoulders.

"But it's what occurred next that I should mention also," he said, with a look of concern that transferred itself at once to Naomi, who's face was now clear of her palms, and to me. "Immediately after the proclamation, Rebecca told me, there were shouts of approval from the majority of those crammed into the main marketplace and the surrounding streets and alleys. Apparently, some men began yelling, and numerous other people in the huge crowd joined in, 'Jews out!'… 'Jews out!'… 'Jews out!'…"

I couldn't help but be reminded of the Nazis shrieking 'Juden raus!' - 'Jews get out!', whilst they cleared the East European ghettos of those destined for deportation to the notorious death camps of Auschwitz-Birkenau, Treblinka, Sobibor and others. It was so unbelievably melancholy for me, to say the least, to know about the six million Jews - men, women and children - murdered by gassing on an industrial scale by the Nazis during the Holocaust, the greatest evil ever committed against the Jewish people; and in the lifetime of my contemporaries.

"What, thankfully, Rebecca didn't witness in the market area before rushing back home… but that we've subsequently learned," Joseph continued, "is that three Jewish men, identifiable as such, were dragged away by a group of thugs and beaten up severely. Fortunately for these brazenly assaulted victims, a few sympathetic bystanders and their neighbours in the Jewry, managed eventually to extract them from the evildoers' clutches and get them, bleeding profusely from their wounds, back safely to our more secure area without further confrontations…"

"How are they now?" I enquired.

Her brother shook his head.

"They're alive still… in one case, only just," he said mournfully. "The injured are being closely attended by our physicians… hopefully, and with the expert attention the doctors can give, they'll all survive their dreadful experience of this violent, anti-Semitic attack."

"We'll pray for that," I contributed, and even though I wasn't usually given to prayer.

Sarah now lowered her hands from her face, but we could all see the reddened eyes. Joseph moved his arm to grasp her nearest hand as it rested on the table. Miriam served the final course, the dessert; but none of us could yet bring ourselves to eat the sweet concoction that cook had prepared so lovingly for the Shabbat meal. Everyone sat in silence for some time, just gazing at the Sabbath candles.

"Don't let's disappoint Rebecca," Sarah remarked suddenly, and with a surprisingly firm delivery. "It looks like she has made something really special for us… maybe to cheer us a little, if that's possible, on a very sad day. So we shouldn't let the fine-looking pudding go to waste."

Without exception, we all nodded our agreement and began trying to enjoy our dessert. Joseph poured some more wine; and perhaps some of us felt the further alcohol intake might be adequate enough to help lessen, even numb our gloomy thoughts.

"You mentioned 'praying' just before, David," he said, after taking a quaff from his goblet. "That has reminded me to tell you we'll be using the tunnel to get to the synagogue in Solomon's house for the service tomorrow morning…"

"Sorry to interrupt, Joseph," I said, "but I remember you telling me the family normally walks the relatively short distance above ground."

"Yes, generally we do that," he agreed, "but, as I think I've told you, much depends on circumstances… and such have now changed, fairly dramatically I would say…"

I nodded, and felt a bit foolish to have raised the point.

"And I have to advise you," my host added, "to be very circumspect, if not exceedingly careful if and when you now go outside the house for any necessary reason."

His words were calculated possibly to send a shiver of apprehension along our spines; and they certainly had that affect on my backbone.

"I was proposing to return to London during the coming week," I said. "Presumably, I wouldn't have any trouble doing that, Joseph."

"You're returning to London this week, David?" Naomi asked, repeating some of my words with a strange tinge of surprise in her voice; and before her brother could reply to my significant question.

241

I nodded towards her pale face.

"You shouldn't have a problem, David," Joseph responded. "Even if there were to be any doubts, I'm sure you can prove you're a Jew living elsewhere than in one of the Queen Mother's dower towns."

"Yes," I said instantly. "I can."

"Well, there you are," he intoned, and added meaningfully: "And we'll be really sorry to see you go… won't we, Naomi?"

She nodded silently, even a tad balefully.

"I cannot find the words to say how grateful I am to all of you," I uttered, glancing around at the three heads turned towards me, each harbouring its own private thoughts. "But definitely I will find and say them before leaving you, probably on Tuesday… and even though your welcome and care have been well beyond praise."

Joseph and his mother readily conjured up a benevolent smile. But I heard a strange resonance escaping Naomi's lips, a sound I couldn't quite construe. It would be a pull to leave her, too. Especially because the sickening experience we'd shared seemed to have created, at least for me, something of a close personal connect between us. It amounted almost to a spiritual feeling, yet another aspect I couldn't find the words to describe adequately in that instant. I needed to tell them about my plans to leave *Cantabrigia*; and not least due to the extremely tight timetable for their forced departure to Huntingdon. There would be so much for them, and the Cambridge Jewish community as a whole, to schedule into the coming days before expiration of the Royal deadline.

I didn't want to be an added burden; though, in truth, I hadn't planned to stay any longer.

Reflecting on that - as we drank our wine and meditated on our individual thoughts - made me think for a moment about when I should be contacting Diva about my return journey to 21st century Cambridge. However, I did possess some more time before needing to concentrate on that crucial matter. I put down my goblet and looked at Naomi. She was staring at me with a dejected, if not rejected look in her eyes. But maybe neither more nor less saddened than her brother and mother; though I wasn't too sure about that. Then an idea entered my mind.

"Joseph," I said, rousing him from a possibly wine-induced mini-trance, which he might not have welcomed, "if I can help you and the family in any way before I go, do please let me know."

The head of the family thanked me; though in such a way as to imply – in the nicest possible way, of course – that my assistance wouldn't really be required.

"Yes, there's much to be accomplished within the period allowed us before our enforced removal," he continued. "I'll be involved in much urgent discussion with others in the Jewry here, and Aaron will again be coming to join us from Huntingdon. Appreciating that this situation could happen sometime or other, and as you know, we've already gone some way down the preparatory road… especially as regards potential land transactions that could well be completed satisfactorily and soon…"

"That's very good to hear," I said reasonably brightly.

"The only… well perhaps not the *only* problem we face is that the actions of the relevant local authorities, in implementing any Royal edict, proclamation, order or whatever, can be unpredictable at times. We Jews, who are entirely in their largely anti-Semitic hands, must hope for the best but bow to such demands as may confront us. To do otherwise, may well have a seriously adverse result. By way of recent illustration, we got to hear that, in relation to other expulsions from the Queen Mother's dower towns earlier this year, houses owned by some of the Jewish families involved were seized, before private sales were completed, and granted to members of her household."

I shook my head, bearing in mind Joseph's words, though not in disbelief.

"Let's pray tomorrow for a more positive outcome concerning the Cambridge community," I said.

"Yes, we'll be doing just that, David," my host reacted then led us in *Birchas Hamazon*.

"So let's now call it a day," he said immediately following the Grace after Meals, "retire to our rooms and hopefully have a restful sleep tonight."

I shook his hand warmly, we all rose from our chairs, exchanged a "Shabbat shalom" again and began to make our way to the bedchambers.

The indomitably adept Miriam, who'd likely been hovering just beyond the archway as usual, materialised instantly and started to clear away the used utensils and tidy up the table.

"Miriam will call you for breakfast, David," Joseph said finally, as we attained the uppermost floor and the women entered their rooms. "After that, we'll make our way down to the passageway and head for the synagogue."

I thanked him for everything again, and ambled off to my room at the end of the hallway.

Twenty Nine

DURING the night, I thought I heard shouting in the vicinity of the house; but I recalled not being able to make out any particular words, or to decipher what was being howled like wolves at the door. When I woke up next morning, I imagined it was all part of a dream that I couldn't recollect in any detail, save for the volume of noise. After being called – by the other young girl, the one that I'd seen assisting Miriam – to join the family breakfast in the main hall on that Shabbat morning, I was shocked to learn that the loud screaming in the neighbourhood of the Jewry, and that I'd taken on board in the night hours, hadn't been a dream at all. Joseph and Naomi, but not Sarah - who told me she was a deep sleeper - were both awakened by the raucous clamour. As Miriam served the Sabbath morning's food and drink, Joseph mentioned that, occupying the nearest chamber to the front of the house, he was able to make out the constant cries of 'Jews out!… 'Jews out!'… 'Jews out!'…

Joseph commented that he wasn't at all surprised; but added that he'd still been extremely anxious about the security of the house, and the safe-keeping of those dear to him within it. He told us of similar anti-Semitic gatherings in the Jewries of other of the Queen Mother's dower towns during the period before their Jewish inhabitants were exiled elsewhere. He noted his confidence about the strongly constructed, securely locked and bolted front and back doors of the house and principal business centre; though he'd been very concerned the thugs might've started throwing large stones at the windows. Fortunately, they hadn't thought about doing that, he said; and doubtless because the choice of shrieked insults was occupying their vile minds. Sensibly, Joseph announced he would ensure all windows were now firmly shut; and that, despite the consequent reduction of natural light, all shutters would be closed and strongly protected.

Despondently, I could sense the feelings of utter consternation around the table. They included, no doubt, those relating to Joseph's statement the previous evening that we would be attending Shabbat morning service in the synagogue via the building's underground passageway. As we consumed our breakfast fare in a languid but befuddled and desolate mood, Naomi – and again, she was sitting adjacent to me – glanced at Sarah, who was saying something to her son, then took the opportunity to whisper in my ear. She said the terrible screaming outside the house during the night - the words to some of which she was able to hear – had really alarmed her. Her body was trembling, Naomi said, so she got up and went to her mother's room, the door to which was never locked apparently in case she became ill. Once inside, and knowing deep-sleeper Sarah wouldn't be stirred by her careful choreography, she got into the bed and snuggled as close to her mother as she could. Although, Naomi added, she wasn't actually being cuddled, the warmth of another close body – albeit through night attire – afforded her much solace. Naomi recalled that she got up before her mother, as she knew she would, and returned to her own chamber. In response to her account, I could only nod a few times.

As we finished breakfast, and prepared to return to our chambers to freshen up before attending synagogue, Joseph waved a pointed finger in the air.

"I'm now thinking it would be best," he warned, "if, generally, we don't leave the house alone or even in pairs… or, indeed, at all at the present time."

We nodded our understanding and concurrence.

"Unless," he noted pensively, "it's absolutely unavoidable or essential to do so…"

Our standing trio nodded again.

"If anything's needed," he added, "its acquisition can be arranged by other means."

After some more nodding of heads, we left it at that.

"See everyone at the top of the stairway very shortly," Joseph said finally.

I followed the mother, brother and sister back down the hall, noting how particularly smartly dressed they were, not that they weren't always very well attired. But especially today, I knew, because it was the Jewish Sabbath and the family were - very much unlike me - regular synagogue-goers. Nevertheless, I was so pleased and relieved to have had the chance to purchase - and before the market had turned dangerously sour – the new clothes I was able to wear now.

Around 10 minutes later, duly refreshed, the four of us met up close to the door of Joseph's spacious room near the staircase. He led the way down, with Naomi helping her mother and me as the tail-end Charlie, to the lobby area on the ground floor. As we proceeded, I couldn't help feeling quite enthusiastic, if not a little excited, to shortly be moving through the tunnel to Solomon's house and its synagogue. We preceded Joseph across his workroom and office then he came up to perform the manoeuvre with the sliding bookcase. I did conjecture, but needn't have, about the level of illumination, if any, in the subterranean passageway. Happily, I wasn't a sufferer from claustrophobia but hadn't been informed about the length of the excavated borehole. I presumed it wasn't that far a distance to traverse; and, thankfully, that proved to be the case. We each now stooped to enter the, necessarily, multi-candle-lit tunnel. Since leaving the lobby area, Joseph was bringing up the rear, with me just in front of him, to ensure that all doors and barrier-devices were guaranteed secure.

Even though the brick-walled passage - which wasn't too low or too narrow, but curved to an extent – didn't possess anything near floodlighting, it was relatively easy to navigate our way along its stone-flagged floor. Looking ahead of us, I could see that Naomi was continuing to hold her mother steady as they walked, using the other arm to keep a balancing contact with the brickwork. But it did seem longer in time to me than probably it took to reach a closed door, rather than a light - I mused, with a misplaced drollness - at the end of the tunnel. Joseph squeezed his way to the front and rapped on the sturdily iron-hinged, wooden portal. We waited only a brief while before it swung open with a squeaky sound.

The man who opened the entryway was at least middle-aged, with a neat goatee beard and wearing a long black and white, woollen *tallit* around his shoulders.

"Shabbat shalom!" he said as we entered a relatively smallish space, though one suitably lit by candles; and the door was shut firmly behind us.

We all responded accordingly, wishing him also a peaceful Sabbath; then I noticed there were no less than three other closed doors. Our greeter opened the one directly opposite our entrance, then beckoned us to climb the few stone steps into the equally bright and slightly vaulted synagogue. I noted there were no windows to be seen, and thus no natural light. Naomi guided her mother into a section behind a ceiling-high partition. I knew this to be a *mechitzah*. In an orthodox synagogue – as, most assuredly, this was – it separated female from male worshippers. I could see that seating in both areas comprised rows of stone benches; with rather more in the gentlemen's than the ladies' section. They were spread with flat cushions, thoughtfully set to assist congregants sit through some quite lengthy services.

I noted also that, as appropriate, the women were able to generally observe the synagogue; albeit through the close-knit lattice-work in the upper part of the wooden room-divider. I'd always reckoned it was installed for reasons of modesty, as well as being an anti-distraction expedient – especially so far as concerned the men. There was only one woman, sitting currently in the second row, behind the screen. She smiled in recognition at Sarah and Naomi when they seated themselves in the first row of benches. As Joseph led me down the not over-lengthy central aisle between the rows of seating for men, he turned and said: "They've now got a minyan, one over in fact." Naturally, I knew that he meant there were present the at least 10-man quorum requisite for having a full service in the synagogue.

We sat in the first row – indicating that Joseph and the other three men seated there were prominent in the community - just in front of the raised *bimah*. This reading desk faced the currently closed and curtained *Aron HaKodesh* or Ark. That cupboard or cabinet would be holding the *Sifrei Torah*, or Scrolls of the Law, containing the Five Books of Moses. The week's *sedra*, a portion of one of the duly mantled and accoutred Hebrew manuscripts, would be read aloud that morning. On the way to our seats, Joseph and I exchanged handshakes and a 'Shabbat shalom' with our fellow, prayer-shawl-wrapped male congregants. Only a couple of them accompanied the customary handclasp and Sabbath salutation with the fairly usual smile. I put that down to the troubles afflicting the community, especially the last night's anti-Semitic ructions in the Jewry; about which, probably, most of the group of more elderly than younger men were aware now.

Before taking our places we shook hands with, I assumed, the *kehillah's* heavily-bearded rabbi – or one of them, as I knew the Jewry had a small rabbinical, learning academy. He was seated on a chair beside the *bimah* and facing the congregation. At his side was a table with several books piled onto it, together with a number of prayer shawls. He reached out and handed a prayer book and a *tallit* to each of us. I emulated Joseph in first covering my head with the shawl then reciting the appropriate blessing before sitting down. I was a bit surprised that there was room for me to perch beside Joseph; though, I reflected as we took our cushioned seats on the stone bench, people might've earlier been told to expect me and rather munificently made the room. In my own day – and because I wasn't, by any stretch of the imagination, an habitual attendee – I was aware that, in some synagogues, opting to take a regular's seat before his arrival could result in the receipt of a very stern glance. I would've been amazed, in this somewhat compact Jewish world within which I was residing temporarily, had more than maybe a few of its indigenous population claimed they weren't *au fait* – practically all the Jewry inhabitants had French origins - with my presence.

The book passed across by the minister was wonderfully unique - to me, anyway - as compared with the *Siddur*, or daily prayer book, that I might've used occasionally in modern times. In those far off medieval days, before the advent of printing, what I held reverently in my palms contained pages of the ancient Hebrew language hand-written by an expert scribe on calf's skin. As a child I'd attended a *cheder*, or religion class for children, after normal secular school. It was held in a synagogue building; though, after reaching adulthood with my *barmitzvah* at age 13, I needed rarely to utilise my acquired ability to read and understand Hebrew. The minister now started leading the Shabbat morning service, while standing at the reading desk and facing the Ark. As soon as I opened my hard-covered book, I could perceive immediately that the calligraphy was superb. Joseph, perhaps assuming this version of the *Siddur* was unfamiliar to a Londoner, found the correct page for me.

The minister *davened* or intoned the Sabbath prayers fairly speedily; and I found it quite difficult to keep up, especially as the prayer book's Hebrew lettering was foxing me more times than not. When, on the odd occasion in my own time, I happened to find a printed prayer book in my hands, I was used to seeing Hebrew on the right-hand page with an English translation on the left. So I was more than a bit bemused. While others seemed to be focusing intently on their own renditions – maybe more so than normal in those uncertain times – I merely turned the soft-feel pages. The officiating rabbi's intonations often reached a fever-pitch of sound.

From time to time - whether standing or sitting, when others did according to the prayers being recited – I glanced stealthily over my shoulder. I was hoping to spot Naomi and her mother between the now slightly increased number of male congregants and amid the separating screen's lattice web. But I didn't. Soon we reached that part of the service when the minister would read the week's *sedra*. That would happen after one of the *Sifrei Torah* was taken from the Ark, paraded around the synagogue then placed in a firm and upright, slotted position on the *bimah*. I noticed two youngish, bearded men approaching a bookcase. From it, they took and distributed to each worshipper a calf's-skin *Chumash*, a volume containing the Five Books of Moses: from Genesis through Exodus, Leviticus and Numbers to Deuteronomy.

A Cohen and a Levi, the ancient priestly classes of the Jerusalem Temple, were automatically the first and second man to be given an *aliyah* or call-up to the reading of the Law by the rabbi. The invitation was extended by a bearded elder – who, I learned from Joseph, was Abraham – acting as a *gabbai* or warden. Each man summoned to the *bimah* intoned the requisite Hebrew blessings before and after the relevant portion was read. Then a mandatory number of so-called Israelites were invited to the reading desk, each to chant the special benedictions. Having been asked beforehand whether I was named for either of the priestly classes, and having replied in the negative, I was called up as an Israelite and read the blessings inscribed usefully on a tablet atop the desk.

After that week's *sedra* reading had been completed, and Abraham had recited the *Haftorah* or segment from the writings of the prophets, the earlier re-wound and re-mantled Scroll of the Law was returned to the Ark; and the rabbi began to lead again for the final part of the Shabbat morning worship. The service came to a close a relatively short while later. We all stood up, the men taking off their prayer shawls, neatly folding and placing them on the benches. Then we moved slowly out of the synagogue, shaking hands with the minister and all the other men present, and wishing each of them a "Shabbat shalom". But I couldn't help sensing - and, I felt, with good reason - that many of the traditional good wishes seemed less meaningfully expressed than one might've expected ordinarily.

I kept near to Joseph, trailing him as we circulated and meandered around the rows of benches in the windowless hall, which was now feeling rather warm and stuffy. He introduced me briefly to one or two of the male members, and particularly to Solomon and his eldest and only son present, Isaac. I could just about see Naomi and Sarah, tracked by three or four other women, disappearing through a doorway at the side of the ladies' section. Some of the men began to infiltrate that area and pursue their close female relatives. The remainder of the male congregants followed suit, with Solomon and Isaac just ahead of Joseph and me as we climbed a flight of stone steps eventually opening out, through an archway, into a spacious and windowed main hall. Twenty or so people - men and women of varying ages, but largely inclined to the seeming middle-years and above - were gathered around a long and white linen-covered, central table, the ladies collecting at one end of its length.

I noted a couple of young girls - about Miriam's age, I estimated - putting the finishing touches to platters of various refreshments, mainly sweetmeats of one kind or another. I spotted a youngish man coming to the end of pouring red wine from a large pitcher into many small drinking vessels, finally filling a large silver goblet to its brim. The rabbi emerged from one group of men crowding around the table and picking up the little beakers. He took up the goblet from its round tray, made Kiddush by reciting a necessary blessing over the wine then sat down on the only chair actually placed at the table, and began imbibing until his vessel was empty. In the meantime, all congregants quickly drained their own, smaller cups of the sacramental liquor. I was standing next to Joseph. We were on the point of reaching for some of the enticing food items, when Abraham and Isaac approached us through the barely socialising and, it seemed to me, oddly dissipating assembly.

"Joseph," Abraham said, "would you be able to join us, and a few others, in the private chamber? And do bring your new friend and house guest, David, of whom we've heard so much about of late."

Joseph looked at me; and in such a way as if to enquire whether I was up for it. I nodded my keen agreement in response to his expressive gesture.

"Yes, Abraham," Joseph said. "We would wish to come along... and thank you for inviting us."

Abraham turned to his son.

"Would you kindly tell Sarah and Naomi to rest here for, probably, no more than a short while... then they can return home with Joseph and David."

As Isaac moved purposefully towards the now small

huddle of women at the far end of the table, Joseph and I followed Abraham, alongside a few other men, to a door in the wood-panelled wall.

Thirty

IT MUST'VE been rather longer than Solomon's 'short while' before the meeting in his private chamber ended. As the half dozen or so community stalwarts, including Joseph, and me trooped out of the large room, we were confronted by an utterly deserted hall, save for the presence of Sarah and Naomi. They were seated on a couple of chairs beside the long table, which had been cleared completely of food platters, drinking vessels and other articles that were spread across it earlier. As the other men dispersed, it appeared to me that Sarah was fast asleep and snoring in softly whimpering mode. Her daughter appeared to be hovering on the brink of nodding off. As Joseph and I approached the two women, Naomi looked up suddenly, probably saved from imminent unconsciousness by the din being made by those now departing. While the son went to wake his mother from her deep slumber, I helped Naomi to her feet after she held out her hand for me to take. I noted with some interest, and perhaps a little grin, that on the table within her easy reach stood a wine pitcher and a cup.

My instant researches revealed that the cup was empty, and that the jug contained little more than some red staining. Joseph noticed this, too; and the expression on his face suggested Naomi would've been drinking rather more than she might've done if we could've left Solomon's house sooner.

"Probably wished to pass the waiting time usefully," Joseph whispered to me and with a touch of whimsicality, as his mother came to a startled wakefulness.

I nodded, and he aided Sarah from her seat. Naomi managed to gain a sense of equilibrium independently of my assistance, and sought bemusedly to focus on her surroundings.

"Although my sister can generally take more than a couple of cups of Kiddush wine in fair order," her brother added quietly, whilst leaning towards me secretively, "more than that will usually make her feel quite heady."

I nodded again.

"Looks like she might've enjoyed quite a number of cupfuls," I added, and with what may've been the hint of a smirk.

"Let's go now," Joseph said, as he took his mother's arm and started to walk in the direction of the staircase, where Solomon and Isaac watched and waited like patient sentinels.

I looked askance at Naomi, who appeared reasonably capable of coping on her own now. She gazed at me in an extraordinarily affectionate sort of way; then, without more and to my astonishment, tenderly grasped one of my hands and took me steadily in pursuit of her close relatives. Solomon and his son, both bearing – and perhaps quite understandably - unnervingly serious demeanours, led us back to the tunnel and bid us farewell as we entered in turn. After shaking hands with them, Joseph accompanied his mother with Naomi and me following on. As we began to make our way along the candle-lit passage, the heavy door could be heard closing shut resoundingly behind us. I assumed the illumination would be snuffed out, one way or another, in due course.

When we were again in home territory, both Sarah and Naomi apologised to Joseph and me. They felt unable to join us for Shabbat lunch. Sarah because she didn't feel hungry at all, having eaten more than she should've done from the refreshments remaining after people had left the hall. Naomi, due to the fact she'd drunk much more than she should've done, said she needed a nap. In turn, Joseph – with my nodding accompaniment – said he was sorry that Solomon's unforeseen meeting had gone on far longer than expected. So while Joseph and I headed into the main hall for some well-earned and customarily substantive nourishment, mother and daughter went upstairs to their bedchambers. Before we separated, however, Joseph mentioned to Sarah and Naomi that he would relay to them the flavour of Abraham's meeting when we all came together for *Seudah Shlishit*, the third Shabbat meal.

As it happened, when Miriam came to call everyone for the final repast of the Sabbath, only Sarah was content to join her son to eat in the main hall. I went down to apologise to both of them, as did a kind of distant-looking Naomi. I didn't have the appetite for any more food that day; and she, apparently, because of a temporary lack of interest in sustenance taking the form of victuals. Naomi said she would now go sit in the social area of the upstairs solar; and invited me to join her and speak of what had transpired at the gathering convened that morning. I agreed readily, and we left Joseph to inform his mother likewise. As we took our leave, I pondered momentarily about the religiosity of all the family members, being aware that the very orthodox wouldn't waver from having the three requisite meals on a Shabbat. Nevertheless, I left it that circumstances can be dictatorial sometimes.

When we reached the informal seating area on the uppermost floor, Naomi said I should sit down and she would return to me very soon. She did just that, having popped into her room for a mere handful of moments. But as she seated herself opposite me, the woman put down on the low table between us a tall and single-handled flagon - filled almost to the rim with red wine - and two bulbous, silver goblets. She stared inquisitively at me for an instant - as if expecting a verbal protest of some sort in view of her earlier drinking bout - then lifted the jug and started pouring for both of us. I was more than staggered by what was happening, but refrained from uttering a single syllable. It wasn't my business to say anything, I felt.

"Please don't tell Joseph," Naomi implored me softly; though rather needlessly, I mused. "He wouldn't understand, David... he really wouldn't."

I nodded then shrugged my shoulders.

"It's nothing to do with me," I commented. "And you are an adult, if I may say so."

"You may, indeed," she said with a worryingly coy smile, while finishing off the equitable wine distribution.

I picked up my drinking vessel and Naomi hers.

"Forgive me for saying so, Naomi," I felt a sudden impulse to say. "But I thought you felt you've had enough to drink today."

She shook her head, reached out to tap her goblet against mine then took a swallow of the red liquid. I copied her movement, and downed half a mouthful of the intense and deliciously fruity-tasting wine.

"But how did you get hold of this, Naomi?" I enquired, as we placed our silver cups on the table.

"Please be assured, David," she opened, staring into my eyes again. "I'm definitely not an alcoholic, but I do like red wine and very much so… it has an extremely soothing affect on me."

"Snap!" I interrupted, and quite unthinkingly.

"Sorry?" she reacted.

"I mean, I agree… it can be exceedingly comforting," I recovered, with an invisible sigh. "I've always thought this and, like you, I enjoy drinking a really good red wine, as this is."

She nodded then took some more of it.

"The family have strong contacts with vineyards in France," she explained. "And you would see, from our cellar below the kitchen, that we stock a lot of imported wine from the old homeland… It almost goes without saying that the barrels will be accompanying us to Huntingdon in the not too distant future."

"But you haven't told me how this particular pitcher came to be in your bedchamber, Naomi," I reminded her, "and together with two glasses, not one."

She appeared to pout, grabbed a few more hefty sips then gave me a charming little grin.

"When we were in the main hall on our return, I quietly requested Miriam to bring them up to my room and without anyone else knowing," she told me. "And, of course, after I knew you weren't going to eat anything more today."

I chuckled wholesomely.

"I do like you, David," she said evenly. "You make me smile and feel good, and I don't experience such attributes very often, especially these frightful days... and nights, for that matter."

"I like you, too, Naomi," I responded, and felt that I wanted to say just that.

She nodded, again with an appealing coyness.

"So tell me what was said at the meeting this morning," she enquired, taking quite a gulp of wine this time.

I summarised for Naomi the salient points of the discussion after the synagogue service. Initially, there had been much vociferous ranting at how and why Jewish communities were being treated so appallingly again. Had they not contributed so much to the English economy and otherwise over many decades, certainly by way of increasingly heavy tax payments to successive sovereigns, financing their military and other adventures? Someone, I reported, advanced a notion that the King wasn't happy with falling profits resulting from a declining Jewish business world; and that the current expulsions could be just a dry run for something even more catastrophic and devastating for the Jews of England. Of course, I didn't tell Naomi that the person concerned was getting really warm.

But I did tell her that Solomon had needed to bring the assembled men to order. And that he'd insisted they needed to be more practicable in their views, advice, comments and suggestions for a smooth transfer of Cambridge's entire Jewish community, whether well off or not, to their new home town. I understood from her brothers, I told Naomi, and even before the meeting, that preparations have been underway for some time now, both in Cambridge and Huntingdon, to help facilitate the anticipated transfer. I added that agreement had been readily reached that those in the community who would be unable or incapable of helping themselves in the forced move, for one reason or another, would be given any assistance required.

Though many attendees already knew, Joseph confirmed to the gathering, I informed Naomi, that his brother Aaron and others previously from the Cambridge Jewry were doing their utmost, in Huntingdon, to reassure its own long-standing Jewish community. And that these Cambridge pioneers had been seeking to make all necessary or desirable arrangements covering, of course, prospective accommodation; and without any imposition or encroachment that might give rise to concerns. Those at the meeting, I said, declared overwhelmingly that they, and others unable to attend that morning, were determined to ensure the transfer progressed well including, naturally, the means of requisite transport for everyone and everything. Naomi was told also that I didn't feel the need to convey to her details given about relevant property transactions; and that she was likely aware, in any event, of much that I was informing her.

I didn't want to mention anything said that could've caused her pointless anxiety; there was enough to worry about, I considered. But finally, though immediately regretting doing so, I reported on two further items. At the end of the informal get-together, Solomon had commented that, despite all the seemingly exhaustive preparatory work being done, which deserved great thanks and a beneficial outcome - may the Almighty hear our words, he intoned - we must be neither complacent nor take anything for granted. Something unpredictable could well transpire, and we needed to be circumspect... on our guard constantly.

Then I told Naomi about one of the attendees mentioning that some of the upper windows of his house, those without shutters, had been shattered by last night's shrieking, anti-Semitic mob hurling stones at them. I noted that, thankfully, no physical harm had resulted from the aggressive assault on ears and glass; and that, just like Joseph, all others present at the debate had taken appropriate precautions in case of a possible stone-throwing repetition or other violent harassment and attack.

During my narrative, we both took breathers – whether from intently listening or reporting – and regularly quaffed amounts of the delectable wine. I did feel slightly put-out that my fellow drinker's intake was somewhat heavier than mine, Naomi having the advantage of being both the distributor and the one with more time to imbibe than the speaker. In consequence, and perhaps bearing in mind also her wine consumption earlier that afternoon, she was looking a tad glassy-eyed to me.

"Is there any wine left, Naomi?" I asked nonchalantly rather than accusingly, being unable to ascertain the contents of a deep pitcher that rested closer to her.

I was also a trifle dumbfounded when she slurped what tiny residue was left in her cup, rose unsteadily from her comfy bench and grasped the jug's handle, staggered to my side of the table, sat down next to me and poured what amounted to a cat's lick into my drinking vessel.

"Y-Yes," she said, a tad haltingly and presumably in answer to my question.

"Maybe you should go to your chamber now… for a bit of a rest, Naomi," I suggested.

"M-Maybe I should, D-David…"

With that, she leaned against me and pressed her lips against my cheek, just for a moment or two.

"T-Thank you, D-David," she said.

I was going to ask her, 'For what?' But then I thought it best to remain silent now, and if at all possible.

We both reached for the empty jug and goblets at the same time, possibly with me being more confident of success.

"I-I'll take them b-back… to my room… for M-Miriam… to collect… in d-due course," Naomi dragged out.

I turned towards her, but her face was so close to mine in reaching for the drinking paraphernalia that my lips swept unintentionally across hers.

"T-Thank you, D-David," she said.

I was about to foolishly explain the accidental nature of our intimate contact, when I remembered my sensible idea to remain mute. I got up from the bench; and, against the apparent odds, Naomi managed to attain a standing position, too. She stooped, would've lost her balance if I wasn't steadying her in the instant, and inelegantly gathered up the jug and cups in her arms.

"T-Thank you, D-David," she said yet again.

I was glad to note that she started to move, encumbered as she was, fairly evenly down the corridor. She must've appreciated I was reasonably proximate to offer any help, if needed. It took a bit longer than usual, but when she reached her chamber she turned, repeated the now almost hallowed words one final time then pushed against the door and entered her room. After that I left Naomi to her own, maybe sleepy-bye, devices and went to my own room, potentially for some reflection on the day that could in itself lead to useful slumber. Immediately after entering my own chamber, the first thought to linger in my mind was of the undeniably enjoyable, if too fleeting, contact with Naomi's soft lips. But I couldn't have anticipated the consequences of failing inadvertently to lock my door.

Thirty One

BEFORE falling asleep later that evening, more thoughts than those of Naomi's soft lips lingered in my mind; though when I actually got under the bedclothes, I needed to admit they may've figured rather significantly. As my head rested at last on the pillow, I couldn't help intuiting that the woman really liked me. In fact, she'd told me so and more than once; but the physical contact could've been down to the wine rather than Naomi.

My tentative perception of her arguably developing feelings towards me – seemingly not frowned upon by her mother and brothers – may've been prompted by her albeit modest, but affectionate, couple of maybe more than gratuitous kisses on my cheek. I could perhaps understand her immediate family's attitude in the circumstances; but I was doing nothing to encourage daughter and sister, and for a quite obvious personal reason not unconnected with the subject of time travel.

Nonetheless, I had to self-confess that Naomi and I were getting on really well together, enjoying being in each other's company. That fact alone, I guessed, could've induced, even advanced certain feelings in a woman whose life, so far, had experienced more than its fair share of emotional isolation. I'd been out of a long-term marital relationship - and thus strictly single in basic terms - for quite some time, I pondered towards the fading of my consciousness. My then judgement about an individual's feelings – including, of necessity, my own - would've become somewhat tarnished. Virtually my closing thought, as I recollected, before drifting away on the ocean of slumber was that my capacity to evaluate couldn't have been that flawed, because I did harbour some inexplicable feelings for Naomi. But my final and perhaps quite understandable reflection, before oblivion overpowered me, amounted to a question: What's the point?

I was awakened, I felt, by a sense of some physical pressure encapsulating my body. As my mind floated somewhere betwixt and between sleep, virtual actuality and complete alertness, what minimum realisation I did possess couldn't decide whether I was in the land of the living or a dream-world. I opened my eyes, both gradually and apprehensively then nearly jumped out of my skin, let alone night attire. In the initial instant of my stunned arousal, I sensed arms firmly embracing me around the rib-cage. In the next moment - and helped by the candle-glow in my dark chamber - I perceived Naomi's pallid but appealing oval face, with eye-lids tight shut, a few inches from mine. I couldn't absorb what my eyes were struggling to register in my brain. But, at the same time, I knew this wasn't a night vision or even a waking hallucination. It was utterly and incredibly real. Whatever may've happened, or was happening now, constituted something way beyond my immediate comprehension. And even though, as I started to think more broadly and perhaps oddly, some things *way beyond* my intellectual capacity weren't totally alien to me.

Having nevertheless assured myself that I wasn't still in the Land of Nod, I was glad not to be engaging in shocked and ear-splitting histrionics on raising my eyelids to behold the absolutely incredible, but somehow increasingly enchanting image before me. Had I done so, the equally hair-raising consequences for Naomi would've been distressingly unpredictable. As I began to speculate, more rationally, about how this unbelievably startling situation could've arisen, I must've adjusted my reclining position to an extent that compelled Naomi to slowly open her eyes and come awake. She didn't scream, thankfully; and even though she was staring at my face with the same substantial amount of traumatised disbelief as, undoubtedly, I was displaying a little earlier. Could be, I mused ephemerally, she was becoming sensitive to the fact that, somehow, she was making one heck of a mistake. During these first few mind-numbing and silent moments, as we facially - and a tad hypnotically - confronted each another, I wondered whether the growing look of dawning realisation in her eyes confirmed my notion that it was all down to her recent inebriation.

"I'm really sorry, David," Naomi said and so apologetically, lowering her eyes but making no accompanying effort to leave my bed or remove her arms entirely from their very close contact with my body. "What must you be thinking of me?"

I was more than a bit surprised that she was speaking so clearly, especially after her wine-incited, verbal slurring and stuttering of last evening. Though, I mused, she could've pre-empted a word-strangling hangover by sleeping comfortably next to me.

I didn't reply by reporting how delighted I felt by her warm and tactile proximity.

"It does seem fairly obvious, Naomi, that you've made a navigational error for some reason," I said, "perhaps one only now becoming known to you."

I detected the hint of another innocent, and not unattractive, smile. But it was difficult to take on board that neither of us had sought to move a single centimetre. We'd known each other for barely a week; and although, unbeknown to Naomi, I'd arrived in medieval Cambridge from the sexual mores of the 21st century, I would've expected a certain reaction bearing in mind her personal history.

"You're right, David," she reacted with a deep sigh that I felt reverberating through me. "I thought I was in my mother's chamber and in her bed... just like the other night."

I looked at her quizzically.

"You remember..." she said, now removing her arms from around my frame and edging away from me, though only slightly.

I nodded with an instant recall.

"Well, looks like it has happened again," she went on. "There were those shrieking anti-Semites outside the house

271

again. The continuously screamed curses, abuse and foul language woke me up and, despite my still rather woozy head, I-I rushed to what I-I believed was my mother's bedroom... but I-I was wrong. I-I'm so very sorry, David."

It looked to me like she was on the brink of tears so, albeit hesitantly, I put a hopefully comforting hand on her shoulder for a brief while.

"Please don't cry, Naomi," I said softly and sympathetically. "It really doesn't matter at all... it wasn't your fault, if it was a fault. If anyone's, it was those loutish anti-Semites... never heard them myself. I must've been more soundly asleep than the other night. I take it they've gone now... it seems quiet outside at present."

Naomi nodded then gazed - quite tenderly and pensively, I thought – deep into my eyes.

"Perhaps this is what was meant to be," she whispered, and quite alluringly.

"What was meant to be?" I asked, possibly feigning bemusement.

"Us... I mean, us being together... like this," she said, blinking a few times as she responded in a hushed but quite a sensual tone of voice.

"Sorry, Naomi..." I said, "I'm not sure what you do mean."

It was only moments after my innocuous, though implicitly probing, sentence that I was made quite certain of what she did mean. I sensed Naomi moving close to me then felt her warm palms on my cheeks, one sliding between my head and the pillow on which it rested. I didn't recoil. She held my face and presented her lips to mine. This time, I received more than a mere peck. It was the start of a long and exquisitely intimate mouth-to-mouth caress; and for which I was as much responsible as Naomi.

Thirty Two

NAOMI and I kissed and cuddled for a while in my bed, but that's all we did. At one point, the woman whispered that she loved me dearly; but, at the same time, I couldn't be sure it wasn't her emotional desperation speaking. Maybe I was being too unkind in my then swiftly distracted reflection. I couldn't judge my own feelings with any real accuracy in the astounding, virtually mind-crushing situation in which I found myself. However, I had to admit, as I ran my lips along her neck, that I did possess feelings for Naomi; and which definitely went beyond mere lust in the prevailing circumstances. But I was unable to assess them, in the instant, as so-called romantic love – assuming she would've been familiar with that concept, and was seeking to convey it with her words and deeds. Not that I was helped by lack of a true understanding of the notion on my part; and this could've been down to my personal history in that region of human life. I recalled a Classics professor advising me that the ancient Greeks, or at least some of their philosophers, advocated that love between two individuals is unlikely to be equal or enduring. But, it seemed to me, these early thinkers didn't know everything… they merely possessed the hubris to think they did.

As we ran our hands up and down each other's night-clothed backs in a - literally and figuratively - moving embrace, I wondered whether Naomi's thoughts were coming on tap as rapidly and eccentrically as mine were entering my head. It could've been that her whispered entreaties of love were somehow exclusive, almost monopolising Naomi's mind. My final notion came just before she announced softly, and somewhat culpably, that she should return to her own chamber now – so as to avoid anyone seeing her leaving my bedroom in a suspiciously dishevelled state. Possibly, I mused, there was some sort of hurdle, barrier, deterrent or inhibition – maybe subconsciously self-imposed, but currently surfacing – that was seeking to prevent me fully endorsing an authentic emotion I may've been starting to feel for her. And despite the exceedingly short period of time I'd known Naomi, in the astounding setting I found myself. But superimposed on all that was a crucial statement that resounded within me… for crying out loud, David, remember from whence you come!

When Miriam informed me of breakfast later that morning, I asked her if Naomi was down in the main hall yet. Apparently, only her mother was seated for the day's first meal; and was, to me unnecessarily though kindly, awaiting my presence before partaking of the repast. The girl also told me she'd called on Naomi, who said she would be resting further and shouldn't be expected for breakfast. On my way to join Sarah, I met Joseph on the stairway. I was a bit surprised to see he was fully attired in outdoor gear.

We wished each other a good day, and he mentioned the noises during the night.

"Yes," I said. "I know."

Of course I didn't say how I knew, not having heard the evidently strident shouting personally. Debatably, he may not have been too annoyed had I done so.

"I assume you're heading for breakfast, David," he said, as we moved down the steps to the hall archway and where we stopped. "I've already had mine. I'm galloping over to Huntingdon with Josce, and some of his men for security, this morning. We're attending a meeting with a number of Jewry elders there... it was arranged through Aaron, who sent a messenger to inform us. We've had a couple of similar get-togethers with these affable stalwarts and, happily, they've been very sympathetic, hospitable and helpful to us in a number of important ways. They've taken wholly on board, and most magnanimously, our Cambridge community's calamitous predicament. I must say that they're doing their open-handed best to assist with the many problems that have arisen."

"I'm very glad to hear that," I said. "Time appears to be quite limited now, and I'm sure there's much to be discussed and organised..."

Joseph nodded.

"When will you be returning home?" I went on, enquiringly.

"We're aiming to be back in Cambridge this evening," he replied, "and, hopefully, in time for supper. Undoubtedly, our Huntingdon brethren would wish to provide us with refreshments before we depart. But I think we'll need to leave them, with our polite thanks, to get here before dusk falls."

"Very good," I remarked pithily, sensing that Joseph seemed anxious to be away now.

Nevertheless, I did add just one more item to our brief conversation before he departed.

"As you know, Joseph," I said, "I've decided to leave town on Tuesday…"

He nodded and I continued, knowing that what I was about to say I'd said previously.

"But if I can assist you in any way before I go, please don't hesitate to ask me."

This time, he was pensive for a few moments.

"Now you mention it, I'll be doing some sorting and packing in the work space downstairs tomorrow…" he mentioned, "and I could do with an extra pair of hands, thanks David."

I nodded with a smile, pleased that I could be of some use to repay the phenomenal kindness I was being shown by him. At that instant, I thought also about how much he must be missing his wife and children; but I knew they were probably on an extended stay in London for good reason. We shook hands firmly, and I wished him and Josce a safe journey and a productive meeting. Then I remembered, with some significant embarrassment, that Sarah was waiting patiently for me to join her in the main hall. Joseph leapt down the stone stairway towards the ground floor; and I hastened to his mother at the table, presenting profuse apologies for my delayed arrival. I did mention, by way of a lame non-excuse, that I was speaking with her son before he rode off for Huntingdon.

We were seated opposite each other as Miriam served, then left us.

"We'll be very sorry to see you go on... on... on Tuesday, I think?" Sarah laboured to recollect, while staring across the table at me.

I nodded confirmation of my projected departure day.

"Thanks," I added. "You've all been so kind, welcoming and helpful to me."

"Thank you, David, and I know that Naomi will be especially sad when you leave us," she said, her head at a curious angle. "I do believe that she has become really fond of you, David... and, in fact, she has confided as much to me."

In the next few silent moments, as I pretended to concentrate on eating my flavoursome breakfast victuals, I fought inwardly to come up with a suitable response, if any. Perhaps I was wondering also what might be coming next from Naomi's mum; and whether the daughter – whose absence from the breakfast table might've been diplomatically deliberate, I reflected also – had encouraged her mother to whatever was going on now. I really did hope Sarah hadn't been informed of, or hadn't discovered by other means, what had transpired between Naomi and me that night. Even though not particularly religious, I prayed inwardly and sincerely that my face wasn't reddening after the salacious reminiscence.

"Yes," I said, "your daughter is a delightful lady, Sarah... and we do seem to be getting along quite well."

I sighed guiltily at *the* understatement of the 13th century, and hoped it would do the trick for the time being. But it didn't.

"Perhaps you would like to keep in touch with her after you return to London, David," she continued. "I mean subsequent to our move to Huntingdon..."

I nodded a trifle vaguely, and Sarah went on:

"As I think you know, we have a number of relatives in the capital... Joseph's wife and children are residing temporarily with some of her own at this time..."

I nodded again, wondering what might follow this oft-repeated information. She wasn't actually posing a question in the context, so I felt it not too impolite of me to refrain from reacting and to carry on munching my tasty bread and cheese. But then, almost inexorably, there came the mother's newly formulated enquiry.

"If Naomi happened to travel to London to stay with our relatives," Sarah stated, bright-eyed and bushy-tailed, "would you be able to meet with her?"

The devoted mum, I pondered, was pressingly accelerating the promotional efforts on behalf of her daughter. I didn't want to upset Sarah, bearing in mind all that her family had done for me. But, on the other hand, I didn't wish to be telling lies perpetually, including about the capital city and me.

"Perhaps I'll have a word with Naomi about this," I offered, hoping - so far as I was concerned - my words were sounding neutral in their purport; though, at the same time, presenting at least a crumb of comfort.

Fortunately, my response seemed to do the trick this time round. Sarah nodded; and rather wholesomely, possibly feeling she was doing her level best for a beloved daughter.

Thirty Three

FOR MOST of the rest of that day there was much on which to meditate. But I didn't feel like being immured in the house, despite Joseph's caveat on leaving it. So I decided to pop out incognito, and take a stroll along another stretch of the Cam to the south-west of the main river crossing below the castle. A sizeable and attractive stone building, which loomed up not far from the bridge, I knew to be the later named School of Pythagoras. In my time, it would be the oldest secular edifice in Cambridge, housing the archives of St John's College. The sun was streaming down, drenching the river with silvery sparkles as it flowed calmly alongside me. My pen-penultimate day in Cambridge was pleasantly warmish and bright; and, whilst ambling at the waterside, I felt quite a contrast with the cold and dark atmosphere now pervading the town. The notion nudged me into thinking I would need, and quite soon, to make contact with Diva regarding my return trip to 21st century Cambridge. And the thought, as usual, induced me also to pat my tunic reassuringly where it camouflaged the body-belt concealing one fundamentally essential smart-phone.

My next idea, as I passed some river-fish anglers, gave rise to a full-blown image of Naomi; though one that had, unavoidably, to be imaginary. Our kissing and embracing of the previous night filled my heady mind. So much so that I needed to sit down on the grassy riverbank, with my back leaning against the trunk of a willow; and then to gape, almost hypnotically, across the Cam to a stretch of honey-coloured fields. Maybe I was searching for the answer to a nagging question. And suddenly it came to me... I really did feel I was falling in love with Naomi; not as an outcome purely of our intimate physical, albeit modestly clothed contact; and in spite of having known her for a mere week. It was an emotion, I sensed, that went beyond these facets. But the feeling wasn't that easy to rationalise, if such a process was at all relevant here. It seemed to me that Naomi might well be harbouring similar notions; though I couldn't be certain of their provenance, having regard to her own contemporary situation.

As I gawped over the sun-dappled water and sighed quite intensely, I knew there was little, if anything, I could do about this mystifying if not incredulous state of affairs. Who would've thought - when agreeing Diva's conditions for my time travel expedition – that, after so many years, I might find love again, and in another era, a love that would appear, remarkably, to be bridging the gulf of many centuries? Then my mind went oddly absent for a while. I was capable of observing everything around me, but I couldn't analyse or evaluate anything. Time passed and, gradually, I began thinking properly again. I considered whether my inner self, maybe my soul, was trying to tell me something I should've taken on board in the real, if not virtual world that I inhabited now. I didn't want Naomi to be hurt psychologically - she'd been harmed enough already — and especially as a consequence of what had transpired between us. Even though I didn't start it, in the sense of what she believed it all meant. But, I asked myself, what could I do to prevent or ward off any potential distress or despair on her part?

So I ruminated, whilst watching some farm animals being herded in the distance. The answer to my question, I concluded diffidently, could be found only in one way. I needed to tell Naomi who I was and where I came from; and that proposal seemed to represent the only rational option. Particularly because Sarah may've told her daughter by now that we could well be meeting up again in London. If Naomi would be up and around the house that coming evening, I was determined we would have a private and personal talk. I trusted that my initial suggestion for such a chat wouldn't raise any false hopes on her part. But what scared me the most, however, was not being able to predict how she would react to my weird and wonderful narrative.

In a real way, I'd been in a similar position when my really close friend from Alpha Centauri informed me that I could go time-travelling. The technological, even philosophical, aspects were far beyond my comprehension; though undoubtedly, I reflected, the scientific theory and practice would be even further ahead of medieval Naomi's credulity. Nevertheless, I knew she was a very intelligent individual. Despite that, it struck me, her reaction to my story could cover — and quite naturally — a spectrum of reactions ranging from shock-horror, through complete and utter absence of comprehension to plain, and possibly amused, disbelief . Perhaps my special fear or apprehension was that her scepticism would derive, and quite understandably, from a suspicion that my highly creative account was no more than a very imaginative effort to call it a day with her. But any attempt by me to randomly forecast the unpredictable, I considered while raising myself from the grass, was doubtless nonsensical.

After a short time, my continuing mixed and haphazard ideas brought me, perhaps a little prematurely, to thinking I was coming to the end of my riverside ramble. So I headed back, slowly and deep in thought, in the direction of the Jewry and attained the house mercifully safe and sound. I went at once to the kitchen, and Rebecca kindly prepared a satisfying snack and a drink for me to take away to my chamber. Miriam informed me, interestingly because I didn't enquire of her, that Naomi was yet resting in her room. I said nothing in response, just nodded and retreated to my own space. I held little doubt – knowing that news travelled speedily around this abode - Naomi would be told, possibly following an earlier request and some time very soon, that I was back at the house in one piece.

Much later that afternoon, Miriam called on me and advised that supper would be served slightly later than normal. Apparently, this was due to the man of the house having only just returned from Huntingdon. The girl said no more, even though I might've been foolishly expecting her to say something about Naomi. Then she gathered up my take-away, fast-food lunch remnants and left the room.

As it turned out, Josce came back to the house with Joseph; and they decided, after all, that others of the household should eat at the customary time. They would have a meal later. After the meeting in Huntingdon, Joseph explained to me in the main hall before he and his close friend closeted themselves in the private chamber, there was much for them to discuss before reporting to the Cambridge community. He did mention, however, that the Huntingdon gathering - which had, of course, included his brother Aaron – was primarily about accommodation in or neighbouring the town's Jewry area. This related specifically to pending completion of property arrangements after the expulsion, whether involving outright purchase, leasehold and rental agreements or other land transfer procedures. Referencing my offer to help him the following day, Joseph explained that the work would include packing up part of the collection - inherited from his late father - of Hebrew, prayer and other books. I knew that, in the pre-printing age, these tomes would be in manuscript format, as I'd seen on Shabbat in Abraham's synagogue.

Some of the sacred and other religious works, Joseph told me, would be donated to the Huntingdon Synagogue's renowned library. It was both intriguing and sad for me to hear this information. I'd learned, in my own day, about the Huntingdon community's extensive archive of Hebrew and other books. Regretfully, I knew – but couldn't tell my kindest of hosts – that these contents would be seized and sold off by the town authorities at an auction held at the synagogue's stone building shortly before it was gutted by a mob in the mid-1280s. As Joseph led Josce into the off-hall chamber, he called to me – after seating myself at the table with Sarah and Naomi – that we would begin the delicate packaging job immediately after Monday morning breakfast. I raised a hand in acknowledgement of the appointment.

Miriam served supper to a silent trio of diners. Sarah was sitting opposite Naomi and me, in the usual dining configuration. Occasionally, she would look up from her platter of hot food, glance across at her daughter and me and smile warmly at what – I speculated bizarrely – she may've considered a *shidduch*, or prospective marital relationship. This potential thought, on the apparently *kvelling* – or happy and proud – mother's part, was kind of endorsed at one point. Naomi performed an act that Sarah couldn't have witnessed directly, but which she may've easily deduced from the direction of her daughter's downward sloping and outstretched right arm. Her mother would've been correct in her ensuing and undoubted assumption; and with apparent acceptance of what was happening.

In fact, her daughter was reaching out to place a slightly gripping but basically tender hand on my clothed left thigh. Soon as I felt the sudden physical contact – though, of course, it was nothing compared to our recent, and fairly intimate, kissing and cuddling – I turned smartly to observe a coyly smiling face. What can I do with her? I questioned myself in the equivocally whimsical instant. Naomi's action almost made me forget my resolution to advise her of my authentic origins at the earliest opportunity.

But it was Naomi herself who gave me reason to remember my determination. It was a brief time after her daughter's tactile laying of hands on me, when Sarah excused herself - probably tactically and tactfully - and announced she was now retiring to her chamber for the night. Naomi and I stood up as she started to walk back down the hall. Sarah turned about half way along it to give us a little wave, though a rather larger grin. We returned the salutation and sat down again. Then Naomi suggested that as, according to Miriam, it was still quite mild outside, we should take the goodly amount of wine left in the pitcher and our goblets into the walled courtyard and have a pleasant conversation. I agreed at once, and for my own specific motivation. Her eyes lit up at my smooth and speedy concurrence.

When Miriam reappeared, Naomi mentioned our intention and requested the dutiful youngster to bring out the wine and, after washing them, our drinking vessels.

Thirty Four

MIRIAM placed the pitcher, together with our well-rinsed goblets, on the wooden table in front of us then said a good night and scampered away. Dusk was descending from a clear sky. Although it was caressingly warmish, a sylph-like breeze would waft above Naomi and me from time to time, rustling the leaves of the wall-hugging tree. Soon the heavens would darken deeply, so that we could both become stargazers again. Though in a sense, I thought, that scenario could take on a kind of amorous ambience for two people who'd become quite familiar in some notable respects. And that, I felt, could play out contrariwise to the planned and beyond problematic exposition to my bench companion.

"Why don't you pour already, David?" she asserted with a sort of comedic frown. "You appear to be star-struck, and even before the tiny points of light have begun twinkling tonight."

"At once, Naomi," I conceded, taking advantage of the usual candle glow – emitted through the kitchen window directly above and behind us – to fill our cups with the highly agreeable red wine. "Sorry for my procrastination, but I was millions of miles away, astronomically speaking, on this lovely evening... please forgive me."

It occurred to me, though only peculiarly and in jest, that I could've then added a note of my being practically 800 years away, too. My thought was somewhat prematurely precipitate... the allusion, I intended, would come soon enough that night. But I needed also to be cautious about my word formulation. My choice of "this lovely evening" might well be unduly misinterpreted. Naomi raised her goblet towards me and I reacted accordingly.

"To us!" she declared, but in a voice replete with an earnest sincerity, then quickly swallowed some of the tasty red liquid.

I could've choked easily had I taken, and simultaneously, more than a sip of my own wine. Swiftly, I set my vessel back on the table lest it fall from my grasp to the stone-paved ground.

"S-Sorry, Naomi," I said, surprisingly faltering only faintly. "I'm not quite sure what you meant by your toast... could you explain, please."

She rested her cup but, at the very same instant, a sudden but transient gust of air spread a sheaf of her tresses across forehead and eyes. Naomi tried pushing her dangling locks back into their erstwhile formal position, though unsuccessfully. The continuing failure seemed to be irritating her - in a playful kind of way, I reckoned – so I did something, impulsively and on the spur of the moment, that really I shouldn't have done. I reached out, gently but unthinkingly, and took her recalcitrant hair between my thumb and fingers then tucked away the wad securely. As I moved my hand on her head, Naomi closed her eyes and adopted an expression bordering on ecstasy at the unintended sensation of my touch. She lifted her eyelids gradually and smiled so sweetly at me, maybe with gratitude at my vanquishing her mischievous locks.

"Thanks," she said - with, and I was certain of it, a definite sigh - and added, looking longingly into my eyes: "And in answer to your question about what I meant by my toast just now, David... I am in love with you."

With that, and before I could physically or even verbally react in any conceivable way, she leaned in towards me and planted a pair of lips tenderly and lingeringly on mine. As she did this, a rapid flurry of reiterated questions transited my grey matter. Was Naomi not living at a time of societal and moral probity? Was this not an era of betrothals, matchmaking, delicate family arrangements and modesty of womanly conduct in addition to that of attire? Was she centuries ahead of her time? I wasn't convinced of the answer to that one... or, indeed, to any of my repetitive posers! Though again I felt, arguably in error, that the intimate kiss I was experiencing amounted to little as compared to our bodily embrace in my bed, despite both of us being clad in nightwear. The qualification to my feeling of debatable incorrectness, I suspected, could've been of material relevance to Naomi's obviously genuine expression of love. I could see the sincerity and legitimacy in her eyes. And it was at that precise moment, in the flood of notions and emotions, that I felt once more something profound and authentic for her. But it wasn't really clear to me whether I could call the feeling, *love*. So I went along with my view – held fairly consistently, I believed – that such a passion is so personal it's virtually indefinable. Though the irrational rationale of my presence in *Cantabrigia* could've been influencing my thought processes.

Our lips parted finally and in mutuality. Although Naomi had initiated the close contact, I needed to admit my own lips weren't at all resistant. In fact, their action evolved into something way beyond neutral as our meeting of mouths developed apace. Now I was hearing and feeling her expression of love for me from her own lips, I needed to come clean and tell her the story that wasn't a tale. But her words and tactility were filling me with an astonishing, and largely uncharacteristic, ambivalence and indecision. What should I tell Naomi now? That I reciprocated her love; or that I came from 21st century Cambridge? Or should I say both? I must've been on the brink of madness even to be raising these aspects as optional choices. Thankfully a sense of reality, even commonsense, dawned and prevailed so as to overcome the confusion in my mind.

"I've got to tell you something very significant, Naomi…" I began, filled with a strangely nervous apprehension.

She gazed into my eyes and, as I'd imagined would likely be the case, quite expectantly.

"Tell me, David," she said, and in a way that was seductively concerning for me.

"You'll find what I'm going to say very difficult, if not impossible to believe," I went on. "But you must accept that it's true… because it *is*."

I couldn't credit she was almost glowing with expectation now. At once, I understood my choice of words could still be taken as equivocal; especially in view of her sad and long-standing condition of barrenness.

"I'm not sure exactly what you may be thinking, Naomi," I continued. "But what *I* mean is that I haven't come to your Cambridge in the year 1275 from London. In fact, I've travelled through time to be here... I arrived in Cantabrigia a week ago from the Cambridge of virtually eight hundred years hence."

Naomi's formerly smiling face transmogrified into one that I couldn't describe accurately; though maybe I wasn't quite on the 'distinct likelihood' ball. The very instant I finished telling her everything, the woman's features erupted into peals of almost hysterical laughter. And it didn't stop until, after my several failed attempts at beseeching her to calm down, she did so finally then stared with sad emotion at me.

"You're just saying all this, David, b-because... b-because..."

In stark contrast to the sound of her frenzied hilarity, I could perceive tear pearls forming in her eyes. But I shouldn't have been surprised at the result of my innovative statement. I placed a hopefully compassionate and soothing hand on her shoulder.

"I realise what you're seeking to convey to me, Naomi," I said with sympathy. "I *do* have feelings for you which, in the circumstances of our meeting, I shouldn't have allowed to happen... for your sake, and for mine. Please try to believe me."

She leaned her head against my shoulder and, perhaps regretfully, I felt the need to wrap a comforting – as well as apologetic – arm around her.

"I'm really sorry," I offered. "But this has nothing to do with… with… I think you know what I mean, Naomi."

I sensed her head adjusting position in what seemed like an awkwardly activated nod. Silence reigned for a while, permitting time for our separate, though likely related thoughts to become logical and collected. Then she raised herself, sat up straight again and, although her eye surrounds revealed tinges of redness, appeared more composed.

"What you've just told me has, naturally, come as something of a major shock, to say the least," she commented evenly. "As you mentioned, it's virtually impossible to believe or accept…"

I apologised for interrupting her flow; and I remembered how comparable my reaction was when Diva, from the very much more scientifically advanced Alpha Centauri star system, had explained the possibility for me to travel back in time. Of course, I didn't mention to Naomi the disquieting pre-condition for my journey; and she continued to look extremely pensive.

"Coincidentally, I've got to confess that my mind has considered the idea of time travel, too," she remarked to my fascination. "I would be really excited to visit the past… say, during a period of the Roman occupation here in Cambridge… when they had a fort and settlement on the hill long before the Norman castle… or even some future epoch, if given the chance…"

I nodded smilingly in acknowledgement of her expressed desire.

"Forgive me for asking, David," she uttered with another of her demure facial expressions, "but can you prove, in any way, what you've just told me?"

I knew that Naomi was a clever and analytical person. So I should've expected her to ask this not insignificant question. The only way I might be able to satisfy her justified request for some convincing evidence, I considered, was to show her my smart-phone.

"Yes, I can give you some corroboration," I responded, not knowing what she would make of my explanation of the device.

I turned away from her, reached down inside my tunic and, with some clumsy effort, managed to retrieve the mobile from my pocketed body-band. I held up the slim, glossy black object in the palm of my hand to an exceedingly curious and intrigued, time-travelling hopeful. Then I told Naomi, in some detail, what the gadget was all about - from communication and the internet to photography, GPS and much else besides. After my discourse, I gave it to her to hold while saying she should be very careful not to drop it. It was pretty clear to me that she was struggling bravely to get her medieval head around all the amazing concepts. But, finally, Naomi indicated she was really taken with the technology's complexity and sophistication, and in such a small object. She listened intently to all my simple, lay expositions. A subsequent Q and A session, which she initiated, resulted in both of us chuckling together. Naomi returned my phone; and the glimmer in her eyes suggested I may've cracked the veracity angle. But she kept staring at me, and I appreciated – from my own experience with Diva – that she was finding everything I was saying virtually impossible to take in, so as to overcome her barrier system of disbelief. I should've wholly anticipated what came next.

"David, it's still delightful out here, and there's more wine remaining in the jug," she said pointedly. "I would be extremely interested to hear from you a potted history of the world, especially our part of it and particularly from the Jewish perspective."

"I can readily understand your desire to know," I observed. "But I've got some real doubts about whether I should tell you, or anyone, about future history... from a kind of philosophically moral viewpoint..."

"I'm not asking for a potentially personal future history of my family and me, excuse my interruption," she said. "But I would just like a general description of salient features."

"Even that's a tall order, Naomi," I riposted quietly and politely. "And I'm not a historian by profession... my knowledge would be fairly broad, in any event."

"Please, David," she virtually beseeched me; and I was beginning to be persuaded of her, understandably or not, compelling urge to know.

"Alright," I conceded, though reluctantly. "But even despite the lateness of the hour, I'll need to be very succinct of course... I'll do my best, Naomi."

She nodded her smiley thanks, leaning back against the wall with her lovely blue eyes reflecting a keen expectation.

So, akin to the title of Cambridge's famous, theoretical physicist in my own day, I presented to Naomi my own take on a brief history of time; though still wondering acutely whether I should've done. I reckoned my lecture – for such it felt to be – endured, uninterrupted save for some wine consumption, for the best part of… who knew. Very briefly, and towards the end of my lecture, I mentioned the Holocaust and the murder of six million Jews by the Nazis, as well as the establishment of the State of Israel in the ancient Jewish homeland. This section of my historical outline had, predictably, the profoundest affect on Naomi. When I ended my talk, she said nothing but merely nodded solemnly then gazed upwards at the sparkling stars in the black heavens.

"Thank you, David," she said after some while. "I don't think you could've made up all that, even if you were the most brilliant fiction writer of all time!"

"So you do now believe what I've told you?"

"Yes… I do," she replied, bunching her lips. "It's all so overwhelmingly mind-blowing and seemingly impossible, but I'm really sorry for ever doubting you, David."

I shook my head a few times.

"There's really no call for an apology, Naomi," I said. "I'd possessed the same, and very comprehensible, doubts when Diva approached and explained herself to me."

"I can't thank you enough," she added. "Now everything is so much clearer to me… and I promise not to say a word about all this to anyone."

"Perhaps we should now retire to our chambers," I suggested, feeling an element of coolness developing in the night air.

Naomi got up from the bench when I did.

"I'm helping Joseph in the downstairs work-space after breakfast tomorrow morning," I mentioned, as we entered the house and she secured the door behind us.

"So am I," she said. "I'll be packing... like you, I think."

I nodded, and then we went to our respective rooms. En route, I could tell from Naomi's intensely contemplative look that she would be doing a lot more thinking before surrendering to slumber that night. At the door of her chamber, and before I moved along the corridor to mine, she touched my arm in a relatively innocent manner.

"Your narrative earlier confirms that nothing stays the same for ever," she opined. "Naturally, I know of such a principle from my own reading of past history. And a good current example would be the enforced and imminent deportation to Huntingdon of Cambridge's Jewish community, after their residence here for well over a century. But there does appear to be one exception to the general rule."

"What's that?" I asked in unthinking mode.

"Anti-Semitism," she replied laconically.

"Though it does morph from time to time," I contributed, "and new tropes take over from, or supplement, the old ones."

Naomi nodded slowly, three times in fact, then entered her room and shut the door.

Thirty Five

SHORTLY AFTER breakfast the next morning, and following a thankfully quiet, calm and peaceful night, Naomi and I accompanied Joseph down to the formerly thriving centre of the family's banking and money-lending operations. As he'd explained to me previously, the business – developed largely by his entrepreneurial father, and alongside many other Jewish ventures in England – had declined steadily over the decades of the 13th century for economic, taxation, competition and other adverse reasons. He'd added that all these detrimental factors were overlaid with a virtually continuous, pervading atmosphere of anti-Semitism that, often and for various spurious causes, became murderously fatal for random or targeted groups or individuals among the Jewry communities.

When we arrived in the mostly underground, extensive and slightly vaulted chamber, Joseph instructed us on what needed to be accomplished that day. Fairly recognisable to me were the three tables, now each with a chair facing the entrance door, holding the centre-line of the room space, the hefty locked chests against the bare stone walls, the wooden cupboards and bookcases, including the one significantly hiding the subterranean passageway leading to

Abraham's house. That well-concealed portal had prompted me to wonder whether there might be other, necessarily and securely concealed objects of value or utility in the chamber; and maybe of especial importance in perilous days. My tentative conclusion without seeing the evidence – and why should I be given any access to such, I mused – was that there had to be at least some items of real worth, even aside from gold and silver coinage of the realm and relevant legal documentation. Maybe, I postulated, they were out of sight in a clandestine vault, safe or niche below floor level or perhaps behind a wall frontage. And that, after all, that's what any banker would have for his dealing with clients.

Joseph said that each of us would have a desk as the base for our day's work, and which he now assigned. He started with me, requesting his sister to sit and wait at the chair nearest the moveable bookcase. I was led to one of the bookcases upright against a side wall. Even at a quick glance, I could see that its shelves were, from top to bottom, choc-a-bloc with Hebrew works including many prayer books. I reckoned my Shabbat at the synagogue in Abraham's home had enabled me to identify them as such. My employer was doubtless watching me peering, closely now, at the books' variety of bindings.

"These are mostly Siddurim, the daily prayer book as you know, David, and other religious works," he pointed out. "Many of them came over with my ancestors from France a long time ago. If you turn their calfskin pages, and compare the writing with versions scribed in this country, you'll notice a distinct difference in the script. My father, may the Almighty rest his dear soul, was an avid collector of such beautifully composed and compiled books. And I've added more to the collection in his beloved memory. For certain of the Jewish festivals, we generally lend some of them to Abraham for use in the synagogue or, in particular instances, to the small rabbinical academy we have here."

"All very interesting, Joseph," I remarked. "What would you like me to do with them?"

He took one of the quite tightly packed works from the shelf directly level with his eyes, and opened it.

"I'm just going to ensure that it's in good condition," he said, gently opening what looked to be a prayer book and carefully inspecting its calf-skin leaves and their attachment to the binding..."

I nodded, observing his careful finger-work intently.

"This appears fine, as you can see," he continued. "But if, for example, the pages are loose and coming away from the cover, or you're uncertain in any respect, please place the book in the lined wooden box over there..."

Joseph indicated the container sitting on a table near to the entrance door; and I acknowledged his instruction with a nod.

"As you may well have estimated," he went on, "this job is likely to take a while to complete. And by the way, you shouldn't have any trouble reaching the top shelf..."

I followed his quick peek upwards.

"So thank you for offering to help us, David... it's much appreciated."

"No problem, Joseph," I responded in the post-modern vernacular, but without repeating yet again my causal refrain about his great kindness and the marvellous hospitality afforded to me.

"So, then... if, after examination, you're content with the current state of the book," he added finally, "please put it in the lined wooden box on your allotted desk. That's the centre one of the three."

"Understood," I said.

Before my temporary boss turned away to give his sister her own assignment, he handed me his passed-for-transit book; and I went immediately to insert it, as the first deposit, in my desk-top box. As soon as I did that, Joseph called from Naomi's position that Miriam would be bringing down some refreshments at an appropriate time. Then I began applying myself keenly, but rather solemnly, to the pre-transport examination of the literature - religious and otherwise - within my allocated framework. Although I'd never had any professional experience of judging a book by its cover or other physical aspect, I mused, I considered that commonsense would play its role during the inspection process. As I brought my desk chair to the bookcase, so that I could inspect the works in some comfort, I noted that Joseph was now seated at his own desk and perusing what appeared to be ledgers of some sort. Naomi seemed to be well occupied herself, seriously active beside a bookcase on the opposite side of the chamber.

I decided to commence my labour, though I believed it would be of love rather than a chore, at the top shelf and work my gradual way downwards. As expected, there was no real difficulty in fetching the higher volumes; and I acquired a routine *modus operandi* relatively speedily... reach for and grasp a book, sit to examine it thoroughly, pass it or otherwise then take the item to its appropriate container. While carrying out my surveys, it became apparent that most of the works would be destined for the box on my desk, or any that needed to replace it when full, rather than the one for rejected items close by the door. A couple of hours must've passed, I judged vaguely, and I was now depositing cleared books in a second box. Naomi also was still heavily engaged; and, patently, Joseph was yet focused unwaveringly on crunching numbers. Now and then, I noticed, he got up from his chair and visited one or other of the large chests to retrieve some manuscript documents.

All of a sudden, I nearly jumped out of my skin... and I assumed, in the instant, that Joseph and Naomi may well have reacted similarly. Like a choreographed performance, the three of us turned in a split second towards the cacophony of pounding noises coming from the reverse side of the moveable bookcase; though 'moveable' only if you possessed the know-how, I believed.

"C-Could it be Abraham, or one of his household?" I enquired – my voice reflecting the apprehension I felt as the banging sounds grew even louder – on turning sharply to an obviously concerned Joseph.

"I wouldn't think so," he replied worryingly; and, I thought, with a distinct hint of uneasiness, if not anxiety in his own delivery.

As the clamorous din persisted, its intent seemingly to beat down the barrier, Joseph rose from his chair; and both Naomi, who appeared understandably fearful, and I joined him at his desk, the one furthest away from the hidden tunnel. The three of us gazed at the bookcase masking the passageway as if mesmerised by the impacting clamour resounding through it. By now, the majority of its shelved books had fallen to the stone-flagged floor due to reverberations penetrating the woodwork. We all appeared riveted to the spot and in a trance-like state.

Then Joseph spoke.

"Doesn't sound too good, does it?" he said, looking like he was deliberating hard.

Naomi and I stared at her brother in stunned silence; but his eyes didn't emulate any sense of the panic that surely must've been displayed in ours. Undoubtedly, we would've looked absolutely petrified. I could see Naomi was very frightened, and almost to the point of tears. At that moment, I felt justified in extending a tentatively reassuring arm about her shoulders. I turned to Joseph, who seemed to be struck with atypical indecision.

"Maybe it *is* Abraham!" I urged, as the unearthly racket persisted. "Isn't it possible that he or others in his household could have a serious problem requiring our urgent help?"

"As I said, David," Joseph observed, "I don't believe so… we've got other agreed means of seeking mutual assistance in a dangerous situation."

In the end, Joseph was proved right and I was proved wrong… very wrong. But at that moment, I was on the point of demanding that we now depart hastily via the chamber's main door. My incipient insistence on fleeing while we could came, however, far too late. That was authenticated, horrifyingly, by an enormous crashing sound followed by a new series of loud, echoing bangs accompanied by shouted threats. The source of this further and unnerving noise was coming from just the other side of the secured entrance to the chamber – our only means of escape from whoever was seeking to invade us from the reverse side of the moveable bookcase. We turned as one to gape at the entry door now being pummelled, Joseph's and Naomi's hearts doubtless pounding like mine.

At the instant we swivelled to face the door, there was an explosive eruption behind us. Again as a unit, we turned back to witness, with sheer terror, the masquerading bookcase burst inwards towards us, its shelves and framework fragmenting, with wood and books flying in all directions like grenade shrapnel. Naomi issued a piercing shriek that penetrated me to the core. Now I could hear the intimidating verbal racket emanating from inside the now almost completely exposed tunnel. As one, we ducked down instantly onto our haunches, hands covering our heads and eyes tightly closed, hoping to avoid being hit by any of the sharp, airborne material.

Next we heard, with horror and dismay, what had to be the entrance door collapsing inwardly. And it occurred to me that, at both ends of the chamber, battering rams of some sort must've been used to smash down the barriers, as well as on the sturdy front door of the house. Moments later – to the new sound of heavy footsteps thumping on stonework – we raised ourselves, simultaneously, to an erect position. We opened our eyes, and I could see Naomi's were pouring tears, to find ourselves surrounded by armed and uniformed men of aggressive appearance. One of them carried a flaming brand; two others carried long and heavy-looking metal objects. It wasn't long before we discovered they belonged to the town's Sheriff and its Constabulary...

Thirty Six

THE SHERIFF'S officer, who appeared to be in charge and responsible for the explosive invasion of Joseph's domain, stepped forward ominously with his sword in hand and confronted my host. Naomi and I stood trembling with fear close beside her somewhat calmer brother.

"Do *not* resist arrest!" the strongly built, muscular official screamed into Joseph's still but now pale face. "Or you'll suffer the fatal consequences… like your moneylender friend Abraham just suffered at the other end of your underground, and underhand, Jewish tunnel!"

I was more than certain that all three of us couldn't believe what we were witnessing and now, tragically, hearing. Unsurprisingly, Naomi began weeping pitifully, and the snarling bully of an officer turned to her quaking figure.

"Shut that bloody row, you…!" he shouted into her crumpling features, and brutally forcing the woman to stifle her pitiable sobs.

But before he could finish the sentence, and in view of his disgraceful though not totally unexpected behaviour, Joseph and I made a tentative, if imprudent move forwards. The official thuggishly raised his weapon; and the several armed men accompanying him, and now corralling us, edged menacingly in our direction. Joseph held me back with a rigidly outstretched arm and lifted his other, palm outwards in capitulating mode.

"Why am I being arrested?" he asked with an enviably heroic firmness.

"In the first place, it's not only you who's being taken into custody today," the officer shouted, his eyes piercing each of us in turn. "All three of you now present in this criminal chamber are being arrested…"

Then he jutted his bullish visage close into Joseph's face.

"And you're all being arrested for the felony of coin-clipping," he went on, "a nefarious activity so beloved of you avaricious Israelites!"

I was horror-struck and shivery now, with Joseph and his sister probably feeling no differently. Wild thoughts of the consequences and implications of this horrendous situation, which were doubtless storming through our minds at that pernicious moment, were maybe of a somewhat different kind in my own case.

"We are completely innocent of the charge!" Joseph declared valiantly. "Any allegations against us are groundless and untrue."

The officer on parade adopted a horribly sullen and sneering expression that critically and ominously twisted his mouth, creasing chin and cheeks.

"The evidence is clear and proves to the contrary!" he retorted, with a raised and contemptuous edge to his delivery. "And lower the tone of your voice… or else!"

At that, a dreadfully shaken Naomi – seemingly on the brink of mental and physical collapse – grabbed her brother and held tightly to him. I felt terrible, too... the scraping of gold and silver coinage of the realm, in order to collect and build up a profitable amount of the valuable metals, was an offence punishable by death. I knew from my reading about the medieval era that, from time to time and especially during periods of heightened anti-Semitism, Jews accused falsely of committing the crime of coin-clipping invariably had been judged guilty by the courts and executed by hanging in a public place. But I couldn't believe, for one moment, that Joseph would've been involved with this source of, to say the least, highly illegitimate income. Who knew what insidiously incriminating evidence might be planted – during an alleged rummage around Joseph's house – to secure a conviction, I pondered painfully.

Coincidentally, the officer continued:

"My men will now search this building thoroughly, from top to bottom and leaving no stone unturned, while you dastardly trio of criminals will be taken to the castle gaol. There you'll be interrogated, and incarcerated to await your trial."

Naomi's body was quaking with fear. My heart went out to her; and both her brother and I sought to comfort the woman, whilst endeavouring to steel ourselves in the dire circumstances that now confronted us. Before the official in control of the operation began to arrange for our armed escort to the motte and bailey castle, Joseph enquired of him – though with maybe understandable reluctance – whether his mother and the household helpers would be allowed to remain in the house. Thankfully, I overheard the reply that she and they weren't included in the Royal Arrest Warrant; and, therefore, they could stay in the building, at least for the time being. That didn't mean, of course, that the health and welfare of the close relative and honorary family folk wouldn't be constantly in the minds of those arrested. But I couldn't help speculating whether the accusations and arrests at this time - imminent to the expulsion of Cambridge's Jewish community to Huntingdon - had some connection with a potential desire to seize local Jewish property, or acquire other financial gain, for the Royal coffers.

Men approached us with chains, grabbed our arms and, making no allowances for female upper limbs, bound exposed wrists behind our backs. The fallen, and heavily damaged, entrance door had been kicked aside by those who'd entered the large vaulted room through a portal that proved not to be that secure. We were pushed forward to the gaping hole of doorway and into the area just within the entrance to the building - the front door of which was lying fractured on the lobby floor - and then to the world outside. I was sure that Joseph and his sister could hear, as I definitely was hearing, the chronic array of search noises emerging from the downstairs chamber; as well as heavy climbing sounds of booted feet on the stone steps leading up to the main hall.

The Sheriff's deputy - delegated by his superior officer to lead us and our guard escort to castle mound - bellowed an order to start walking, with Joseph just ahead of Naomi, then me. What else could we do but obey, with varying degrees of terror filling our minds. As we commenced our march or trek to prison – and whatever horrible prospects awaited us there – I focused on my own personal equation, notably from whence I'd come and to where I was hoping, now praying, to return. I'd been proposing to contact Diva this very day, in order to arrange for my journey back to 21st century Cambridge on the morrow. But I was now unbelievably aghast at the likely want of an early, if any, opportunity to communicate with my crucial, Alpha Centauri travel-manager. I barely comforted myself with the thought that I would need to wait and see. And with hands bound behind my back, I couldn't even feel the reassuring solidity of a mobile phone beneath my tunic. Now flanked, led and backed by the posse of sword-brandishing guards, we progressed along the medieval High Street and turned left into Bridge Street.

En route to the main river crossing adjoining the quayside, and our ultimate and dreaded destination atop its commanding hill, we three chained prisoners were jeered by a number of individuals and small groups of pedestrians, a drover herding some cattle, a few horse-and-cart drivers and even by a couple of conspicuously well-heeled horse-riders. As we trooped past the busy dockside area with its moored, river-cargo craft, I happened to espy Josce supervising the unloading of goods from a barge. I detected that Joseph was aware of him, too. My erstwhile host glanced over his shoulder and gave me a quick, but rather ambivalent shake of the head; though I believe the drift of his meaning was clear to me. Then he looked again towards Josce who, perhaps alerted by the harsh sounds of mocking and derisive taunts, looked up to gaze quizzically at the roadway then recognised the three of us immediately. His incredulous eyes, gravely questioning, met those of Joseph, whose further surreptitious headshake in the direction of his close friend demonstrated – and clearly, I felt – that Josce shouldn't interfere or get involved at that moment in time. I could see the shocked family friend was closely following our prominent procession; and I was certain he knew we were headed up the hill to the castle and its jail. He acknowledged me also, his face an image of stark disbelief, with a single nod; and I returned it. Next, I noticed Joseph gazing furtively around at our guard-escort; and, apparently resolved, he looked again towards Josce, who was clearly noting his close friend's every move. I could just make out Joseph mouthing emphatically the name 'Abraham'; then shaking his head with the saddest look he could muster. My attention turned again to Josce, who placed his hands behind his head and lowered it.

Thirty Seven

CROSSING the principal stone bridge over the Cam, I took a swift backward glance towards quayside and spotted Josce staring after the three of us being escorted by armed Sheriff's men and constables towards the castle. I couldn't help but absorb the continuing look of horror on his now fully exposed face. We trooped onward, beginning to take the gradually rising gradient on the old Roman road, Via Devana, in the direction of the hill-top fortress, its wood-constructed keep, round towers and palisades dominating the river and surrounding countryside. I recalled it wouldn't be until the next decade in the reign of King Edward that work would start on reconstructing, mainly in stone, the currently fairly neglected and weakly defended castle. I was aware also that within the keep were the Sheriff's offices, dungeons where prisoners were held and a court; though I couldn't remember whether it was a civil or criminal forum.

Our grim convoy followed a rightward curve of the inclined highway toward a steeper climb to the motte, or mound, on which the fort loomed above us. As we progressed upwards, I could hardly credit it being just a week or so back since I'd ventured down, using the same route, from my time-travelling arrival point; and after being confronted by the two venomous sentinels. Now bunched together, armed men and prisoners transited the short span over the moat and funnelled a way through the sentry-guarded gateway in the high wall to enter the open ground of the bailey. Joseph, Naomi and I were to be led now by only a few of the Sheriff's men, the others dispersing – across the expansive space enclosed by the lofty palisades – in the direction of a low building. I spotted a couple of soldiers patrolling the battlements, and another guardsman on sentry duty at the massive door to the towering keep. As we approached this entryway, the guard banged with his pikestaff on the really solid-looking, iron-hinged portal. After it was opened, quite slowly and with some effort from within, the three of us were individually pushed inside.

Two of the escort squad accompanied us into a reasonably spacious chamber – well illuminated by candles and some natural light entering through window slits in the walls – and stood guard by the door after it was secured. Just to the left of the entrance, I noted a desk with various documents atop it and a bench-seat behind. Beside the writing table stood a tall slim man, who introduced himself – in a not impolite manner, I considered with some surprise – to the three fearful prisoners arraigned before him, as one of the Sheriff's chief clerks and jailors. But by the look on his face, I knew the adjective 'fearful' in my mind applied now also to the normally indomitable Joseph. Then I noticed a short and stocky man - probably another jailor, I thought - in the large room. He was located at its other end to the main door, near the open gates in two adjoining but wall-divided cages, their bars extending from floor to ceiling. The clerk beckoned to him and he approached with a noticeable limp. In turn, he asked one of the guards at the door to accompany us and him to the pair of cages. As we moved forward, I perceived a closed door on the left side of the cells and another similar entryway on their right flank. I merely assumed that one of them would have a stairway leading down to the dungeons; and that the other could possess steps heading upwards, possibly to the Sheriff's office and a judicial forum, of whatever status.

When we were halted in front of the cages, the limping jailor indicated - with a flailing hand - that Joseph and I should enter one of the barred cells, and Naomi the other. After we complied and were finally incarcerated, he closed and locked each gate with a long iron key that hung from a wide belt on his brown leather apron. Both he and the accompanying guard moved back, the soldier returning to his colleague at the main entrance and the jailor disappearing through the door he now opened to the right of our cells as we looked out. Joseph and I took in the sparsely furnished cell. Against the back wall, there was just a low wooden item of furniture covered with straw; and which, we supposed, was intended as a bed. In addition, there was a wooden bench against a side wall; and in one rear corner stood a kind of half-barrel set-up, the aim of which was achingly obvious to us. Then the clerk picked up something from his desk and walked purposefully towards us, a document of some sort now clearly clasped in his hand.

Joseph and I held onto the bars, peering through them with apprehension doubtless marking our faces, and awaited the man's imminent arrival. Before that, I sneaked a quick glance to my left. I thought my ears were noting a sound of low whimpering coming from the other cage, but I wasn't certain. I did feel that, at a more apt time, it would be manageable for me to reach an arm through a gap in the bars nearest the dividing wall and possibly attract Naomi's attention with a wave. Perhaps, I thought with optimism, it might even be practicable for us to hold hands, the partition between us being not much more than a brick's width thick. Now, however, my attention was drawn to the clerk standing on the other side of the bars. I didn't know what Joseph was thinking; though, so far as I was concerned, the official appeared to have a demeanour that I wouldn't have described as aggressive or disdainful in any way. But, I reflected instantly, it was early days yet; and his maybe superficially benign attitude could've been a devious ruse for his own objectives. We needed to be extremely wary, I considered.

Then the man spoke, in a position from which he could see and address all three of his prisoners.

"I regret to confirm," began the clerk, "that you've been arrested for clipping coinage of the realm, or for aiding and abetting such clipping. These are serious criminal offences and, if you're found guilty, the punishment is death by public hanging or, in certain circumstances, imprisonment."

We could hear Naomi's piteous wailing; and Joseph placed a comforting hand on my back.

"But we're totally innocent of these crimes!" Joseph declared.

"The prisoners will remain silent!" came the surprisingly booming and echoing voice from the junior jailor standing behind the clerk, who just nodded evenly at us.

"You would need to prove your innocence, of course," he said and continued, pointing a long and skinny index finger at Joseph. "You are indicted for a crime sanctioned exclusively by capital punishment. Very shortly, you will be removed to the dungeons… and, tomorrow morning, you will be transported to the Tower of London, where you will be incarcerated with others of your ilk to await your trial…"

I could see that, on hearing this announcement, my dear friend was now gripping the bars so tightly that his whitened knuckles seemed on the point of bursting out of his skin. I noted also the clerk's reference to "others of your ilk". But I couldn't be certain whether he was alluding to alleged coin-clippers generally; or if he was proving me wrong in my 'gentlemanly' thoughts about him by his sardonic implication of a 'Jewish' connotation.

"As for you… and the woman," the clerk went on, transferring the direction of his now waving finger to me then Naomi, "you are both charged with the lesser, but still heinous crime of assisting a felon. You will remain here for the next day or so, for interrogation, and we would welcome any information you can give us... Depending on that, and subject to the judge's decision, there could be a reduction in your very lengthy sentences when both of you are found culpable."

I didn't know what was going through the mind of my fellow inmate in the adjacent cell, assuming sadly that her mind was moderately operational. But I noted for sure the clerk's manifestly deliberate use of the word "when" rather than "if". So was this yet another example of my mistaken belief that this official could've harboured a more sensitive mind-set, I wondered. Certainly, I hoped the terrified Naomi wasn't thinking that the suggested welcome for any information supplied by us would be subject to the prior application of some cruel and painful medieval tortures. However, there was nothing I - and doubtless Naomi - could've said.

Next, the clerk turned and called one of the guards and the limping jailor to his side.

"You will now take that man down to the dungeons," he said, indicating Joseph.

The jailor unlocked our cage and the soldier stepped in; he seized my good friend by the arm, pulled him out and the gate was secured again. Before Joseph was taken below, he smiled wanly at me and also at his sister, whom he may've been able to see directly now. I could still hear Naomi weeping as if her heart was breaking into tiny pieces. Then the clerk spoke again to his two remaining inmates.

"Soon you will be brought some bread and water," he said, "you must be feeling hungry and thirsty..."

I couldn't speak for Naomi but I felt a bit thirsty, though without much of an appetite.

"Thank you," I managed to force myself to respond.

The clerk nodded then announced something that, at last, brought me to my senses. Or awakened me from a numbness of mind induced, undoubtedly, by the overwhelming nature of this dreadful situation, of which I was now an integral part.

"After you have eaten and drunk," he said, addressing me to my face, "you will be taken upstairs to the interrogation room, where first your person will be searched… that is, searched meticulously."

With that, he returned to his desk and had a word with the other jailor, who left through the main door opened by the guard; and possibly to fetch the items just mentioned. Any thoughts I might've been entertaining about watery refreshment evaporated instantly. Why hadn't I anticipated that I would be searched, and very thoroughly at that? Prisoners generally would be subject to such a detailed examination. Clearly, the delving inspectors would find – and no doubt retain - the coins in the purse attached to my belt, as well as the money in the holder on my body-strap. Such articles of value wouldn't be considered out of the ordinary here. But what would happen when, in a container on the other belt strapped around me, my smart-phone was discovered? My mind was suddenly ablaze with panic. Immediately, I thought that - when drinking and maybe eating shortly - I could sit on the wooden bed and hide the device under the straw covering; or possibly conceal it in the toilet-barrel. But what if I were to be seen? I pondered hopelessly. Then I speculated whether I could pass the mobile to Naomi. But, again, that would be an awfully obvious movement for those instructed to watch us closely; and, besides, I didn't want to involve her.

If I couldn't secrete the gadget in any way before my search and questioning, how should I explain it? I asked myself with the deepest angst. For certain, I was prepared neither to repeat the narrative I'd given to Naomi when informing her about Alpha Centauri, nor to attempt an enlightening explanation of my time-travel journey from the 21st century to medieval Cambridge. Above all, and with my heart beating abnormally, I wondered how I was going to survive; let alone contact Diva to rescue me from this hell on earth.

Thirty Eight

THE CLERK looked up at me, his features a picture of bedazzlement.

"What in heaven's name is this infernal object?" he asked, his amazingly intrigued eyes locked onto mine as he turned in his hands, over and over again, my slim-line smart-phone.

I was standing, more or less to attention and now fully clothed again, directly in front of a desk behind which the Sheriff's officer sat in a high-backed chair. My head was spinning with the outrageously extraordinary and virtually unbelievable situation I was experiencing first-hand. Not that my mind, to varying degrees, hadn't been whirling with incredulousness since my arrival in *Cantabrigia*. A while earlier, and by then I would've lost all practical sense of time passing, I was taken forcibly from my cage by the squat and snarling jailor, who made up in strength and viciousness what he lacked in height. Accompanied by one of the guards to the rear, we followed the clerk up a steep, narrow and winding stairway to the next floor. As I began my ascent, I could yet hear Naomi weeping in her barred and confined space; and, quite emotionally, I felt my heart go out to her.

At the end of the climb, I was led into a chamber through an arched entranceway. With the jailor and guard escort now in position behind me, the clerk ensconced himself at the room's single table on which - I could just make out - there lay some articles of writing paraphernalia. I noticed also a couple of substantial chests, side-by-side and close to a wall. But I couldn't properly assess the approximate measurements of the chamber in which I now stood, quivering with fear at what might befall me here. Behind the seated official were drawn and heavy-looking, black drapes. Through a slight chink where the two halves met, I perceived we were separated from the rest of a possibly much larger room. My lack of knowledge concerning its extent or, maybe more relevantly, its content filled me with a scary apprehension. Did the unexposed area hold a court of law or, more horrifyingly, a set of torture implements, including thumb screws and other crippling bone-crunchers? I pondered, sending icy shivers rippling along my spine. Our divided section of this floor in the Norman keep, which was receiving some natural light through arcing window holes, was no doubt considered adequate for present purposes.

As soon as the clerk settled himself at the table, and there were no other seating arrangements, he ordered me to undress completely. I could scarcely take on board the command; but the other jailor's hard prod in the middle of my back confirmed, somewhat needlessly, that I was being given no choice in the matter. There was nowhere to heap my shed attire other than on the floor; though I was told by the official to place my outer belt and purse, and my pair of body-belts, on his desk. I wasn't concerned, in the main, about the money; nor, for that matter, regarding the coinage I'd left inside the bag in my room back at the house. I appreciated the tidy lot of valuable cash would be confiscated without more. But then came what I was dreading since the clerk stressed, in the chamber of cages, that personal searches would be "meticulous".

Entirely naked now - with street clothes, underwear and shoes scattered around my feet – I was forced to stand astride, bend over and allow myself to be intimately violated by a gloved jailor. The two other men in the room must've been looking on as if this was commonplace, I thought, feeling quite nauseous from the painful invasion of my body. Instantly after that deeply shaming and physically nasty experience, I was nudged to adopt an upright position again. While seeking - aching with soreness - to attain it, I noted the brutal violator of my person shaking his head in the clerk's direction. Then I was told by the jailor to put back on my garments and footwear, and stand to attention before the officer, who was on the point of emptying the contents of my belts onto his desk. But before he asked me, with maximum inquisitiveness, to explain the thing that was my mobile phone, he enquired about a number of other matters.

He demanded to know my permanent place of residence, the nature of my profession, why I was present in Cambridge, when I'd arrived in the town and the reason for my residence at the house where I was arrested. He didn't need to ask me whether I was Jewish. After taking a few moments to try and compose myself, and gather some rational thinking capacity, I responded to the clerk's need to know. I considered starting by saying I was absolutely innocent of the crime of which I was charged; and that there was nothing I could add. But a quick peek at the sinisterly dark curtains ahead of me definitively ruled out the dubious non-option.

"I live and work in London," I began, as the clerk dipped his stylus tip in an ink pot. "I'm self-employed as a private tutor in various subjects. I arrived in Cambridge a little over one week ago, entirely with the aim of having a short break from my teaching duties. I was making enquiries about available accommodation for a visitor when, by pure chance, I was offered a room at the house you mention. I didn't know any of its occupiers, or indeed any other Cambridge inhabitants, before that time. When arrested, I was helping my kind host and his sister, both of whom you hold as prisoners, to package books for transportation to Huntingdon. To which nearby town, I've been told, the Jewish community of Cambridge is being expelled shortly and in pursuance of a recent Royal decree."

The official continued writing for a while longer after I finished speaking.

"Where exactly do you reside in London?" he asked.

I was also dreading being asked this supplementary question; and my slight hesitation in replying, I gauged at once, could've given this interrogating officer significant pause for thought. Although I was half-anticipating such a query, from anyone, I wasn't prepared to – and couldn't – answer it by the book. But I needed to say something, and immediately.

"I reside near Cripplegate," I replied, naively expecting the clerk to leave it at that. Needless to say, I was seriously mistaken.

"I asked you for your *exact* place of residence in our capital city," he stressed, and in a pointedly elevated tone. "So do give me your precise address… and now!"

I held my breath for a few moments.

"M–my… m–my address is… is…" I stammered, "I–I'm s–sorry, s–sir… I–I'm inn–innocent… a–and in a t–terrible s–state of s–shock n–now… a–and a–all this a–aggravation has c–caused m–me to… to f–forget it…"

The officer raised his eyebrows, frowned then grinned alarmingly.

"That's a good one," he said, leaning back then forward. "But we'll leave this matter for the time being, and return to it in due course."

It was then that he picked up my smart-phone, turned it over in his hands – more than once – and, his eyes bulging with an acute case of curiosity, asked me: "What in heaven's name is this infernal object?"

Despite my disastrous quandary, the almost whimsical thought crossed my mind that many smart-phone owners might well ask themselves the very same question. But how was I supposed to respond to the clerk's understandable need to identify this, to him, unique and mystifying "object"? I wondered in that critical, heart-hammering instant. I was sure about one thing, however: I most assuredly couldn't endow the clerk with the kind of explanatory account about the world-changing piece of hardware that I'd related to Naomi. I might've been despatched to an asylum for the rest of my life! Nevertheless, time was passing; and my feeble delaying tactic was - from the half sceptical, half cynical look monopolising the official's penetrating eyes - perceptibly endorsing the suspicions he would be harbouring about me.

Then he spoke further.

"Shock and aggravation got your memory again," he enquired with a callous slice of sarcasm, "and your tongue now?"

I merely nodded.

"Right, then," he remarked sternly. "Tomorrow you will join your former bed-provider on the transport to London. Hopefully, and for your sake, the feelings of shock and angst will disperse very soon, and a good memory with a strong and truthful voice will return before you reach the Tower..."

After hearing all that, my traumatised mind virtually switched off.

"And tomorrow morning," the official continued, "we will interview your ex-host's sister... perhaps she will be more sensibly inclined and forthcoming, and tell us what we want to know."

With that, he got up from his chair, walked to one of the chests, opened the lid of the storage container and withdrew a metal box. He went back to his desk and placed all my personal belongings, together with his manuscript notes, inside the tin then returned to the big coffer. Actually, I must've been approaching total madness even to have nursed the idea of asking the clerk if a particular article could be given back to me. The box was put inside the chest, which was closed and locked with one of the keys suspended from the official's broad, leather waist-belt.

Before sitting down, he addressed me one more time.

"You will now be escorted back to the cage, in which you will spend your last night here in Cambridge," he said. "Guards and jailors will be changed before long, but I will be here again early tomorrow morning. In the meantime, if you happen to enjoy a speedy recovery of recollection and vocal cords, do not hesitate to inform the fresh personnel in my temporary absence overnight. Do you understand me?"

It seemed impossible for me to recover my sane mind from the clerk's earlier pronouncement on my personal expulsion from Cambridge to London on the morrow. But I managed to recoup just enough mental capacity to nod slightly. Next, he barked an order directed at the guard and the limping jailor.

"Take this animal back to its cage!"

When returned to the ground-floor chamber, and really surprisingly in view of the profound shock on learning my impending destiny, I felt slightly more mindful. I noticed Naomi sitting, head bowed but now quietly, on the bench in her cell. I did wonder whether she might be sleeping; and if she were to be, I would've readily understood. But just in case she was only resting wakefully, and as I came closest to her cage, I called in a fairly soft voice:

"Naomi... I'm back."

I was so glad when she looked up towards me and nodded an acknowledgement, albeit with the most desperately melancholy expression I've ever had the misfortune to witness.

"We can hear you've got your nice voice back, then..." the jailor chortled mordantly, as he and the guard virtually hurled me into my cell, slammed shut the gate after me and secured it.

Thirty Nine

I SAT DOWN on the bench in my cage, my bottom still achingly sore; and I felt thoroughly exhausted, both physically and mentally. I adopted the identical bodily position Naomi was using, head buried in cupped hands. There was so much in the way of my pending future for me to mull over; and yet so little that was within my control. Unfortunately, my fate seemed to be sealed. I was soon to be transported, alongside Joseph, to the notorious prison in the Tower of London. How had I got myself into this terrifying mess? I posed superfluously, knowing full well how my mind-stunning dilemma had come about. Its apparently final straw, the confiscation of my smart-phone, became manifestly the most significant factor contributing to the foregone conclusion that was now my ultimate fate. Why hadn't I seen fit to contact Diva earlier that day, and before I began helping Joseph to package up his library? I asked myself inconsequentially.

I started to think of my son in New York, and whom I loved dearly; then I felt tearfully emotional. I was beginning to comprehend that I would never see Michael again. In those same moments, I knew something else… something that I was sublimating or suppressing for whatever reason, and consciously or subconsciously. I was truly in love with Naomi, and that was the something. I couldn't but be aware that we'd exchanged some mutual thoughts of love in a certain ardent situation. Maybe, I reflected in my classically contemplative position, I was withholding any final, formal and confirmatory declaration of my love for Joseph's sister in order to protect her. But I was blameworthy also of seeking to overcome, if not obliterate, my feelings. In the end, perhaps it took the traumatic happenings of late, in which I was inescapably immersed now, to compel the acceptance of my staunch feelings for Naomi. I needed to speak with her, and at once.

I got up from the bench and went to the front corner of my cage most proximate to Naomi's cell. Very softly, I called her name. No sounds were coming from her side of the barrier wall, whether of weeping or otherwise. Possibly, she was slumbering now, her body sadly wracked with an all-pervading weariness. It seemed quiet enough on her side of the partition; but there was no response to my restrained call, at least from my fellow inmate. Even though I kept my voice as practicably low as possible, the two guards standing by the main door and the jailor, now seated at the desk, peered in my direction with daggers in their eyes.

"No talking!" the warder shouted at the top of his voice.

I sat down again and, only when doing so, spotted underneath the bench a pottery bowl of water with a chunk of bread floating in it. Just as the food and drink might've been set out for a dog! Admittedly – the realisation then came to me – I *was* a trifle thirsty and a bit peckish. It did seem like the rats, and I was almost certain there were rats about, hadn't got to the receptacle as yet. So I lifted it, hesitantly removed but held onto the soggy rustic hunk of loaf, and imbibed some of the liquid. It looked fairly clean, save for some suspended fragments of crust, but it tasted brackish. I placed the vessel beside me on the wooden seat and started nibbling – my mind almost a blank canvas – on the over-moist, half-brick of wheat. Mainly because, with Naomi being non-contactable at present, I had nothing better to do.

It could've been the tedious racket of my teeth chomping on the damp but yet crusty, or maybe very stale, bread portion that was keeping me awake. Then other sounds entered my ears that served to rouse me from my thankfully monotonous and thus mind-numbingly distracting, chewing routine. First, there was a loud rap on the main entrance door. I peered through the bars then observed the shift change mentioned earlier by the clerk. The portal was unlocked by the jailor and opened by him. At the same time, the Sheriff's official came into the chamber from upstairs. On exiting the room of cages, accompanied by the two guards and his short assistant, he looked quickly over his shoulder and – somewhat to my surprise – cast a witheringly caustic, even hostile glance in my direction.

However, the departing quartet was replaced on duty by one guard only. The hulking sentinel secured the door, stared neutrally at me for a moment or two, unsheathed his sword, placed the shiny weapon on the desk and sat down behind it facing the cages. I took some more munches on my bread whilst eyeing him in a secretive manner. After a mere few moments, to my astonishment, he began to blink in a less than normal manner; his head appeared to shift forward and slightly downward. Following that movement, his eyelids started to lower gradually, like they were hung with many tiny and invisible weights. I could hardly credit the bulky but youngish soldier was nodding off; but that clearly appeared to be the case, and before my very eyes. Just for a jiffy, I thought his helmet-less head would come crashing down onto the solid table and definitely knock him for six. But that didn't happen. Instead - and in a sort of robotic mode – the guard's arms came up and folded themselves atop the desk, as his face turned about and descended onto them.

My hearing joined my vision in the strange and unexpected scenario I was observing. The heavy-set warrior began snoring suddenly, and quite loudly. I knew Naomi and I didn't pose, or represent, any kind of real threat to the guard. We weren't in a position to cause our watchdog any trouble; and, inevitably, we were incapable of fleeing from custody. Perhaps, and I was ruminating idly, our guard had come off another long duty recently and was extremely fatigued. But I did know that - at this period in its history from 1068, but before its reconstruction in stone during the 1280s on King Edward's orders – the Norman castle had been ineffectually garrisoned. So I concluded, though

331

uncertainly, it was quite possible the available personnel were obliged to perform double duties. But what if an officer dropped by to check on the vigilance of the sentry? I asked myself. Shouldn't be a problem here, I considered. In all likelihood, our guardian would be rapidly awakened by a loud and sudden rapping on the door. His superior would never know of the 40 or so winks!

It occurred to me, however, that I could take some advantage of the slumbering bull, and seek again to communicate with Naomi. Immediately, therefore, I set about doing just that; and from the most beneficial position. I called her name, initially at low key. When I received no reaction, I tried again at an increased volume but with a really chary eye to the seated, sleeping and noisily snoring sentinel. Then a faint sound emanated from the neighbouring cage. Happily, it was Naomi's albeit restrained voice.

"Yes?" I heard her enquire. "Who is it?"

"It's *me*... David," I responded enthusiastically, so grateful that we were now in dialogue together. "Please come to the front corner of your cell and nearest mine, Naomi."

I just about detected her near-soundless approach. I pressed my body against the dividing wall and stretched my right arm through the bars, curving it towards her cage.

"Take my hand, Naomi," I virtually pleaded; and I felt so uplifted when she made contact. We clasped each other's fingers awkwardly, and I heard what sounded like a fresh bout of weeping.

"Please don't cry," I enjoined tenderly, my heart bursting with compassion for her undeserved plight; as well as for her feelings regarding Joseph's perilous situation and probable lot.

"W-What's been h-happening to you, David?" she asked, with a voice seemingly hovering on the brink of emotional breakdown.

I told her about my interrogation, the clerk's changing attitudes, my forthcoming removal alongside her brother to the Tower of London's infamous jail, the loss of my mobile phone and, with it, the last chance to communicate with Diva. On absorbing my sorely depressing information, Naomi burst into tears again; and squeezed my hand so tightly that I thought, momentarily and oddly, it would be lost as well.

"I-I love you, David," she pined through her sobs.

I didn't hesitate this time.

"And I love you, Naomi…" I responded, "with all my heart and soul."

I could still hear the sound of her crying but, somehow, the tone seemed to have altered. It felt like there was a distinctive but strange element of implicit joy in its makeup.

"R-Right now," I went on, feeling quite sensitive myself, "I-I would give my life just to be able to hold you close to me one last time."

The weeping increased in tempo.

"Please don't cry any more, Naomi," I begged, hoping to calm the torment for her own wellbeing, and added – for me, abnormally and out of the blue:

"We're in the hands of the Almighty, and can but pray for our salvation."

Naomi persisted in gripping me. Gazing across the chamber, I was so grateful that the guard was still entrenched in his guttural slumbers. I closed my eyes, thankful now to have been able to clearly express, and absolutely genuinely, my deeply-held feelings for her. I kept them shut as we carried on holding each other's warm and consoling hands. Until a moment arrived when, without prior warning, Naomi's hand loosened its clutch and fell away from mine. In the instant before I opened my eyes again, I heard the most unfathomable ever gasp coming from the adjacent cage; and I feared my loved one was collapsing with the incalculable hurt she was suffering. Then, with full visibility again available to me, I too emitted my most intense intake of breath of all time; but one combined with a startling jolt to the system. Just a metre or so from the bars of our cages stood facing us a woman, a woman I recognised immediately. It was the woman from Alpha Centauri… Diva!

Forty

THERE WERE so many things I couldn't believe were happening at this time, but Diva's sudden and amazing appearance, in the clothes of the era, crowned all of them. I supposed that the ongoing series of bizarre and unexpected blows to my mind were virtually conditioning me – akin to one of Pavlov's dogs – to become oddly though acceptingly immune to their affects. But seeing Diva poised just in front of my cage could've constituted an astonishing exception to the apparently developing, habituation rule. She stood before us, staring first at me then at Naomi – who I knew was now up against the bars of her cell – and finally at me again. I fought to find, extract and convey some suitable words from my brain, via my vocal cords to my mouth. After possibly just a few moments that certainly felt a lot longer, I did.

"Diva…!" I exclaimed aloud, feeling my eyes, as well as my head, popping. And I added the nebulous and meagre statement: "I don't understand, Diva."

She edged closer and grasped one of the bars, adopting a fairly casual stance.

"Let me explain, David…" she said, in a tone of voice more serious than her seemingly relaxed, physical deportment might've suggested.

I nodded, but before the extra-terrestrial — and, in the instant, I nearly forgot about her status — went on, I pointed to the still sleeping and snoring guard slumped over the desk behind her.

"Don't worry about him," she said with the tinge of a grin. "I've ensured that his snorting slumbers will go on for longer than might otherwise have been the case."

I nodded with a half-smile.

"But how did you get inside the castle and, in particular, this chamber?" I enquired with a compelling but silly curiosity.

"You, of all people," she answered with a telling frown, "should well know I have my ways and means of doing things."

I nodded again, this time with an acknowledged recognition of my idiocy and her Alpha Centauri methods of operation. Then she gave me the explanation from which I was distracting her by my superfluous queries.

"I was becoming very concerned about not having heard from you," she began, her eyes fixed on mine. "And I was anxious that you may be in need of some help, for whatever reason. So here I am, David, as a witness to the fact you have indeed got yourself into a bit of trouble, just to be more than a little euphemistic… a spot of bother, I see, that does appear to require my urgent, remedial assistance…"

"When did you arrive in Cantabrigia?" I said, realising I was again being needlessly disruptive of her word flow.

"A few hours ago," she answered. "As I'd intended, my landing here was close outside the Jewry area…"

I didn't have the time or inclination to inform Diva about my own time travel set-down, at a location somewhat off course. So I just nodded, yet again.

"How did you get to know I was incarcerated on the mound?"

"Well, I needed to make enquiries, of course," she replied. "But it wasn't difficult... bad news travels fast, as you well know. Grapevine reports of your imprisonment up here have been circulating like wildfire. I was telling the Jewish folk I met that I'm a friend of yours, and they directed me to a certain house."

Before she related any more information, I introduced a silent Naomi to her - though rather belatedly, I felt. I apologised accordingly to both of them for that error on my part. I explained to a more than surprised Diva that Naomi knew about her true identity in all respects; and I mentioned my fellow prisoner's relationship with the house to which, undoubtedly, she was referring. For the first time, Diva heard Naomi's voice.

"D-Did you speak with my mother, by any chance, Diva?" she asked in a fraught timbre.

"Yes I did, Naomi," Diva replied, addressing my inmate neighbour directly whilst releasing her hand from the bar it was grasping. "And I was aided in doing so by a very adept young girl whose name, I believe, is Miriam."

"H-How is m-my... m-my m-mother taking this dreadful situation?" Naomi enquired, audibly fighting to keep her emotions in check and remain rational. "Though I hardly need to ask... I can easily imagine."

"Yes…" Diva reacted with great sympathy, "your mother is, naturally, overwhelmingly distraught and fearful of what may happen to you, your brother Joseph and, of course, to David… and she expressed her heartfelt grief and sorrow at the death of a community elder named Abraham, who will no doubt have been known to you. But you will be reassured to know, Naomi, that your mother is being well cared for by Miriam and her mother Rebecca, I believe, until her son Aaron arrives."

With a deep sigh accompanying my next thought, I could readily comprehend the reason for Naomi becoming tearful again. I noted Diva reaching out a hand to comfort her. At that juncture - and wholly mindful of our immediate circumstances - I felt Diva deserved being told, but very succinctly, of why and how I came to be in my current dreadful tight-spot; and to have a concise summary of what it meant. After I completed the summation, Diva spoke with a resounding finality.

"We must leave this place at once," she said, taking a step back.

I knew precisely what she meant, but I was absolutely certain that Naomi hadn't a clue about the real import of Diva's announcement.

"I agree entirely, of course," I stated firmly.

I reached out through the bars to attract Naomi's attention.

"Give me your hand," I said quite audibly. "I want to tell you again how much I love you."

On hearing my words, Diva gazed at me with some initial bewilderment and Naomi grasped my waving hand.

"I love you so much, Naomi," I gasped. "And you must leave here with me, of course."

"I love you so much, too, David," Naomi responded, filling my heart with gladness. "But leave for where?"

"To my own time... to Cambridge of the 21st century," I answered. "The time and place I've described to you..."

I could hear Naomi breathing very heavily now, virtually hyperventilating, with the kind of thoughts that I knew must be deluging her mind.

"I-I love you so dearly, D-David," she gasped. "But how can I abandon my family in the terrible situation that afflicts us now?"

I could see Diva looking at Naomi with an equivocal expression, perhaps undecided as to whether she should nod with approval at what was being said. Or shake her head with the understanding that, if the woman remained where she was, something dreadful, if not fatal could happen to her. If Naomi was resolved on staying in *Cantabrigia*, I knew that my unalterable decision would be to stay put with her. But I really wanted her to survive... for both of us to survive this terrible ordeal.

"Regrettably, Naomi," I started my effort to convince her to depart with me, "there's nothing that can be done for Joseph. He'll be transported to London tomorrow, and I'm scheduled to go with him... quite likely, and I have to say this, to our deaths..."

There again the pitiful sound of Naomi weeping, but I needed to continue with my appeal.

"Look Naomi, your mother and the rest of the family cannot help him or us… nobody can, despite our pleadings of innocence. I believe you know that. But I, rather Diva, can help you to outlast the pain we can understand, and to have a full life with someone who loves you more than anything. Think of it this way, Naomi… if you leave with me now, to time travel to a future Cambridge, your mother and the rest of your loved ones will know at least that you've escaped somehow from this hellish place, one that may well cost you your life needlessly. They will never see you again, and you will never see them. But they will know for sure that you and, indeed, I have got away from this evil and survived it. The alternative, I say with great sadness, is that your family will, sooner or later, be informed of our likely deaths at the hands of the King's authorities. To me, there's no contest between these options. And I'm sure that your, rather *our* getaway, to wherever they might think, would be a greater consolation for your mother and other beloved family members…"

At the end of my plea, I could hope only for the best outcome. Doubtless to Naomi's surprise, but not mine, Diva merely touched her hands to the locks on our cage's gates and they swung open. Each of us staggered free from our cells, turned slowly then fell into each other's arms and embraced, undoubtedly, with every fibre of our beings.

"What *is* your decision, Naomi?" Diva asked with a due emphasis. "The time has now arrived."

Naomi and I parted, and looked so deeply into each other's eyes.

"We must go now, David," my beloved said to me.

I bunched my lips then kissed hers. Diva smiled then requested us to stand side-by-side. After she was satisfied with our positioning - me to the right of Naomi - the woman from Alpha Centauri instructed us to close our eyes and hold each other's hand tightly, which was certainly no problem for us. Then I felt Diva place a finger on my right temple, as Naomi must've likewise felt a finger on her left temple. Before we departed, I think I understood why neither Naomi nor Diva raised the question of rescuing Joseph from the dungeons.

Forty One

DIVA, NAOMI and I duly arrived - all necessarily garbed in appropriate modern attire at which, to my delight, my darling gazed adoringly - in 21st century Cambridge. Dusk was falling when we turned up at precisely the intended location outside the lofty, crest-topped gates of St John's Divinity School, where I'd begun my almost catastrophic personal adventure to *Cantabrigia* little over a week earlier. I congratulated Diva on her successful, pinpoint navigation.

My attention turned now to Naomi. She was staring about and appeared utterly stupefied by her surroundings, almost falling over with fright at - to her, of course — the unique sight and sound of a motor vehicle. The car was being driven along St John's Street, past the eponymous college and towards Trinity Street flanked by its own college of that name. Of course, it was more than obvious to me that Naomi would be vastly more unprepared for her new environment — and in countless different ways - than I was when entering the medieval life, and everyday context, that had been familiar to her. It would've taken many hours just to mention them to her. Clearly, there would be a need for Naomi to travel a steep and lengthy learning curve, a journey I proposed to start with her almost, but not quite, at once. In those first and seriously mystifying moments for her, I wanted to ensure she wasn't flummoxed to such an extent as to make her regret coming along with me to post-modern Cambridge. Suddenly, Naomi smiled at me; and I felt so relieved at her evidently revealed emotions that I held her tightly in my arms and pressed my lips zealously against hers.

"I should leave you two now," Diva remarked discreetly. "But, in any event, I've got to be somewhere else."

I took both her hands in mine, and - so wonderfully, I felt - Naomi placed a hand on each of Diva's shoulders then hugged her warmly for a few moments.

"On behalf of Naomi and me," I said, "I've got to say you have our undying thanks, Diva… and for everything, not least by saving our lives."

"I want to give Diva my own personal thanks," Naomi said, unbelievably to her and not so surprisingly to me, in perfect modern English.

"My pleasure," returned Diva, grinning broadly. "And maybe we'll meet up again some time."

"We hope so," I said, at the same instant pondering whether she or others from her star system would've been interacting, in any way, with other Earthlings.

Finally, Diva said a fond farewell – which we reciprocated with sadness at a poignant parting of the ways - turned and disappeared into the narrow, building-flanked section of All Saints Passage. Naomi and I followed her with, I sensed, quite moving expressions until she vanished between the high and dark-brick walls. I clasped Naomi's hand and kissed it to her delight, mentioned how near we were standing to where her house had once stood then led her on the short walk to my apartment beside the river. En route, I spoke of the places we were passing; and I wasn't at all surprised she could roughly identify with some of them and specifically with others, like the iconic Round Church.

When we reached my flat, I knew I would have to ask the next-door neighbour for my spare key. Fortunately he was at home and I was able to gain entry to our new home, to which I welcomed Naomi heartily. I and my dearest one would have so much to discuss; and she would have rather a lot to learn about modern-day life. But I knew her to be a highly intelligent woman who would absorb fast, because she appreciated the necessity to do so.

But I was aware, for certain, that the study curve wouldn't be transited overnight; and especially in relation to the everyday ingredients of our species' lives today. Like reading books, newspapers and magazines, watching television and going to the cinema, riding in cars and public transport vehicles, using a mobile phone, getting familiar with time-keeping wristwatches and clocks, drinking in coffee houses, shopping at supermarkets and – in Naomi's particular circumstances – at clothes boutiques for a completely novel wardrobe. But I knew also that it would take a long time, if ever, for my dearest love to come fully to terms with the loss of her beloved family. I vowed to myself that, so long as we lived, I would devote myself to making Naomi as happy as I possibly could, in the hope that her hurt and pain wouldn't damage her or our soul-linked relationship.

* * *

After a year had passed, a year so full of learning and loving, the now 'regularised' Naomi and I decided to get married. We tied the knot at a synagogue in London. It was Naomi's third or fourth, stupendously eye-opening trip to the capital. But well before we wed, I confessed to the terms of my agreement with Diva that had enabled me to time travel to *Cantabrigia*. On hearing my story, Naomi's tranquil attitude - for which I was more than glad and grateful - was that *All's well that ends well*; and that was the first and last occasion on which the matter was mentioned.

Of course, I was in continual contact with my son as normal; though, sadly, his relationship had broken down and he was single again. Ours was a small private wedding party, and he came over from the States to be with us. It was so good to see him, and he and Naomi were anxious to meet. Shortly after my return from *Cantabrigia*, I told Michael that I'd met her in Cambridge. I felt uncomfortable about the half-truth; and, across the year since then, I was always contemplating the possibility of someday telling him the honest truth about Naomi and me. However, I did tell my son there was a fair gap between Naomi's birth year and mine; but I believe he was well aware this wasn't so unusual these days. In Cambridge alone, I was noticing so many youngish Chinese girls with rather older men. The wedding and the reception that followed were delightful; and I was overjoyed to see that Naomi – who'd borne so much distress in her former life, especially concerning her barren condition – appeared to be really content with her new world.

Then one day, and nearly half a year or so after Naomi and I had wed, it happened… yet another incredible moment that changed our lives again for ever. Naomi and I didn't go on honeymoon after the wedding; but on the afternoon in question we were at home, snugly ensconced on the settee with some holiday brochures and discussing where to go – in the present day and age, of course – on a belated trip. Suddenly, there was a ring at the doorbell. I went to see who it was and, on opening the door, couldn't believe who was standing on the doorstep. It was Diva! I called to Naomi who, with a concerned expression, joined me quickly. But together we smiled so joyfully, opened our arms and somewhat inelegantly – for the two of us at the same time – embraced Diva comprehensively.

"What are you doing here?" I asked, though my words sounded wrongly phrased. "I mean… it's really great to see you, Diva! Any particular reason why you're back in Cambridge again? Please come in…"

"In a moment," she responded, recomposing herself after the overwhelming caress. "I'm sorry that I couldn't attend your marriage ceremony… yes, I was aware that you've wed and I'm so happy for you both…"

"Thank you so much, Diva," my wife and I intoned, almost in chorus.

Naomi had just beaten me at the post.

"But why…" I began, and that was it.

"I've come to give you both an overdue wedding gift," Diva interjected. "It's just along the corridor by the lift… I'll go fetch it now."

Naomi and I looked at each other in bemused anticipation. What might the present be, I wondered with an aching curiosity, that it couldn't have been brought by Diva immediately with her to our front door.

The pair of us almost fainted with bewilderment when, just seconds later, Diva arrived back with a large perambulator, a trendy double buggy holding two gorgeous babies.

"They're for you," she said with a smile, "a boy and a girl, twins actually."

Later that day, when Diva had left us and Naomi and I were sitting together on the sofa, the boy asleep in my arms and the girl slumbering in hers, we each meditated silently. The children were, naturally, the result of my arrangement with the woman from Alpha Centauri. Naomi, who knew all about that unbelievable deal, and I adored Diva's gift to us at first sight. We appreciated it was vital for us to find the best legal way to 'adopt' the twins, and eventually we did. We named the boy, Joshua Joseph Aaron Josce, and the girl, Sarah Ruth Rebecca Miriam.

The little ones are dearly loved, and we've devoted ourselves to them. I didn't feel too old to become a father, far from it; and knew I possessed loads of energy to spare. Naomi was ecstatic and just couldn't take in her good fortune and, as she said quite emotionally, the answer to her prayers. Now, she felt so thankfully, her father, mother, brothers, sister and others would live on in the lives of their namesakes.

One fine-weather day, Naomi insisted I chauffeur her and the twins on a private-hire punt along the River Cam. When first we glided beneath the famed Bridge of Sighs at St John's College, our eyes met meaningfully and – after glancing at the children, then back at me – she said, with a touching little smile: "It is water under the bridge now, David."

Forty Two

WHEN DIVA, Naomi and I arrived in 21st century Cambridge from medieval *Cantabrigia*, and as I was congratulating our time travel manager on her excellent course-plotting, I remembered that my smart-phone remained at the old Norman castle. It occurred to me that the vast majority of those who forget to take their mobile phones with them, on leaving home for work or other activity or vice versa – and, apparently, that happens quite frequently nowadays - do retrace their steps automatically on realising its absence from pocket, purse, bag or case. The indispensable communication device is now considered to be almost as crucial as a limb.

Diva didn't bat an eyelid when I informed her of my loss, telling me that the mobile's absence made no difference in any way; that it was no longer of any significance in the time-journeying context; that I could acquire a new and updated model the very next day, if I was so desperate. And, albeit politely, that she was definitely not travelling back nearly 800 years to retrieve it from the box within the chest in the upstairs chamber at the keep on the castle mound. Then I smiled at her, at last having the real freedom to breathe the fresh,

Cambridge evening air and to curve the corners of my mouth upwards.

But from that day on, I became an even more avid reader of publicly available reports – especially any lists of finds in them – relating to archaeological excavations or investigations in the Cambridge city area. I've yet to note, however, any reference to what would be the world-shattering discovery of a mobile phone in the relevant medieval strata. If it ever happens, Naomi will be the first person I'll inform... well, virtually the first person.

Praise for

"The Shtetl
and other Jewish stories"

"Humorous, sad, thought-provoking and relevant to each
of us and our life-style today... I enjoyed this book more
than I could ever have thought possible."

Reggie Ross, *Belfast Jewish Recorder*

"Mark Harris follows brilliantly in the tradition of a writer
with a gift for descriptive narrative and the ability to paint
his characters so accurately that you can see them in your
mind's eye... The author senses he is building a pipeline
for the thoughts and emotions of the characters that walk
through the pages. And he does it with style and feeling."

Manny Robinson, *Essex Jewish News*

Praise for

"The Chorister and other Jewish stories"

"Mark Harris' style makes for easy reading and comprehension. He paints the background to each story with a delicate, gentle and at times humorous touch. The subjects of his stories are seldom light-hearted, dealing with sensitive issues... but they are all worth reading."

D J Coppel, BJR

"The author meticulously outlines the theme of love, an emotion that weaves like a piece of tapestry through the pages... In many of the stories there is a twist in the tale. And that perhaps is Mark Harris' greatest strength... having the ability to describe a seemingly everyday scenario and make the reader sit up at the surprise ending."

M Robinson, EJN

Praise for

"The Music Makers and other Jewish stories"

"The third of Mark Harris' trilogy of his Jewish short story anthologies carries, in the main, a theme of Jewish suffering that extends across the Holocaust of the Second World War, the persecutions before that period and, indeed, anti-Semitic attacks subsequent to it. The author invites the reader to use his or her imagination to visualise the dialogue-based stories... Mark Harris writes with clarity, and his knowledge of Jewish custom and practice is lovingly transmitted through the pages... There are stories that are sombre and stories that are horrific, but also some lighter tales. Many of them carry in their words both faith in the Almighty and a belief in a better future for the Jewish people."

Manny Robinson, *Essex Jewish News*

Praise for
"Last Days in Berlin"

"Mark Harris' debut novel is a serious story about a married, retired professional man and fiction author in his early 60s, who is on a creative journey in Berlin. Being Jewish, he harbours some ambivalence for a city he has visited many times; and he has sought to understand its complex and enigmatic character. But he embarks also on another kind of voyage of discovery with two fellow passengers – both of them women, other than his spouse – that could end in tragedy. The capital of the Federal German Republic has a fascination for many people. And in this well-written, meticulously observed book, Mark Harris presents a unique perspective of Berlin as seen through the eyes of a man whose personal dilemmas seem to mirror the city's own uncertainties."

Manny Robinson, *EJN*